Books by Aram Saroyan

POETRY

Aram Saroyan (1968)
Pages (1969)
Words & Photographs (1970)
Cloth: An Electric Novel (1971)
The Rest (1971)
Poems (1972)
O My Generation and Other Poems (1976)
Day and Night: Bolinas Poems (1998)

PROSE

The Street: An Autobiographical Novel (1974)
Genesis Angels: The Saga of Lew Welch and the Beat Generation (1979)
Last Rites: The Death of William Saroyan (1982)
William Saroyan (biography, 1983)
Trio: Portrait of an Intimate Friendship (1985)
The Romantic (novel, 1988)
Friends in the World: The Education of a Writer: A Memoir (1992)
Rancho Mirage: An American Tragedy of Manners, Madness, and Murder (1993)
Starting Out in the Sixties: Selected Essays (2001)
Artists in Trouble: New Stories (2001)

EDITOR

Selected Poems by Archie Minasian (1986)
Selected Poems by Ted Berrigan (1994)

Aram Saroyan

ARTISTS IN TROUBLE

new stories

BLACK SPARROW PRESS
Santa Rosa • 2001

ACKNOWLEDGMENTS

Some of these stories first appeared, in whole or in part, in the following publications, to whose editors and publishers grateful acknowledgement is made: *Beat It Up a Little Bit, Disturbed Guillotine, Fell Swoop, Long News, Los Angeles Times Book Review, Navasart Monthly, Structurally Sound,* and *Zyzzyva.* "The Genius" was printed as a Keepsake of the 14th Abraham S. Burack Lecture, April 26, 2000, by the Friends of the Libraries of Boston University.

Black Sparrow Press books are printed on acid-free paper.

LIBRARY OF CONGRESS CATALOGING-IN-PUBLICATION DATA

Saroyan, Aram
Artists in trouble: new stories / Aram Saroyan.
p. cm.
ISBN 1-57423-171-5 (paperback)
ISBN 1-57423-172-3 (cloth trade)
ISBN 1-57423-173-1 (signed cloth)
1. Manhattan (New York, N.Y.)–Fiction. 2. Beverly Hills (Calif.)–Fiction. 3. Artists–Fiction. I. Title.
PS3569.A72A88 2001
813'.54–dc21 2001043736

To my family and friends

Note

A love of form may play as decisive a role in life as it does in art. We want to bring the design whole into the fabric of our lives, we want closure, understanding, balance in our affairs. Life, as often as not, has another agenda. What mistakes we make! What turns of fate await us! Yet the artist in each of us struggles on, calming us with stories and pictures of an ordered world, or at least a world in which we learn from the fates, from our mistakes, and honor the love of form ingrained in us.

In the end, these novellas and stories are about the generations—man and woman, parent and child, the imperfect circuit of love, the trials of work and money—and the way the world is there, somehow a tender medium, in the dark when we discover we are lost.

A. S.

Contents

Love Scenes	11
Double Fries	77
Traffic School	83
The Genius	87
The Musician	89
Jobs	93
Bicoastal	103
My Literary Life	107
M	197
Hollywood Lessons	201
Grand Street	209
Chloe	215
The Dead	221
The Shape of Jazz to Come	223
The War	229

ARTISTS IN TROUBLE
new stories

Love Scenes

1

AN ACTOR NAMED Wesley Sender was at a Hollywood party, in the kitchen getting a beer, and he could hear another actor, Tony Warrens, in the living room talking about what a star was. Wesley knew he wasn't a star, and neither was Warrens anymore.

What was that Western, tail-end of the sixties, when he was still riding high—every pun intended? Tony always had some kind of crisis being in the saddle, and in a long shot in that picture you see a sheriff riding the range with a languorous Valium habit.

And now he'd been shot down. This was just a little backwater of a party, the Hollywood variety on one of those little streets in the flats where the sky seems to begin about two feet over your head. Hollywood was a company town, a magnetic force-field, everybody's lives slanted toward the money.

Wesley stepped carefully outside the kitchen door—he was wearing a walking cast on his left ankle—into a little alley-driveway with his beer and stood there for a moment in the darkness punctuated by the light from the kitchen window.

He'd been divorced for about a year from his wife of seventeen years, an actress named Annie Ray. He had had an automobile accident months ago; his cast was supposed to come off any day now. His son, Stephen, was going to Taft, a prep school in upstate New York. And there was nobody at his house except a dog he no longer paid any attention to.

In the darkness at the front of the driveway was a woman. Wesley couldn't tell whether she was facing the street or was turned toward him. It was like a little Cracker Jack toy puzzle to occupy his mind while he stood in the windless, temperate evening and listened to the muffled tinkles and voices and laughter from inside.

"Hello," she said, clearly, out of the darkness.

"You know," Wesley said, "from where I am I couldn't tell whether you were turned around to the street. Sorry, I should have said something."

"Oh," she answered without moving out of the darkness, "and I thought we were having a very Tibetan moment together."

It was very musical, the way she said that.

"Tibetan?"

"Nothing–nothing at all."

That was unusual too. People who had religion in L.A. were ready to loan you their secret mantra just to get you started meditating before you could pick up one of your own for $79.95 the next morning. So different from the New York crowd. And then she still hadn't moved. Maybe the voice wasn't an actor's instrument? Maybe it was a person from another business out there? Actresses tended to move quickly out of the darkness or create an immediate bonfire in the area. This person was still being quiet.

Wesley walked toward her. "I guess we had the same idea. You know, when you're an actor sometimes you only talk to other actors, and I think it may not be healthy."

He had come up beside her now and looked to see any response. She was holding a small liqueur glass of something, and he could make out a smile in the dark but didn't look too hard.

"Could be."

"Are you an actor?"

"Oh, no. I'm here from New York doing the costumes for a picture at Warners. I came to the party with Cynthia." Cynthia Roberts, whom he'd said hello to inside, was a voice coach.

"Oh," Wesley said, surprised.

Her name was Janet Heller. Later that night at Joe Allen's he sat opposite her at an outside table and watched and listened to her. She was beautiful and intelligent. When she smiled her face suffused with an inner light. Did she know it and was she having little moments with herself, with her own beauty, as certain actresses did? Her voice, her smile, the light that came into it—Wesley was a man in his middle forties with a back-log of suspiciousness.

Three weeks later, ankle cast off, he was making a Western in Mexico. He had the third or fourth part and there was a good poker game every night but he kept getting distracted. He'd drop out and go back to his trailer and try to remember the exact intonation and tenor of her voice, the smile she had, and the light that came into it. Early one morning he got his son, Stephen, at Taft on the telephone.

"We gonna spend some time in Yosemite during the break, Steve?"

"Dad, I don't want to go camping."

"Okay—well, you name it."

"How 'bout a car?"

"A car? ... Well ..." He considered the perennial question again. Why not? "I guess you can have a car."

"Thanks, Dad. That's what I really want. Thanks. A lot of my friends have them. Really, thanks."

"Sure. We can find you a car. I guess you're getting too old for me now. From here on it's just sex, drugs, and rock 'n roll, right?"

He didn't know what to say about the divorce. He should have said something before now, but he didn't know how to discuss it and was afraid he was going to upset Stephen. He got dressed in the trailer, periodically going back to the memory of the woman he'd seen in Hollywood a few weeks before.

2

"I need to *do* something about this," Wesley thought in his Hollywood hills house, looking up from the *Los Angeles Times* on a sunny morning as he ate a bowl of Kellogg's Common Sense.

Later that morning he called Cynthia Roberts and managed to get Janet Heller's unlisted New York phone number. He told Cynthia he had a scarf of Janet's, discovered in his car just a week ago, and wanted to return it.

"Sure," Cynthia said.

Wesley stood next to the wall phone in the kitchen next to a David Hockney poster of a pool with a big splash in the air above it. "Strictly honorable, Cynthia."

"You're telling me you're in love, right?"

"In love?" He'd lived with the feeling, mined it, pushed it and pulled it, sat with it, acted with it, waited with it, looked out the window with it, showered with it, even polished his shoes with it, but that didn't give Cynthia the right on the basis of one casual phone call–Cynthia whom he'd known for ten years and never talked with for longer than ten minutes – to tell him, just like that, that he was in love. He studied his shoes, the brown antiques he liked to polish, against the white linoleum floor. "Cyn, give me a break."

"Wesley, I didn't mean anything by it, hon. Honest. It's just that Janet's like that. She does that to certain men."

"Does what, exactly?"

A shadow had crossed the room. He looked up through his skylight and saw white instead of blue. He was going to go to Manhattan about a movie soon and it would be a relief to live for a while in the density and ferocity of that city. Hollywood was good in its own way. But it needed to be countered, talked back to, refinanced emotionally, once or twice a year. Otherwise, you turned into a William Morris agent or, like they said, an orange.

"I don't know," Cynthia answered, "ask a guy. She's not *that* good-looking, is she?"

"Janet?"

"No, Cybill Shepherd. I'm sorry, Wes. We shouldn't be having this conversation. I've got to go. I have a lesson arriving in five minutes."

"I love ya, Cyn."

"Tell Janet hi, OK?"

"Will do."

He hung up. So maybe Janet Heller *did* know, and *was* having little moments with herself, knew all about it. But he'd been over this ground before, maybe a hundred times. At a certain point it had come to him that whether Janet was a four star phony or not didn't really matter. He would see right through her–the smile and the light that came into it. He would see right through it all, but then would come back to the other part, which seemed to be a gift of the world, of life, and not to be quibbled with. Then again, on the basis of one evening it was a little hard to tell.

Wesley had lunch at Angeli on Melrose with Tony Warrens, who was suffering the AIDS epoch with uncharacteristic chastity.

"So I told him," Tony said, raising a fork of pasta in the air, "... I said, '*Fuck you!*' " Here he seemed to forget both the pasta on the fork and the preceding narrative and broke into a smile that was both arrogant and bewildered.

In Wesley's scheme of things, Warrens had said "Fuck you" way too loudly so it was now necessary to get Tony into a more secure frame of mind. An actor couldn't handle all the ego necessary to go in for auditions and be rejected by people half his age without occasionally making an arrogant spectacle of himself. Wesley looked down.

"I know what you're thinking..." Tony added.

"I'm thinking you need to lower your voice or we're gonna be in trouble here."

"Oh," he said, and as Wesley looked up he saw him put the fork into his mouth and look wide-eyed at him, as if to say, "Honest, I didn't realize."

Warrens was a natural actor, mostly untrained, who was,

at bottom, in spite of his famous polymorphously perverse sexuality, an innocent. Wesley liked this about him but suspected himself of slumming, a sign of his own battered ego. The problem in Hollywood, as in New York, was that people who considered themselves more intelligent than Warrens, and maybe were in certain ways, tended to be mean pricks.

"Hey, let me ask you something."

"Shoot, Wes."

"Seriously."

"Tell me!" Tony said loudly.

"All right. I met a lady awhile ago at a party and I..."

"No kidding... Who?"

"Her name's Janet Heller."

"Janet... She does costumes..."

"Right, you know her?"

"I did a picture with her. Nice, but not my type."

"What d'you know about her?"

"Nothing... I don't know... She's married, isn't she?"

"Is she? She didn't mention it, and neither did Cynthia Roberts, who's her friend."

"So what's the problem? She's a good-looking woman, a little too old for me."

"So is Drew Barrymore."

Warrens laughed in an exaggerated way that was both falsely hearty and reassuring. He was back at the controls of his personality.

That night, alone in his house with Rocky, his combination Collie and Golden Retriever, Wesley watched the news and then put his channel-changer through its paces, lingering guiltily at the Playboy channel. The latest of the Hefner empire's selections: the fixation with woman as innocent mammary phantasm—the cantaloupe school of beauty. Fabulous babes, fabulous cars, a silk bathrobe, a pipe, and a decently liberal political outlook—because if the ACLU goes, after all, so does Miss November.

But the reason he felt guilty about the voluptuous, homiletic Miss November—"My Mom means more to me than anyone else. She's my role model"—was that he noticed she intercepted the romantic current Janet Heller had given a focus to over the last six weeks of his life. The hazards of soft porn. Wesley switched the TV off and sat in the dark with Rocky.

3

He had a sparsely furnished one-room studio on the fourteenth floor of a high-rise on West 53rd Street, the window of which turned out to be visible, at least in theory, from Janet Heller's floor-through apartment in a brownstone on West 52nd Street.

An almost full moon was rising, and New York seemed a sort of gigantic sound stage. He had brought Janet over an impulse present, spotted earlier that wet chilly December day in the window of Sam Goody's on 48th Street and Sixth Avenue: the reissue of the Ray Charles/Betty Carter album. Janet put it on her stereo and suddenly the apartment was engulfed by the romance of Wesley's first years on his own: the two's classic duet on "Every Time We Say Goodbye."

They had dinner at the Szechwan Corner on Eighth Avenue and then took a taxi to the Village. Janet's about-to-be ex-husband was a television writer. They had a daughter at Vassar.

"So what went wrong?" Wesley asked as they walked down MacDougal Street in their overcoats. There was a single dirty running shoe on the sidewalk.

"Nothing—or rather it would take me about a day to tell you everything."

"Let's go to the Figaro."

"OK."

They found a table on the second level and ordered espressos.

"We were just going in different directions," Janet said.

"I'm not really an L.A. person, and if you live out there you damn well better be. People don't pass through there, like they do in New York. They're there to work. Period."

"I guess so. But this town is pretty heavy for neurotic obsession."

"How?" she asked and looked up from her espresso so Wesley saw her left eye and some freckles. He felt aerial, as though the night, and their lives, were young.

"You can come up if you like," Janet told Wesley at the steps of her brownstone late that night, "but I don't want to ... do ..."

"Neither do I ..." he offered.

"So," she said after a long moment. "would you like to come up?"

"Yes. If you'd like me to."

"It's your decision," Janet Heller said and now looked at Wesley with obvious unease after what he took to be a wonderful, intimate evening.

It seemed that everybody in the world who had passed the age of forty had suffered injury and it was now a question of forming alliances based on damage control and maintenance. He wanted to hold her in his arms, that was all.

"Look, I can see you're nervous about me as a man wanting to get involved or something ..."

"So?" Janet said.

"Look, I'm trying to tell you I'm not thinking like that."

"Why not?"

"I have a different kind of feeling about you. I feel all your sadness, anger, and everything. It makes me sad, maybe because I already am sad. I'm probably still not over my own divorce. I know I'm not. So I didn't immediately jump into thinking about jumping into bed ..."

A car went by in the street. The moon was on the other side of the avenue now, but there was still the thin-edged fineness of a full-moon night.

"I guess I can invite you up," Janet said.

"Great."

She walked up the steps to her entrance and opened the

front door and Wesley followed her in.

An hour later, sitting on the floor of the living room again, Wesley was sleepy. Ray Charles and Betty Carter had been replaced by Haydn's *Piano Sonata* number 33. He was also slightly tipsy now. He had had a little brandy.

"Don't get upset," he said, standing up. "I want to sit down next to you on the sofa."

"That's it?" Janet said smiling.

"That's it–what?"

"That's all you're going to do?"

"Yes. After that, you have to make the next move. I'm falling asleep."

"Do you want to go to bed?"

"With you?" It was nice being tired; one's deeper anxieties became a sort of nocturnal toy-basket from which to pluck and toss.

"I'm not inviting you to make love. I have a big bed." She got up and walked into the front room. "It's in here," she called. "Make yourself at home." Wesley heard her shut a door in the front room.

He went into the room. There were white shutters across the lower half of the windows overlooking the street. She had gone into the bathroom. He walked over and looked out the top of one of the windows. There was still a light or two on in the brownstones across the street. By her bed a clock said it was nearly two. He needed to meet his director, Harold Sterns, tomorrow for lunch. Wesley's service had taken a garbled message but he hadn't gotten hold of Sterns to find out what it was about.

4

Harold Sterns, large and darkly brooding, had a table in the window of Truffles on Madison Avenue and gave Wesley a wave as he got out of the taxi and headed inside. It was one of those odd days–seeming to grow more common by the year–

that have nothing to do with the season. It was sunny and up in the sixties.

"How 'ya been?" Sterns said to Wesley as he sat down on the other side of the little table. "You look happy, for Chrise sake."

"Hi, Harold," Wesley said, sitting down in his chair.

"You happy or what?" Sterns said.

"I don't have to be–whatever mood you want..."

"I'm making an observation," the director told him glumly. "Ever since the thing went down with Annie you've had this cast to your face. I don't know, man–it was like Byzantine. Now, it's like–French, you know, very Truffaut." Sterns laughed gutturally.

"It's probably love." It was involuntary. Wesley wasn't a person who liked to get personal, and neither was Sterns, who now looked up sharply at him as a waiter came and handed them menus.

Sterns disappeared behind his for some time. He was doing the studio rough-and-tumble, Wesley reflected, putting his picture together, and had no time for the finer feelings stirring into being in an actor who was just another piece of his big puzzle.

"Ya see what I mean?" Sterns had lowered his menu and was looking directly at Wesley. "How did I know that? When I said you look happy?"

"An actor's an open book..."

"Well, guess what, kid? Now you're gonna think I'm a fucking genius–"

The waiter came back and they stopped to order.

"How am I going to think you're a genius?" Wesley asked when the waiter left.

"Because I keep thinking I should put you in the lead in this picture," Sterns answered, staring abstractedly into deep space.

"The studio won't buy it." This was old territory.

"That's not the issue right now," Sterns told him, refocusing and exercising his prerogative as director. "We're talking, that's all. You've never been an obvious leading man, we know that. You're too fucking Byzantine, like I said."

"So what's the deal?" Wesley asked, curbing an impulse to laugh. The man wanted him for the lead. It was a beautiful day and New York was going by outside in full regalia.

"Did you read my script?"

"Of course." Wesley was supposed to play the female lead's father. She falls in love with a man his own age whom he eventually confronts outside the man's brownstone and threatens to kill.

"You could do the other guy."

"You asking me?" He has an affair with a woman in his office half his age. It was the big part in the movie, Gold himself.

Sterns nodded and didn't say anything, but continued to eye him like a man in a poker game. Lord, it was time.

"I can play the role. I could give a lot to it." Janet and Wesley hadn't made love, in the end, the night before. Or rather they had made a little love, far short of intercourse, and he had fallen to sleep holding her, which was close to unprecedented in his nocturnal history.

"So," Sterns asked him, smiling, "do the words Jungian synchronicity mean anything to you?"

"Sure, but how come you suddenly..."

"Well, look, I'll be honest with you, I saw a rough cut of Roland's Western the other night and you and that Mexican babe sure raised the temperature. She the one?"

"No... No kidding. I haven't seen it."

When Wesley entered his studio apartment, it was almost dark out and he sat down in the black leather contour chair keeping the lights off. The window, unobstructed by any nearby skyscrapers, gave him a darkening sky that seemed to resonate with the urban tumult below.

Something had happened to him. Just what it was, though, was hard to sort out. As it had ended with Annie, precipitated by the knowledge that she was seeing the director of the film she was doing, Wesley's emotion had come up out of his own dormant depths with painful piquancy. He had woken up one night in the Hollywood house, having heard her voice in his dream pronouncing his name "Wesley" with that combination of delicacy and urgency which had always held him.

He had woken to find she was still gone somewhere–by now he already suspected the whole story–and his heart was suddenly raw with grief. But it had taken the circumstance of Annie betraying him for Wesley to register his love for her, which he otherwise kept buried and expressed only with a routinized sexual impulse. Yet his tenderness that night seemed virtually infinite and centered in the small of her long-waisted back. He loved her deeply, he had learned too late and in the wrong place. Wesley got up from his chair and walked over to the window and looked below to see if he could find Janet's windows, a simpler proposition than yesterday's search for his own from her apartment. He thought he had the ones he wanted, which weren't directly lit but had a faint interior illumination so he couldn't be sure whether she was home or not.

He moved away from the window now and, in the darkness, stretched out full length on his bed. Maybe he could decipher out of the swarm of the day's information some further installment.

What had moved Wesley most about Annie was her willingness–both of them just back in New York from Cambridge, Massachusetts and students of Bill Hickey's downtown–to kiss the whole business goodbye and start over. Make a new world. It had been the sixties, of course, so they had company. But that time had more to it than the psychedelic cartoon show–with the same three or four tired stills from Woodstock–the media was eternally flashing. Their playwrights–Shepard, Lanford Wilson, Horowitz, and the rest–would maybe never measure up to the heights of Albee or Tennessee Williams or O'Neill–but wasn't that because, as they had all known at La Mama in the early days, the play was only half the thing? The other half being to build a new world. And Annie, the daughter of a music professor at Bennington, raised under the most genteel circumstances, was as eager as any of them to put her delicate shoulder to the wheel. Ideally, she was a Shavian heroine, someone who could hit all the high notes in *St. Joan,* but she was ready, willing, and able to crawl out of a beat-up Chevy and wail Sam Shepard...

Wesley woke out of a brief nap and went through the odd moment of the veteran traveler who must re-establish his whereabouts by the red flags of recent memory. Then the telephone rang again.

5

Tony Warrens was at The Gorham, a few blocks uptown and several more east, and coming out of his building, nodding to Sam, the taciturn young night man who was a weight-lifter, Wesley decided to walk. The city at night took on a different character. Each person you passed had a more pronounced singularity, which you in turn seemed to have for each of them, if only because of the threat of violence. Off the main thoroughfares things took on the heightened chiaroscuro of a dream or a Dickens novel. But even on the West Coast things had changed. Just that fall, driving home one midnight from a party in Glendale, he had started to turn down a street in the middle of which he suddenly saw Asian and Mexican figures with baseball bats clubbing each other under the street lights. It was a turn into stark nightmare and he quickly veered off.

At the Gorham, Wesley picked up the house phone in the shiny wood-paneled reception area.

"Tony?"

"Yo, Wes. Come on up. It's 1202."

He took the little elevator up. He knocked at Warren's door and it opened fast, Tony bare-chested and barefoot in a pair of jeans.

"Hey, Dude," Warrens smiled. "Come in."

"Tony..." Wesley smiled and stepped in as Warrens patted him on the back, then rubbed his shoulder.

"How's the boy? I'll be a minute more and we can hit the streets. Jesus, man, Allen Schweitzer?"

"What?"

"I don't know, I guess I should be grateful he hasn't got me and my dick swinging from the chandelier."

"I thought he'd lightened up with the Brat Pack. That last picture was a hit."

"Man, I'm supposed to make out with this guy in one of these elevators in a high rise, gambling that every time it stops we won't be found out."

"In the AIDS era?"

"Tell me about it. I told him up front I wouldn't do any soul kissing. Plus the guy he's got me in there with is this giant Dolf Lundgren clone..."

Wesley gazed out the window at the half-built tower where construction work was in progress even after dark. He turned around as Warrens, now in a blue workshirt, zipped up and sat down on the bed to put on his shoes.

"The guy's an original, I guess," Tony added.

"I guess so."

"So how *you* been—when do you start?"

"Well," Wesley said, walking over to lean against the writing table, "I've got to read again and maybe test now, since Sterns thinks maybe I could play the lead..."

"The lead?" Warrens stopped tying his black Adidas and looked up at him.

Wesley raised his hands in the air as if to say, "Don't ask me." He realized suddenly that Tony was going to find this information a bitter pill.

"What's with that Western you made, man? I heard about it. You do something great or what?"

"I haven't even seen it."

When the two left the Gorham, Warrens began walking at a tremendous pace, as if, Wesley thought, he was trying to get away from his impending stardom.

"Hey, would you slow down or something."

"Oh." Warrens eased up. "Sorry, guy. It's just"—and now he broke into a small voice he sometimes used as an alter-ego, a melt down. "It's just that I'm so eager to see *Gorby*."

Wesley had glimpsed banner headlines all day and occasionally noticed heavily policed intersections, but his own schedule had carried enough momentum that he'd ignored Janet's *New York Times* that morning and not picked up a paper since. It was nice that she wasn't in the business. Warrens would freak; so would anybody else he knew who was an actor. And he didn't even have the part yet.

Fifty-Seventh Street was lined with police; pedestrians had gathered along the sidewalk to witness the passing in a limousine of a man who might change the world, make it a better place. They stood just east of Carnegie Hall, waiting with everyone.

"I *love* Gorby," Warrens said in the small voice. A middle-aged woman turned around and looked at him, her curiosity turning to a glimmer of recognition. Wesley was touched by the turnout. New Yorkers, tough as nails on the outside, had generous hearts. This Russian wanted to stop the Cold War, they'd welcome it and treat him like a hero. After several minutes, there was a ripple in the crowd and suddenly a movement toward the street, the mounted police reinforcing the blue wooden saw-horses from the other direction. A black limousine passed, slowly, and then another. The third had Gorbachev in it, history with a birthmark, smiling at the limo window, with his hand up. The crowd cheered and waved.

Then the Russian leader was gone and they walked east on 57th Street. Wesley would call Janet after dinner. They decided to eat at the Carnegie Delicatessen around the corner. It was getting cold again.

"You know," Warrens told him as they ate pastrami sandwiches, "my mother actually worked here for a while. God, what a broad. No wonder I'm a fuck-up. She tells me my father—did I tell you this?"

Wesley swallowed. "I don't think so."

"She tells me my father was some kind of French journalist. Warrens is *her* name, you know, coal-black Irish. This guy's name is Edward Boubat, very chi-chi. They had this big affair. I see trenchcoats and love notes. Written with *fountain* pens, you dig. This is World War Two."

Wesley set down his sandwich and sipped a glass of tea.

"...And then he went off to the war and got offed under circumstances I could never quite figure—he was supposed to be a journalist, not a soldier. But he got some kind of illness, and he was gone. I didn't tell you this?"

"I don't think so."

"So I'm making *Strange Adults* last year here and I get a call at the Gorham. And this guy with a heavy old-country accent says, 'Anthony?' I go, 'Yeah.' He says, 'This is your father.'"

"You're kidding?"

"The guy's a goddamn Greek—his name is Kostakis. Tommy Kostakis. And he's got like a shish-kebab place, like a take-out, lunch-counter place in Queens. I always wondered where I got this beard, you know. I need to shave twice a day and my Dad's this French aristocrat? Think again. My mother and him had just run into each other again for the first time in decades and she tells him, 'Oh, by the way, we have a son. You've even seen him in the movies.' "

"It must have been a shock—for you, I mean."

"Oh, and then dig this: I take him and my Mom out to dinner at the Deux Magots. A little showing off for the old man. Frankly, I don't think the sucker had seen an offset menu in his life. And would you believe it, my mother starts juicing, and they're both getting hot and bothered right in front of me. So later I say to her: 'Mom, I mean I'm not mad or anything, but why did you lie to me?' And she tells me: 'Anthony, I wanted you to be proud of your heritage.' "

6

Janet held an arm straight up and Wesley's hand went up its length, slowly, and took her hand, which was warm and light, and then let go and rode slowly back down her arm again.

She loved to kiss and do quick or slow things inside the kiss. She had an erotic identity that was playful, mischievous, and he would get caught up in her and then discover some mission of his own.

"You feel so light," Wesley told her in the room's semi-darkness.

"You're like this dark forest I get to dive into," Janet said.

She and he would kiss and not kiss and kiss again and not move at all. Then they would roll over and not move and kiss again.

A car went by outside. Wesley rearranged himself.

"I don't want to just do it now," she said.

"Fine."

"Tell me about your day," she said.

"It looks like Harold Sterns is giving me the lead in *Gold*..."

"Oh, no."

"Why?"

"You'll go berserk and our little romance will end."

"I'm counting on you."

"Don't. I don't want to be counted on."

Wesley turned all the way on his side to face Janet. "You're as bad as me."

"I should be worse. I'm a woman. You're an actor. You're already a narcissist. If you become a movie star..."

"And you're not a narcissist? I've heard about you, the little gangster of love."

It was silent for a moment outside.

"Ask me about *my* day," Janet said.

"How was your day?"

"Well, I went to the Metropolitan to sort of shore myself up after our date because you're such a big bundle of vibes. I go to the Met with my notebook..." There was the noise of a truck downshifting on the West Side Highway. "I've got this sort of futuristic thing coming up for Fox but the Renaissance is just this great index of ideas."

"We definitely get to make love after this."

"Don't interrupt. Then I go to lunch in the cafeteria, which is fun and the food's pretty good actually. And I'm on the balcony next to this table of women, who are–I don't know–mid-sixties."

Wesley rested his head on one hand supported by his elbow. He looked at Janet in the room's dimness. She caught his eye and turned back to the ceiling.

"And I can't help hearing what they're saying. They're talking about the soup. 'This is spicy.' 'Umm-*hmm*, it's got a tang to it.' '*I'll* say. It's *hot*.' Then another woman joins the table and takes a spoonful of hers and says, 'Oh, that's got a *bite* to it, doesn't it?' "

He laughed and brushed a strand of hair from Janet's face and let his hand linger for a moment at her cheek.

"I mean the most inane, sort of brain-dead moron talk, and it just went on and on–soups in foreign countries..."

"Well, they're old ladies, right? Rich old ladies."

"Then it came to me. Stop interrupting. I suddenly realized these ladies were all my age *now* back in the sixties, which was like yesterday, and I'd better get very busy..."

"You *have* a career. And I'm not about to crush your identity, by the way, if that's what you're suggesting. Then again, you do have that sort of bruised fruit look..."

"What?"

"Like some of the sugar has spilt but there's more. I've noticed it among red-heads. It's very erotic."

"Jesus." Janet turned on her side away from Wesley.

7

Isabel Hawkins, the young actress Harold Sterns had in mind for the lead in *Gold*, was from California, and the director had asked her to fly to New York to read with Wesley. His agent had left a message with his service. Wesley heard it late that morning sitting at Janet's breakfast counter by the kitchenette between the bedroom and the living room. He had a day to kill now. He put the phone down and went back to his coffee, glimpsing Janet's naked back as she meditated in the lotus position on her bed in the front room.

"Confucius say, 'Woman never meditate naked with guy around in morning. Plant seed of spiritual havoc.' "

Janet didn't answer and he went on reading the *New York Times* report of the Armenian earthquake. His father, Walter Senderian, was half-Armenian, and Wesley had grown up with a vague sense of the history of that beleaguered, ancient people. This earthquake had cut short Gorbachev's New York visit and seemed to be a catastrophe on a biblical scale. People swallowed by the earth? A whole town swallowed? Wesley's father had an uncle named Krikor, the only Armenian he remembered personally, a man who liked to play backgammon and tell loud stories in Armenian. His mother had disliked him and by the time Wesley was a teenager he was no longer a visitor in their Park Avenue apartment. Although he'd scarcely exchanged a word with him, Wesley had felt something sad and displaced in the man, who always greeted him with a curious, smiling, eager gaze–as if to say, "Hello, hello, what is it *you* see when you look at me?"

Janet came into the room wearing a dark blue robe. She poured herself a cup of tea.

"So, tell me more about the accident," she said, taking a stool beside Wesley at the counter.

"That comes later. With a house in the suburbs, a dog, two and a third children."

"Why are you talking like that?"

"I'm probably nervous. They just gave me a free day."

"Oh. Well, I've got an appointment at Fox. Do you want to meet later? It's cold again."

"I guess so. I don't want to study," Wesley said.

8

One of his New York stops when he was in town was an acting class run by an old friend, Red Harris, who had been used in a lot of crime pictures, for the movies and television, and now occasionally popped up in a horror movie, always as the neat and clean, straight-arrow side-kick to the good guy. As Red got older, Wesley thought, his performances were more interesting for what was now constitutionally askew in him. His head seemed too large and, with his close-cropped thinning hair, naked as a prize-fighter's; his shoulders were big but hunched, and he always made his moves a split-second too fast, which seemed to betray some deep-seated insecurity. As a young man he would have been the perfect Gregor Samsa in Kafka's "Metamorphosis," a bureaucrat with some erratic, ecstatic strain just below the neat-necktied surface. But the business was the business and he had done his turns instead as the partner of Steve McQueen, Clint Eastwood, Sinatra, and the rest, and somewhere along the line discovered teaching. He loved and gloated over each of his students. The nurturing side of men that was supposed to kick in after forty had appeared like a Samurai in Red.

Wesley liked to sit in on his class and sometimes took an impromptu exercise assignment. His studio was on Lexington Avenue between 57th and 58th Streets, a second floor walk-up one-room apartment, and he'd designed the day around a stop here. Wesley sat now in a green upholstered chair near the front door and watched two actors, a man and a woman, both in their early twenties, do a scene inspired by Mickey Rourke and Kim Basinger in *9½ Weeks*. The young man was Puerto Rican, the young woman black, and they were each giving it everything they had. Wesley admired the young man's composure, giving the young woman, blind-folded, a sip of a drink; letting her, now lying on a red rug in her slip, feel a drop or two of the drink on her neck, and all of this while Red, Wesley, and half a dozen students a few feet away looked on intently in their chairs. Going for their edge was what they both were about, and would need to be about—to survive. But that edge could cut both ways. Push it too hard and you ended up—say, having a car crash.

There must be a way—was the young man there, or Wesley himself in his career, finding it?—to relax and at the same time be alert to all the nuances possible in a performance. It was, a lot of it, in the timing, in not doing a thing too quickly, letting the action or the lines play just long enough to make the moment open and come alive, and making those moments happen one after another, stringing them together so that they *were* the performance. It took craft, yes, but it was rooted in something else, an animal self-possession you could see in the young man. The young woman, on the other hand, beautiful as she was, was less certain of herself, at moments retreating inside the current they were passing between them.

At Trinity School as a junior Wesley had had a small role in *You Can't Take It With You*: A house servant with an air of innocent insouciance. There were a couple of high-powered Moss Hart/George S. Kaufman set-ups where he got the payoff in laughter. Opening night, he had walked out onto the in-the-round stage and a couple of his classmates in the first row had snickered in recognition. For a split second Wesley might have given everything away. But in that same instant there was something deeper and stronger that kept him inside his performance, what he would later learn to call concentration. A half-minute more and his classmates were laughing at his lines.

In effect, a strong instinct he hadn't known he'd had came to the fore that night. In the climactic scene of his performance, Wesley came upon the young lovers home from a movie and the lines built to a crescendo of hilarity of which he was the radiating center. By now his classmates and the rest of the audience, which happened to include Moss Hart himself that night, were, he knew, in his pocket. At the same time, his instinct kept him inside each moment, one at a time, until now, when, at the center of the laughter, Wesley could feel the audience as a whole identity waiting for him, in fact *wanting* him, to crack up himself, to admit he was loving getting the laughs, and let the high school play be the high school play.

He was a mediocre student, never one of the truly favored among his classmates, and now a moment was unfolding that seemed, in retrospect, to have contained the very muscle of his life's destiny. The audience wanted him to laugh. Wesley sensed he was slightly frightening to them now with his concentration. They weren't expecting professionalism but only a good time. He could feel in the rise of their laughter beyond its previous peak a good-natured dare, the all-but-articulated threat of engulfing him, bringing him down. They would love him for breaking up, too, he knew. But something in him clung to the power so suddenly vested in him and wouldn't surrender it matter-of-factly.

It was his own muscle, then, that he was discovering in that moment. And then, abruptly, something broke–on the other side of his performance, in the audience. It wasn't mere hilarity anymore, it was pandemonium. In effect, Wesley had waited them out, convinced them, and they rewarded him with a moment that seemed to engrave an identity into his restless, wandering sixteen-year-old self. When he exited, there was prolonged applause.

Afterwards backstage Moss Hart, whose son was in the lower school at Trinity, singled him out: "Your timing was so good," he told Wesley, "that I know you're lost to the theater now forever." Even at the time it was hard to miss a rueful note in the way Hart phrased it.

Wesley watched another exercise, a scene from Tennessee Williams's *This Property Is Condemned*, heard Red's and the class's second commentary, and then whispered to Red that he was going.

"OK," his friend whispered as the actors were getting up for the next scene. "Call me. Let's talk."

"Great," Wesley said, with a hand on Red's shoulder. "Good teacher. Good class."

"Thanks, buddy. Don't be a stranger."

Wesley walked up Madison Avenue in the afternoon cold. He was going to meet Janet at five at the Whitney and that gave him another hour, but he'd wanted to let go of the sharp focus of Red's class. He would be meeting Isabel Hawkins and reading with her tomorrow and he needed to rest and recharge his battery, not necessarily the same process, simultaneously. People watching now replaced scene watching; maybe it was a matter of keeping proportions, of switching channels. A young woman in a red overcoat gave him a smile that might have meant many things but, Wesley knew, meant only that she had seen him in a movie. He smiled back at her.

After his performance in the Trinity school play, he knew he was an actor. The school itself assented. He was noticed and talked to by boys who had never noticed or spoken with him before. William Claxton, as a junior already the editor of the *Trinity Times* and the intellectual terror of the upper school, had even told him the girl he was just then breaking up with—and Claxton's sexual precocity was legendary—had seen the play and thought Wesley was sexy. In the flush of his newfound success, he boldly ventured to call the girl, Genevieve Rolland, whom he had seen with Claxton several times in Hamburger Heaven after school, and invite her out to the theater, his future, as it were.

His father was seldom at home now, working late into the night setting up real-estate deals in a development in New Jersey; and his mother, still beautiful in her late thirties, was heavily into the pill-taking that rendered her a seductive X-factor in Wesley's adolescence as the marriage went bad. When he'd announced he was taking a girl to the theater she'd given him one of the exaggerated looks he found embarrassing, as though he were on the verge of some epochal venture, and, rushing up to him in an all but transparent white silk nightdress, slipped a crisp fifty-dollar bill into his hand at the door.

"Thanks, Mom," Wesley said, bewildered. Maybe after the play he was to supposed spend the night with Genevieve at The Plaza?

He took her to the Living Theater's production of *The Connection*, which he had seen before. It was a play Wesley felt comfortable making his intellectual and spiritual calling card. Junkies and jazz musicians waiting for their heroin connection in a pad somewhere in Harlem. It was the late fifties and these were the people the artistically inclined prep school boy wanted to be recognized in the midst of. In fact the actors and musicians, each still in his persona in the play, mingled with the audience in the lobby during intermission.

Wesley and Genevieve didn't know each other. Claxton, a sort of self-styled sixteen-year-old combination of Albert Camus and Mickey Spillane, had explained wearily that he and Genevieve had eventually just "grown tired of each other's bodies." Standing in the lobby during intermission with this dishy French girl, Wesley found it hard to make conversation. Not only was he a virgin, he had never kissed a girl. Genevieve was as tall as he, striking and statuesque, with a MacDougal Street address and a twinkle of knowing in her eye that had him so intimidated he was tongue-tied.

Afterwards they walked from the Living Theater west to the docks on the Hudson River, and Genevieve, evidently expecting a sexual denouement, dared to put her head in Wesley's lap as they sat side by side on a piling by the water's edge in the darkness. He had begun the evening at A, and as the evening was advancing to its conclusion, without any intermediate stops along the alphabet, had come abruptly to Z. This girl was ready for midnight abandon, she wanted sexual high-flying, right then and there, and might even have mistaken the unusual, expensive character of the first date for a different sort of investment than it signified.

Wesley was trying to find out whether his nascent personality would fly with the Claxton/Rolland crowd and the theater tickets were invested not really in a romantic impulse, but in a stop-gap, last-minute panic effort at self-definition he hoped might give him the boost he needed to get through the night. It was absurd; *he* was absurd, with this knowing French girl's head on his lap, directly over his shriveled-in-terror member. It was not going to be possible for him to make love with this young woman, A) Because he knew nothing about how to do it, and B) Because he was a strange *tabula rasa* sort of person, one with virtually no self-knowledge and no personality.

Wesley passed the Whitney–there was still another half-hour before he would be meeting Janet–and kept on his course up Madison. Hamburger Heaven was long gone at the corner of 79th Street. There were women's clothes on mannikins now where once his heart would catch in his throat on spying one or another Upper East Side schoolgirl at a table through the picture window.

Genevieve raised her head from his lap after a few more minutes and he walked her home to MacDougal Street where she lived with her mother. They parted civilly, without even a kiss. Sorry. Wrong Number. Then he walked all the way uptown to his parents' apartment building on 81st Street and Park Avenue, mortified by life, by not being ready for it, by going too far into what he had no working knowledge of, by overmatching himself his first time out, by being completely out of his league. It was, Wesley realized now, going by the empty P.S. 6 playground, just that instinct for over-shooting his mark that would prove both difficult and useful to him as an actor.

9

As five o'clock approached, Madison Avenue was suffused with twilight, and Wesley's thoughts went back to Janet, to the night before, when he and she seemed to change places, melting into and out of each other, the way the sunlight touched the side of a building or an overcoat or a face and gave each the moment's translucent unity.

Janet was a woman he was just getting to know, with a history, including a marriage, he knew only in vague outline. He was someone she knew in more or less the same way. And yet something else had intervened, as if his coming across her in the little alley driveway at the Hollywood party that fall had inaugurated some kind of powerful magnetic field which Wesley had done his best to steady himself inside. Then he'd come to New York and seen her again and now they were letting it play through them.

Janet seemed to know more about it than he did. Or was that only the power of rumor? He caught her eye as she stood beside the front pillar at the Whitney. She was dressed up for the cold like anyone else.

"There's something you should see," Janet said, smiling at him.

"What's that?" Wesley said and bent down to kiss her. Her lips were cold and a little wet, and she gave him a little bite.

"Eric Fischl."

"Let's go home. We can see this later."

"Don't be silly. I want to share my mind too, you know. And you've got to share yours."

"I'm an actor," he said. "I don't have a mind."

"Well, if that's what acting's about we've got to let all the Buddhists know right away."

She started walking to the glass doors. He caught up with her and they went inside, bought tickets and checked their coats, and went up to the third floor.

Wesley remembered seeing a big Franz Kline abstract black-and-white painting one Saturday afternoon with his mother and sister years ago at the Museum of Modern Art. It gave him the feeling that the artist had gone out of his way to create something awkward and ugly, something that made you cringe inwardly when you looked at it, and paradoxically this had made Kline fascinating to him.

Eric Fischl's paintings reminded him of Kline. A pubescent boy jerking off in a plastic swimming pool in the backyard? It was ugly, yes—but now Wesley was forty-five instead of thirteen, and fresh from Los Angeles, so he looked at each painting, suspending judgment. An attractive woman sitting outdoors naked holding a mirror in front of her face. It was called "Vanity."

Suddenly he felt Janet's hand take his arm. "So," she said, "what do you think?"

"Interesting."

They were confronted with a painting of a room with a sweeping view of Manhattan at night, a room with a large bed upon which lolled a voluptuous naked woman and nearby on the bed a not yet fully grown boy. The title was "Birthday Boy."

They went through each room and viewed each painting, sometimes quickly, sometimes lingering over one. Wesley felt again more than once the visceral revulsion he'd known with Kline, but then there was some loose strand of tenderness waving through each vision.

In the street again, he was no longer clear on his destination. Janet took his arm and they walked downtown. It was dark now.

"He's amazingly vulnerable, isn't he?"

"He's the only one I really like–of the new people," she said.

"Are they all sort of like this?"

"Not really. Superficially, maybe. But this is somebody with a whole body, not just their mind or their hand or arm."

"So you're in love with Eric Fischl?"

"With what he does, un-hunh."

"What does he look like?"

"He looks healthy, I guess. Sort of full-bodied, but buoyant."

"I feel kind of wounded and lit up."

"That's what the Metropolitan does for me too. Art is good for you."

"Yeah, Brando used to do that to me. De Niro does it sometimes."

"Meryl Streep?"

They were standing at 72nd Street waiting for the light to change.

"Meryl Streep reminds me of you, especially when she turns herself into pure light."

"Thank you. Let's go into Ralph Lauren. I think it's still open."

Wesley hated shopping but being with Janet after seeing the Fischl show made it easy enough to wander through several floors of clothes and housewares.

"It's the English Country Cottage look," Janet told him.

"We could go to the English countryside if I didn't have a job."

"I've got a job too," she answered.

In the street again, Janet took Wesley's arm. "Have you had a lot of affairs?"

"No."

They were walking downtown again, the streets still full of people going home from work.

"I didn't think so."

"How come?"

"You just seem sort of skittish, I guess."

"I love feeling this way," Wesley said, looking at the oncoming lights of the traffic, "but I don't exactly know where it leads."

"Men always want to know where it leads. You should just enjoy what you feel."

"OK."

"Were you ever in love?" Janet asked.

"I guess. I can't really remember. What about you?"

"None of your business."

"Your ex-husband... So what's he like?"

"I told you, he writes for television. Constantly. He's made a lot of money and everybody adores him."

"Except you."

"He doesn't really have time for me–or himself."

"Yeah, I know all about it. I was with ICM for five years. They ride herd over talent. It's how they make a living."

"Well, why do you *let* them?"

"Because they buy you lunch and answer your phone calls and most of us desperately need the ego boost."

"But they literally eat people alive and then flush them down the toilet."

"Remember when Richard Pryor came out naked, just wearing a body stocking, on his first special and sang 'There's No Business Like Show Business'?"

"I missed that."

"It sort of summed it up."

"Well, you're the new movie star. Don't say we didn't warn you."

"Listen, it's not like that. I've already stood for years on different rungs of the ladder looking up, looking down, looking all around the town. I'm making a living and I'm not that way."

"What way?"

"I'm an actor; I'm into acting. It's much bigger than ICM. Ask De Niro. He's the one who sort of made it clear."

"Is it fun?"

"When you get into it it's the second best thing in the world and actually it's the same thing as the first best thing."

They turned west on 57th Street. "Yes?" Janet said.

"I don't like to think about it too much. I just have the job staked out, like now I say 'Good morning, sweetheart,' or whatever, you know."

Janet was looking in the window of Laura Ashley. Wesley stopped talking as she looked, and then they continued walking.

"Go on," she said.

"Well, it's all staked out, I know it by rote, so all I'm doing is keeping these appointments, moment to moment, and then something kind of kicks in—with me being sort of inside out; with another actor also being that way; in a play, with the audience, which is like another person there too. You get everything down pat so you can get lost."

"Like trust."

"Trust..."

"I mean in a relationship."

"Oh, right," Wesley said. "Let's go by Doubleday's."

"Sure."

"So you and your husband didn't trust each other?"

Janet held his arm as they crossed Fifth Avenue. "We had

some great times together but, well, I just really loathe that sort of speed-demon television scene."

"I guess it's his job."

"Oh, sure. That's his job. But–"

"It wasn't great for you ..."

"He made all this money, you know, but it was hard to figure out what was supposed to be happening. Once Rain got to be a teenager, I had to start working or go crazy with her."

"My son is sixteen."

"Where is he again?"

"At Taft prep school upstate. He'll be here soon for part of his Christmas break."

They had come to Doubleday's and went through a moment of not knowing whether or not they'd go in, looking at the book display in the window, and then continued to walk downtown.

"You didn't trust him then?"

"It got to be so there was no 'him' there anymore."

"You feel sorry for him?"

"No, not really. I guess they have geniuses who know how to do it, but it's a lot of locker room crap, everybody's super macho and at a certain point that means they fuck each other over. And if you're the wife, forget it. They really haven't heard of you."

"It's funny. I've had this thing floating around in my mind for years. I don't know where I picked it up, maybe on an acid trip twenty years ago with Annie and this other couple ..."

"What?"

"Well, I got this sudden clarity at some point that the way you relate to men is also the way you relate to women. I don't know if it's true or not, but I got this idea that, you know, if you have this competitive, fucked-up thing going with one sex, your own or the opposite sex, underneath everything, however different it may look, it's going to follow suit in your relationship with the other sex."

"I don't know," Janet said.

"Me either." Wesley stopped at the corner of 53rd Street and Fifth Avenue. "It was one of those blinding flashes from the sixties. I don't have them anymore."

10

Isabel Hawkins turned out to be a dark-haired twenty-year-old woman, quite small, with pale luminous skin and wonderful eyes. She had star quality falling off her in every simple movement. Wesley sat beside her on the sofa in the eighteenth-floor office at the Twentieth Century–Fox building on 57th Street where Harold Sterns set up the meeting. Along with Sterns was a Fox vice-president in packaging named Laura Truitt, a tall woman whose every eye-lash was picture perfect and who radiated chic and poise and knowing sympathy for everyone.

Sterns was standing in the middle of the room. Truitt was on the phone behind her desk.

"How do you like New York?" Wesley asked Isabel.

"I don't know," she answered, looking straight ahead. "I've looked out the window and gotten into a cab. It looks fun, I guess."

"Where are you staying?"

"At the Pierre. How 'bout you?" She turned to him.

"I have an apartment. You're from California, right?"

She nodded. "Death Valley."

"Death Valley? Really?"

She smiled back mildly and let her gaze return to the room at large. "It sounds funny, I know. It just happens to be where I come from."

"I'm sorry. I've never been there, actually."

He had caught some turn at that moment, a little corner of fright in her, so young, so far from home, about to be the biggest thing that had ever happened in the history of her family and, who knows, maybe the whole wide world. A young Cleopatra, a nascent Helen of Troy. They wouldn't fight a war over her this time; they'd use her power at the box office. She was still inside a man's world. He could see how the Trojan war could take place–someone very similar to other women but this time everything had set so flawlessly that the parts added up to a seamlessly luminous, fluent being, the same size as the others, only perfect.

Truitt hung up the phone. "Dan's coming," she said to Sterns, who nodded.

"OK, kids," Sterns addressed Wesley and Isabel on the sofa. "The studio producer's gonna be here with the casting director to get a sense of how some of the smaller parts could be cast to go with you. So we're going to read a little, okay?"

"Fine," Wesley said, and then looked through the window behind Truitt's desk at the building across 57th Street half in sunlight.

"You okay, baby?" Sterns addressed Isabel.

"Sure," she said.

"Whataya need, babe, a Coke?"

"Some water, maybe?"

"Wes?"

"Water. Great."

Truitt picked up the phone and talked to somebody about it and then a thirtyish man and an older woman, the producer and the casting director, came into the office and there were introductions. Sterns called Wesley and Isabel into the center of the room and laid out two chairs. The water arrived, a pitcher and glasses, and Wesley and Isabel, holding a glass each, discussed the scene with Sterns. Gold walks into her office at the end of the day.

Then they started, with Isabel in a chair.

"Every beautiful woman has a secret, right?"

She turns around to him, her boss, and blushes. She's been watching him since she took the job.

"Oh, Mr. Gold..."

He smiles at her. "Sorry. I didn't mean to startle you. Everybody's gone home. Can I offer you a lift anywhere?"

"No, thanks. I'm just finishing up."

"I've been wanting to say hi, and to thank you for that presentation..."

She looks gratified. "Thank you."

"It was wonderful. And, well, you know you're young and smart and beautiful and everybody around here has fallen in love with you, and so I've wondered what—you're all about… Boyfriend picking you up?"

She is staring at him now. He puts up his hands. "OK, back off, right? Sexual harassment?" He moves away. "No offense intended. I'm outta here. One thing, though—I could have sworn you've been giving *me*…" He stops himself, shakes his head. "No problem…" He's on his way out of the office.

"Mr. Gold."

He turns back to her. She stands up and walks over to him. The girl had a perfect pitch of frailty and swagger. Slowly she reaches up and touches his neck and pulls him into a kiss.

Wesley could feel Isabel trembling as he put his arms around her and kissed her lightly in the middle of the midtown office.

The summer after the disaster of his date with Genevieve Rolland, Wesley got to know an Irish Italian girl named Linda Di Maria who lived in a brownstone on East 82nd Street opposite the apartment where his best friend at Trinity, Rick Jarrells, lived with his parents.

Rick was an only child, a tall boy who towered over both his parents, social workers who had found their rent-controlled apartment a decade or more earlier, and gotten their son a scholarship to Trinity. Rick's IQ was supposed to be very high. Wesley had dinner with the Jarrells once or twice and was bewildered one night when he said something at the dinner table and caught a slight undercurrent in the way he was regarded by both Rick's parents. In another instant he realized he was stealing time between them and their tall, wondrous son.

Rick was a sort of spoiled boy-genius. He was sweet-natured, not at all stingy or mean-spirited but too bubblingly garrulous. Very early on, he took to drinking quarts of Ballantine Ale, and liked to throw instant parties whenever his parents took off for their beach bungalow on the Jersey shore.

Diana Di Maria lived across the street, and Rick was in love with her. She was a tall, taciturn, effortlessly stately sixteen-year-old who lived in an apartment with her mother, a frazzled newspaper-woman who wore a permanently amused expression and whose stockings always seemed to have run. She wrote a weekly column of fashion tips for *The Daily News*. Like any goddess, maybe, Diana took her beauty for granted, and she felt no need to cultivate female wiles. She and Wesley got acquainted through Rick and then she indicated she favored him over Rick.

At Coney Island one night, in the darkness on the sand beside the Boardwalk, she rolled over on top of Wesley. This time his member went into its traditional response sequence. He was delighted. Rick, beside them in the sand, cackled hysterically. Something was up for him too. Or down.

They were a strange threesome, a teenage Manhattan version of *Jules and Jim* that summer, if you didn't look too hard. Wesley had so little sense of himself that he virtually tagged along after his hardons with Diana.

Once she confided to him about Rick: "He's one of those people I have trouble listening to, do you know what I mean?" He understood, which made it poignant when every so often he would tune in and discover Rick going on rather wittily about something or other. He was a person who liked to use archaisms like "forsooth" and comic book words like "pshaw."

As the summer wore on, Wesley and Diana inevitably began to meet more by themselves, and these times, with no court jester in tow, gave them a graver sense of their own individual identities. They weren't a good match. They walked into a party together one night on the upper East Side and Wesley, mostly for something to do, tried to join a circle of people and was pushed casually out of the circle by the arm of a Trinity graduate. He wasn't certain what had happened and approached and joined the circle a second time. The boy repeated the gesture, more boldly and firmly pushing Wesley outside the circle's parameter.

He was bigger than Wesley but not that much bigger. Wesley wanted to destroy the boy, to pulverize his face. But his identity ran thin; he had some illness of the personality, rendering him a tattered, fractured self. They left the party soon after, Diana not having noticed Wesley's humiliation.

One night in Greenwich Village she started crying as they waited for a bus back to the Upper East Side. The tears just began, provoked by nothing Wesley could identify, and he couldn't do anything to stop them.

A little later that summer, they made the clinical decision to go through with intercourse. Up to now, they had only made out, sometimes he had gotten her top off, but he hadn't pressed very hard to go further.

Diana was beautiful, with cool, alabaster skin, but there was no pull between them. She had no self-esteem, which seemed to be the currency of sexual magnetism, and Wesley had none either. The day they were going to do it—in her apartment, her mother at work at *The Daily News*—she stopped him, left the room and came back with a wrapped condom. Wesley had never seen one before. In the process of trying to put it on, he lost his erection and couldn't get it back.

He was, Wesley reflected with absurd finality, impotent. He was sixteen years old and his life was ruined. That afternoon he walked home through the streets in a gentle summer rain that smelled of stale city steam from beneath the manhole covers. Welcome to Hell.

Janet lay in bed with her hand on Wesley's chest. "What does it mean again? If I love you?"

"That's it?"

"Yes."

"It means we're in love. You're supposed to know these things."

"I guess so," Janet said.

"I realize love is very young," Wesley said. Outside a car moved through the wet snow. "I'm a lot younger than forty-five."

"I'm younger than you are."

For a while they were quiet.

"When this stops, I'm going to be very disappointed."

"You're so sensitive," Janet said, looking at him.

"Your interior color is deep blue."

She kissed him.

"I know I can do a good job because I haven't smoked marijuana in years."

"Why?" Janet asked.

"Because no one on marijuana actually falls in love."

"Have you noticed our conversations seem not to work properly?"

"Our dialogue is on love," Wesley said, looking at the white shutters in the room's dimness.

Being in Hell in New York City at sixteen was like living in slow motion. Time stretched. He watched with disembodied eyes, seeing everything that went on, minute nuances of behavior that spelled out big and little revelations about everybody. Wesley studied the absent-minded sensuality of waitresses. He fell distantly in love with all sorts of young sirens of the Upper East Side, grieving at his luck of having ruined his life before it began. He observed *endlessly,* having been called out of the race to sit on the sidelines of adolescence. He had died this huge death at the threshold of real life and didn't have any idea how he was supposed to spend the rest of his days.

There was a movie theater on 86th Street between Lexington and Third Avenues called The Grande, a repertory house that showed anything that was at least a year old. After the disaster that summer Wesley became a regular, sometimes going in for the first show at noon on weekdays: The red upholstery and baroque decor in the half-light and only two other customers: a thirtyish woman wearing a red scarf on her head in the dead center of the orchestra, and another teenager, in a black leather jacket, up close. He took an aisle seat about three-quarters of the way back and the lights went down, and the three of them watched *From Here to Eternity.* Wesley saw that Montgomery Clift had the same thing inside him he was walking around with in New York, some kind of gap between him and all the real goods of life, a short-circuit.

One afternoon at The Grande he watched *On the Waterfront* and saw Brando at the pool table with Lee J. Cobb, the big overlord of the waterfront, the crooked boss, and his underlings. Cobb was looking out for him, taking a special interest in the young boxer, and Brando gave him a look that said thanks, Johnny, and at the same time registered his uneasiness at being made an exception–and for the first time Wesley saw *acting*: With one look Brando had said two things at the same time.

11

In a dream Wesley saw a mountain–its one hump by the side of the road. A very simple place he might live in a simple cabin. His mother and father had parked and now he couldn't find them. He woke up in the middle of the night with a strange contentment thinking of the mountain. There were things in the world that could make you feel complete just by looking at them if you were a certain kind of man.

"Are you awake?" Janet said beside him.

After getting his mind over to her from the half-dream, Wesley answered, "Yes."

"I feel very uncertain and happy."

"What are you uncertain about?"

"Guess."

Wesley and Janet decided to pick up Rain, who had come home for Christmas vacation, at La Guardia. She turned out to be blond, taller than her mother, with an athletic bounce to her walk. As Wesley–at the wheel of Janet's maroon Astin Martin–drove them home, Rain told them she'd been " 'shrooming."

" 'Shrooming?" he asked, turning to Rain beside him, Janet having elected to sit in the back seat.

"You know, mushrooms. You all must have taken them during the sixties."

"Oh," Wesley said.

"*I* never did," Janet said.

"Well, didn't Dad?" Rain said, turning around to her mother.

"I don't know. You'll have to ask him."

"Mom," Rain turned all the way around to Janet. "Don't do that, all right? Okay? I mean, *Can-You-Deal*?"

"I once tried psilocybin," Wesley said.

They had gone through the Queens midtown tunnel and come into a nighttime Manhattan. Suddenly the night seemed full of possibilities. "Anywhere I can take you?" Wesley took a right on Fifth Avenue. They could see the giant crystal snowflake above 57th Street. Then they could head over to Madison. "Maybe the Carlyle? Want to hear some jazz?"

"Wait a minute. None of us are dressed," Janet said, her head suddenly at Wesley's ear.

"Well–there's the Brasserie, I guess–"

"What about The Plaza? ... Oh, it's so pretty," Rain said as they approached the big white crystal *objet d'art* suspended over the avenue.

"Oh, it *is*," Janet said. "All right. Wait a minute, the Tea Room at the Plaza's closed, isn't it?–but, wait a minute ..."

And then, simultaneously, Janet and Rain said: "Rumpelmayers!!"

"OK," Wesley said. "It's heart-attack city, but that's fine."

"You can have my water," Rain told him. "I want to hear all about philocybin."

"Psilocybin."

"Whatever," she said, and then, looking back at her mother, "Hey, that's great, you guys. No, really. This is nice."

It was during the summer of 1965 in Woodstock, New York, where he worked in the summer theater, that Wesley belatedly said goodbye to his virginity one night with a fellow internist named Trudy Winslow. Trudy was pretty and adventurous, a member of the avant-garde out of East Orange, New Jersey, and Wesley's future was glorious and assured in her eyes. They played Nick and Honey in *Who's Afraid of Virginia Woolf?* and the parts had led into an off-stage companionship.

That changed one evening in August when his roommate Chris Chasen, who later got very rich in four seasons on NBC as a computer criminologist named Rutgers, announced that sugar cubes of LSD were being sold by a girl at the Espresso Coffee House for five dollars a cube.

Nobody knew what was going to happen, but the writing on the wall might have been clear enough. For five dollars, the invitation was extended to experience approximately eight hours of a state of consciousness alternately described as ecstatic and as the equivalent of Buddhist enlightenment.

It turned out Wesley and Trudy weren't particularly compatible twenty or thirty minutes after ingesting their blue-stained sugar cubes. Wesley would rather have looked at Kim, Chris's blond girlfriend of the moment, a Woodstock townie who sat wrapped in a poncho on their living room sofa and seemed to be purring.

"Harold says he's going to shoot all the interiors first on the coast. Will you come with me?"

Wesley and Janet were lying on Wesley's bed in the middle of the night. He had been told that day that he had the part in *Gold.*

"What's the point? How long will you be gone?"

"Weeks. I want you to see the house and be there with me so I do well..."

"... so you no longer have any idea what's real and everybody wants to go to bed with you."

He turned to look at her to find what it was about her that reassured him. She had been confident about somebody's love once upon a time, her parents' most likely, before getting all racked up with her real lovers, her husband; before *real life* hit–and it showed. She was bemused at times, but fundamentally strong.

"I only need *one* person."

"Are you sure?"

"Yes." Wesley looked at Janet. "*Yes.*"

During the summer of 1967, the Summer of Love, Wesley appeared in Frank O'Hara's *Try! Try!* at the Poet's Theater in Cambridge, Massachusetts. He shared a row house in Central Square with another actor and a poet, and had begun to see the play's set designer, a painter named Lorry Stover, who still had her bedroom in her family's big house in Brookline. Mr. Stover was a textile tycoon. Lorry was a voluptuous Jewish American Princess who was also kind and intelligent, and Wesley felt an immediate sense of largesse in her presence and environs.

Early one June morning he woke up in Lorry's childhood bedroom on the second floor of the house, both of her parents off on a summer trip, and looked out the window over the fog-bound garden toward the Charles River and discovered himself fantasizing that he was the Laurence Harvey figure in *Room at the Top*, the young interloper who gains access to the house on the hill, who attains the bed of the boss's daughter and fondles her breasts and looks into her gentle, not entirely comprehending gaze.

As he had once fancied himself among the junkies and jazz musicians in *The Connection*, now he imagined himself a tough young lower-class man who had sussed out the moves to make it up the class ladder. But looking into the fog-laden distances that early morning, Wesley realized he'd crossed some threshold in himself as an actor that made him not want the comfort Lorry, in her person and place in life, proposed. The house was filled with built-in fixtures made out of processed wood. Industrial wealth had extended itself into sensibility of a kind. Poor Lorry's intelligence and taste were held hostage in her childhood home.

The night before, their first night in bed together, things hadn't even opened into sexual play, let alone love-making. Wesley sensed Lorry's large breasts were an albatross to her; she came to bed with a gray shapeless sack over herself and immediately turned away from him. He had already noted that during the hot Boston summer days she kept herself inordinately covered with high collars and long sleeves. She was the Playboy ideal in his own generation, with brains, most likely smarting from the mindless hormonal assault from the opposite sex that had awaited her. If she was plainly spoiled, she wouldn't or couldn't exploit herself, nor would she in any way exploit him, except, Wesley feared, to spoil him.

A day or two later, he met Annie. The Poet's Theater had begun to cast a new play and she came in to audition and Wesley was her reading partner. She was, in contrast to Lorry, blond and lithe, and there was a sensual slowness in her responses Wesley immediately connected with. After they got down off the stage he invited her out for coffee in Harvard Square, something that usually took him longer.

As it turned out, the play was not produced and the theater suspended new projects for the summer and kept up its bill of *Try! Try!* and Edward Albee's *The Zoo Story*, in which Wesley eventually took the role of Jerry when the actor who had been playing the role moved to Los Angeles.

Annie happened to be in Cambridge because she was ending a love affair with a young man at M.I.T. graduate school named Harold Sims. Wesley immediately saw in her the definition, perhaps the edge of hurt, he had missed in Lorry. Then too, it was the summer of *Sergeant Pepper's Lonely Hearts Club Band*, and before long Wesley and Annie took acid together. In a literal sense, it was their marriage sacrament.

They took it one afternoon in the little apartment Wesley had moved to over a diner in Brookline. They made love on the bed and then lay together on the bed looking out the large front window at a church steeple and listened to the Rolling Stones' version of "My Girl" on the radio.

Later they took a walk down the little street by the train depot and sat in the swings in an empty playground that was a psychedelic wonderland that mild afternoon.

12

Janet finished meditating on her bed: no mind turned back to her mind, and she sat for a moment levelly observing her own room, the clock and the telephone on the night table, along with the issue of *Mirabella* and the one of *Elle*. Wesley was gone off somewhere in the complications of his life. Her room was her own, for the moment, along with the rest of the house.

She pulled off her long pink tee-shirt, trying to think of how to dress for the evening, in case there was to *be* an evening. She had a video of *A Man in Love,* directed by Diane Kurys, whom she'd almost worked with once. Wesley would be phoning at some point or maybe just coming back. He had the extra set of keys now.

She put on her blue robe and strolled into her living room and looked at a drawing she'd done that afternoon for *Q*, the new futuristic punk comedy she'd been hired to do the costumes for. It was snowing outside, the dark distances out her living room windows pitted with white, mobile.

The phone rang and she put the drawing back on the glass-topped table and walked over to the kitchenette and picked up the wall receiver.

"Hello."

"Hi, this is Tony Warrens. You may remember we did a picture called *Paperback Writer* together..."

"Of course. How are you, Tony?" Tony Warrens was contiguously involved in two affairs on that picture, one with the casting director, Judy Russ, and then one with a co-star, Dennis Farns.

"OK. I'm doing a movie with Allen Schweitzer called *Buddlies* and it's deeply strange, but otherwise fine. Yourself?"

"Pretty good, thanks. But Wesley's not here and I'm not sure where he is. Does he know how to reach you?"

"Yeah, I'm at the Gorham. I thought you all might want to join me and my friend Nancy Terry for a bite tonight. Nothing fancy. There's a new place up the street, lots of glass and nouvelle light..."

"Sounds nice. Shall I have him call you? The writer?"

"Yeah, great. Nancy. Right. I'm gonna be here for an hour or so."

She put the phone back in its cradle and looked out at her living room again. The phone rang again. It was Wesley.

"Tony Warrens just called and wants you and me to meet him and Nancy Terry for dinner up the street from the Gorham."

"Nancy Terry?"

"She's very chic right now. You know there's a whole Brat Pack of these novelists now too. And she's the punker."

"Oh, yeah. *American Insane Maniac*."

"*Psycho. American Psycho.* Do you want to go? Where are you?"

"In Grand Central, what a story."

"What?"

"The homeless, wall to wall homeless."

"Oh, I know. And it's snowing."

The restaurant was candle-lit and elegant. Nancy Terry was a blond-haired vamp and wore something white and tight on top and was harsh in a way Wesley found both repellent and sexy. She referred to a situation in which she enjoyed having her breasts played with, but said it wasn't something she wanted done by just anyone.

"Well, I should hope not," Tony answered jovially. "Not everybody *deserves* to..."

Janet seemed to have gone into a deep meditation, hoping, Wesley imagined, for an out-of-body experience. He decided to try to bring to the discussion an element of dignity.

"What are you working on now?" he asked Terry.

"A new novel," she answered, "called *Screwing*."

"Oh, an autobiography," Janet said, looking at her.

"You have a problem with that?" Terry asked, smiling. Wesley noticed for the first time that she had a tiny gold ring through her tongue.

"I have a problem with *you*," Janet said, her face now flushing.

"Oh, there, there," Nancy mocked, still smiling.

Janet picked up her water glass and gave it a quick flick: water covered Terry's face and top.

Then Janet was up and gone from the restaurant.

"*Bitch!*" Terry yelled, wiping herself with her white linen napkin and standing up now, maybe to go after her. Tony looked alarmed. A white-jacketed waiter rushed over.

Wesley stood up, holding Nancy Terry's eyes. "Listen, please. I'm really sorry about this. Tony, I'm going." He put a twenty-dollar bill on the table for their drinks. "I'm sorry, Nancy," he said. "She's upset. She's going through a divorce."

"Look," she said, "she wants to rumble, let's rumble. I *love* girl fights."

"Yeah, thanks," he said.

Out on the sidewalk, he saw Janet way down the block, walking toward Fifth Avenue. There was a light veil of snow. It had stopped again for the moment.

"Where are you going?" he asked when he caught up to her, his breath in the air.

"I don't know. I don't want to have dinner with that stupid bitch."

"I don't blame you. Where would you like to eat?"

"Nowhere. What are you doing here?"

"What am I doing here?"

They had come to the corner of Fifth Avenue and Fifty-fourth Street.

"Yes," she said.

"I'm here because I want to be with you."

The light turned red and she walked out into the street.

"Taxi!" she yelled and turned to him.

Fifth Avenue was momentarily an almost empty throroughfare. He looked at her and then spied the top yellow light of a taxi headed their way.

They got out at the local deli and brought home smoked salmon and bagels and a six-pack of Miller's.

"I wanted the role so badly," Wesley said in Janet's kitchen, "I turned blind, deaf and dumb. I was a sort of human bullet."

"Hmm," Janet murmured and checked the bagels in her toaster oven.

"So," he said, "I'm coming home from the dentist one Friday afternoon and, there's this rise just before it levels out..."

"Yes."

"And when I get to the crest of that hill, there's a motorcycle, passing this van at the top of this blind hill. So he's in my lane, coming at me at about seventy miles an hour, about a car's length away from me when I see him."

"Jesus."

"Yeah, so I think, 'Oh, I may be about to say goodbye to the world."

She turned off the toaster and put the bagels out on a plate.

"So, I sort of edge over the center line because the van is almost past me, and then the motorcycle edges out, I guess, and ends up glancing off the side of my car and I skid across the lane and go right into this flagstone embankment and fracture my ankle. I'd braced my foot against the floorboard, which is the worst thing you can do."

"Was he killed?"

"Abrasions up and down his back, and his bike totaled, but he was walking. Wired and pissed, all coked up."

"Oh."

"So, anyway, the deal was: He's playing Russian roulette, passing on a blind hill. And I've turned myself into a human bullet, right?–aimed at this part, which I've got to get. The way it worked out, though, I was *his* bullet."

"Shall we eat?"

Janet had everything on a tray and Wesley followed her to the round white marble table beside the kitchenette counter and they sat down.

"But here's the end. My ankle's like jello but there's no puncture, just fractures, so it's not bleeding, and I haul myself out of the car. And suddenly, for the first time in weeks, I'm noticing, oh, the sun is shining. Over there in the bushes are these birds, chirping. There's this little breeze ruffling the greenery, and I can smell honeysuckle on it. And I'm breathing in and breathing out. I'm alive and the world is alive. I'd had to almost get killed to be able to see that again, to be alive again."

"The career got too important," she said.

"A man, at least, has this tremendous love of form."

They were walking in Soho. It was cold and overcast, and Wesley had a sudden sinking feeling, as though his happiness might be only a matter of his having forgotten something critical.

"Oh, come off it. And women don't?"

"Well, I guess you being a designer, a painter..."

"Yes?"

"Well, maybe you do. Do you want to go in?"

They stood at the threshold of an exhibit of canvases covered by words.

"No, I loathe this sort of thing."

"Did I tell you I finally understood what this movie needs?" Janet said in the middle of making love that night.

"No. Your movie."

"Yes. My movie. The costumes need to be 'tubular.'"

"Tubular."

"Rain used the word, as a joke. It's perfect."

"That's great..."

"Your sense of form. My sense of form is you don't want to talk about my movie costumes..."

"I *do* want to. It sounds great. Really. I just have a question."

"Yes?"

"Don't you just love the powerful way I make love to you now?"

"Don't talk like that," Janet said.

13

"We made a major mistake in the sixties," a short man named Evan with a gleaming bald pate and an athletic bearing told Wesley as they stood together at the Starving Artists bar.

"We made a lot of them," Wesley answered. He was drunk, and it was clear to him that collecting his mistakes from that decade would involve more than one trip.

"Yeah, OK, but one major one," Evan, who was a commodities trader, answered. "We forgot the shadow side."

This struck Wesley as overwhelmingly correct. "That's right."

"OK," Evan said. "The expression 'Nature abhors a vacuum'—?"

"Sure." Wesley put down his beer.

"OK, the sixties, right? Flower Power. Make Love Not War. Hell No We Won't Go. Love Peace and Happiness. The Summer of Love. Correctamente?"

"Sure."

The bartender, a graceful brunette actress named Gretchen Street whom Wesley knew slightly, signaled him for a refill and he nodded. He got out payment.

"All those Love Generation rallying cries," the stock broker told him. "OK, I give you nature's retort."

"What's that?"

Evan had lots of brand new crisp dollar bills on the bar beside his brandy. Like play money. "Very simple. Here's your beer."

"Thanks," Wesley said to Gretchen.

"Mmm-hmm," she said, smiling and moving down the bar after collecting his money.

Maybe he was too drunk now to encourage collegial exchange. Was Gretchen being slightly professional with him?

"1968," Evan said.

"1968?"

"Think about it," Evan answered.

"Think about 1968," Wesley reiterated.

"That's right. Nature didn't agree, you might say. And so it responded with a year that played havoc with every goddamn slogan and button we had in our parade. 1968."

"1968."

"Think about it."

Wesley drank from his new beer and then put the glass down. "I will."

"All right. Martin Luther King and Bobby Kennedy–both murdered that spring. Andy Warhol almost died too. Then, that summer, the Chicago Convention where the police rioted and bloodied the heads of middle-class kids. All in about three months. And the Love Generation was down for the count, totaled, *fini*."

That spring and summer Wesley and Annie had been living in a communal loft on West Broadway and acting together in an off-off-Broadway play. Wesley was no longer even calling his agent, who at the time was Carol Stevens at the William Morris Agency. In three years with that agency, while a lot of people got their acts together, he did two *Mod Squads.* Annie did three months on a soap opera but wanted to quit after a few weeks because they both felt she was making much more money than they had any use for. For about a year and a half, it really had been a revolution–at least if you asked them.

"You're an actor, right?" Evan said now.

"Yes," Wesley answered gratefully. People recognized him. They knew what he did. He had found his niche in civilization. A little too late not to have caused a lot of pain, but he'd found it.

Evan nodded. "I've seen you. Hey, nice talking with you."

"Leaving?"

"I'm heading downtown. Share a cab?"

"Thanks. I think I'll stay a while longer."

"Later, then." He squeezed Wesley's shoulder and walked toward the doors.

Wesley turned back to the bar remembering running into De Niro one afternoon in Central Park at the height of the sixties. Bobby had been studying the bears at the zoo for one of Stella Adler's exercises. De Niro had never really gone very far into the period's mystique; he'd smoke a joint like everybody else, but he knew what he wanted, where he was going, and kept to his path. Scorcese knew, too. So did Di Palma. Meanwhile, Wesley and Annie and a lot of others took the trip all the way into the mythical garden of Eden. He let his hair grow beyond any possible relevance to the William Morris Agency. He appeared in *General Electric,* a play by James Redding that contained a long speech about rendering money obsolete by *looking* at it.

Gretchen came by and picked up the dollar bills Roger had left her.

"How's it going?" Wesley asked her.

"I'm OK. I'm sure reading about you, Mr. Big." She smiled.

"Really?"

"By the way, Tony Warrens came in with that writer chick. He's... There they are." She waved.

In a moment, Tony and Nancy Terry were standing before him. Terry was wearing jeans and a white, crisply ironed man's shirt unbuttoned so that her breasts were visible.

"He looks cute tonight," she said, smiling at Wesley.

"Oh, he's cute," Tony answered, appraising him like a casting director.

"Hi, guys," Wesley answered.

"You're drunk," Tony told him, smiling at him now with surprise.

Wesley lay naked on Tony's bed at the Gorham while Nancy, naked, sat upright on top of him with his half-hard cock in her hand.

"When I come toward you, lick this," she told him. She held one of her breasts in her hand, moved in his direction, and he did what he'd been told.

Tony stood naked by the side of the bed, observing them, with his own cock in his hand.

"I'm not gay," Wesley said.

Nancy and Tony both laughed.

"I know you're not," Tony told him, "but a little affection between guys is okay. It's good. You know that."

Tony reached out; Wesley tentatively put his hand out. He kept thinking about other things. Tony's cock seemed big and as he held it he wanted to take hold of his own cock with his other hand to compare his with Tony's.

"Lick and then suck this now," Nancy told him, bringing herself to him.

While Wesley was doing it, Nancy said to Tony, "Where are the rubbers?" And then to Wesley: "Umm, that's nice. Now let go of Tony's dick."

Wesley walked from the Gorham toward his apartment building in a pinkish gray dawn full of the banging and roaring of garbage pick-ups. Midtown Manhattan had that slightly wasted aura it had in the dawn. These streets had been pounded and pounded and were only momentarily at rest before another onslaught.

He had woken up between Nancy and Tony with a strangely relieved feeling, as if the worst had surely occurred and each breath from here on was either for pleasure or for nothing at all. Both Nancy and Tony were heavily into Safe Sex and they'd treated him generously and solicitously the night before. Nancy was into her extraordinarily explicit instructions, and he wondered how much of her pleasure had to do with being exactly obeyed. In any case, it seemed to be a relatively harmless procedure. Tony gave every evidence of enjoying being directed and performed with obliging vigor. He himself was drunk enough to enjoy Nancy's regimentation too. It was like being in the army, naked. It was like being an actor.

Had he and Tony gone over a particular threshold with each other into being gay? Most likely they had, and it seemed, if anything, more of a letting go than a beginning. They were old friends who had now lain naked together. Somebody else would have to call the police.

Walking toward the blue awning of his apartment building–sunlight beginning to splinter into the street–his step felt light.

"Morning," Sam the nightman said as he held the door for Wesley.

"Morning," Wesley answered smiling and entered the building's peach-pink faux marble lobby.

14

With his father and mother as the giant stage phantoms of his post-adolescence, and the shallowness of his identity as a beginning actor, Wesley knew he'd been scarcely capable of any of the larger emotions, and blamed himself for the failure of his marriage to Annie.

He and Stephen saw the tail end of a wedding dispersing onto Fifth Avenue from the Pierre Hotel as they walked toward Central Park in an overcast day close to Christmas. The bridesmaids, who wore purple flowers, trailed the couple to the waiting limousine.

"Dad, can I ask you something?" Stephen said as they entered Central Park.

He knew he was about to speak about the divorce and even welcomed it. The day, with its deep winter browns in the park and Stephen's sturdy profile and high complexion beside him, was as good as any to finally set things straight.

"Please. Just say it."

"Is Tony Warrens gay?"

Wesley turned to see Stephen's expression, which was only perplexed.

"I think he's bisexual. Why?"

"I just wondered. I mean I like him and all, but I mentioned him to Nick Rayers at school and he starts in about—you know, this whole gay thing..."

"So what if he is?" Wesley asked.

"Well, I mean, nothing."

"Look, are you worried *I'm* gay?"

They passed an old married couple, the man with a cane

and a golfer's hat pulled down over his eyes, walking in close tandem.

"Geeze, no, Dad."

"Let me say something, Stephen. This issue about being gay–it's really not that simple unless it happens to be."

"Meaning what? You think I'm worried *I'm* gay?"

"No. Take it easy, OK? You wanna check out the zoo? Grandpa's seals?" Wesley's father liked to visit this attraction whenever they were in the neighborhood.

"Sure."

"How was he?"

"Grandpa? He's OK. He's got this lady cooking for him and taking care of him."

"Margie," Wesley said.

"I guess so. Pretty well preserved."

"Yeah, that's his lady except in name. He won't marry her. It's a little cruel."

"Is he still–active?" Stephen asked.

"Ask Margie."

"Great, Dad. Let me give her a call." There was a phone booth at the threshold of the zoo, and they both smiled.

"I was trying to say that, for most of us, the real issue isn't homosexuality versus heterosexuality..." Wesley caught himself feeling an urgency to communicate something maybe not relevant to Stephen at all. "It's a question of bringing together attraction and love, sex and tenderness. It's a lot more complicated than straight or gay."

"So you feel you're getting a better balance with Janet?"

He knew he'd already crossed over into a lecture. But why not take the rap and give Stephen the little information he had, just in case he could use it. What else were fathers for–but to get their information, hate them for a while most likely, and move on?

"I want to say one thing."

Wesley and Stephen approached the seal pool with its group of spectators at various vantages along the rail.

"What?" Stephen said.

Wesley stopped before they reached the rail and looked at Stephen, who had stopped beside him. "Your mother is a fine woman, a really fine person, and I'm very happy I was married to her and that we had a son."

"OK, Dad..."

"The divorce doesn't change the fact that we're your family–whatever problems it might make. I hope it doesn't."

"I never thought it did, exactly."

They stood together at the rail and watched the seals bark and swim, disappear and re-emerge. There was a subtle hypnotic pull in this spectacle of another species in its strict parameters in the middle of Manhattan. Wesley felt close to Stephen yet conscious of the limits of their relationship at this stage. He wanted to give him something, but didn't know exactly what it should be. After a while, they broke away and continued walking.

They walked further uptown in the park, observing the endless, random configurations of old people, groups of the young, couples of every variety, parents and children. It was the kind of dull winter day Wesley had known all his life and somehow liked. They were no longer talking now, but Wesley was conscious of some companionship in each of them.

At the corner of 72nd Street and Fifth, coming out of the Park, they both followed an unspoken impulse to the ice-cream stand and bought Good Humor bars, and continued to walk uptown on Fifth Avenue on the wide cobbled sidewalk under the stripped trees, eating the Good Humors in the cold.

"Are you enjoying any subjects this year?"

"You mean do I know what career I want yet–like when you did that play at Trinity?"

"No, just if you have any good teachers."

"Physics is pretty good."

"Good." Wesley stopped and picked up a quarter from the crevice between two cobblestones. "I hear it's very interesting. Quarks and all..."

"It's true. Grandpa says it's good luck to find money and I guess you believe him."

"It is." Wesley handed the quarter to Stephen, who took it with a half-smile, and they continued to walk up Fifth Avenue.

15

That night in a dream Wesley saw a new-born baby and studied its expression for a moment and then pointed out to someone how it was exactly Annie's look: open-eyed, direct, yet with the edge of a question in the eyes, some strain of uncertainty in them.

The night before they left for Hollywood Janet lay on her stomach in bed with her hand on Wesley's chest.

"I had an interesting dream this morning," he said.

"Good for you."

"I was lying in bed with my father, only he was a young man, or no older than me, just about my age I guess, and strong and handsome. Both of us were naked..."

"Oh, no."

"It's all right," he said.

"Okay," Janet said.

"So I feel like we're supposed to make love, but I'm repelled by the idea, though my father seems like a good man ... And I say to him, 'Look, we can't do this because we're not men.' "

"Seems like it should be because we *are* men," Janet said.

"Yeah, it does. But I think I get it. What I'm saying is, I'm not a whole man yet because I haven't totally accepted and loved my own power as a man. See, my father and my mother got all skewed and it was hard for me to get into either of them. My father was pretty tough in certain ways. But what it's about is I have to accept his power in me, let it become part of me, to go on now."

The next afternoon, at home in Hollywood again, he lay on his stomach on his maroon towel with his wet head on his arms. "What about *your* parents?" he asked Janet absently.

"Come again?"

"You know. I'm Armenian Italian Jewish, two genocides flanking the bon vivant. What are you?"

"My parents are both Jewish, German Jewish."

"Straight genocide. What are they like?"

"They're old, very old, and I'm in this period of watching them lose their marbles. It's very strange." Janet lay on her back now and closed her eyes as Wesley looked over at her.

"Like what?"

"Oh, my mother, who was once upon a time *the* big woman in my life, has shrunk into this very tiny person. Sometimes she seems not to know where she is. When she drives a car, which we only let her do now in the summertime on the Vineyard, you can't see anyone behind the wheel. A car goes by with nobody in it. She's just so little."

Wesley laughed. Janet sat up and hugged her knees in the hazy sunshine and quiet of the Hollywood hills, punctuated by an occasional fluttering in the nearby palms, an occasional bird trilling. It was surely the most blandly boring place on earth.

Wesley sat beside Janet in the Ashs' Bel Air screening room with only Roland and his wife Gabby and watched *Wanted Man* unfold. He had only met Janet and taken her out to Joe Allen's from the Hollywood party when he went to Durango to make the movie in early September. His big scene was with the female co-star, Maria Fontes, who decides to make the lead jealous by seducing his right-hand man. It was an existential Western, full of implicit feminism though set back in the time of William Bonney.

When the movie ended in the screening room, Roland, a short man with counter-culture length red hair but an easy interpersonal style, the kind of social efficiency useful in a director, said to Wesley, "You know that scene with you and Maria is so good I think it may have skewed the picture."

"I hope not," Wesley said. "What did you think?" he asked Janet.

"I enjoyed it," she said, smiling at him.

"Really?" the director said. "Well, good. Gabby and I have seen it too many times to know."

When they came out of the screening room and went into the living room with its glass-domed ceiling, there was another couple seated on a gray sofa together and Janet and Wesley were introduced. They were casually but expensively dressed—it was a new unisex look, Janet reflected. It made them look a little like ambulatory pieces of camping equipment. He was a screenwriter named Ellery Seabrook and she was his young and pretty wife, Hilary. They both had more pockets than they could have any possible use for.

"I got a chance to hang around Danny De Vito for while. Movie stardom is beyond far out," Ellery reported to them, radiating what Janet strongly suspected was unqualified wonder.

Janet took Wesley's hand while they sat side by side on another gray corduroy sofa. Though she hated Hollywood, here she was again with the very people who made it go.

"Good or bad?" Wesley wanted to know. Whether he knew it or not, he would be a New Yorker till the day he died. Good or bad?

"I mean he can do anything he wants. Anything."

She gave Wesley's hand two squeezes, personal code for something, "moron" maybe.

Gabby Ash sat in a blue leather-backed chair that could have been a Regency antique. She seemed puffed out at the chest, like a cross between a queen and a cannon-ball. The story was she'd struggled before meeting Roland but she'd been taking Hollywood wives lessons. Her husband was, Janet supposed, a good steady Hollywood hand. His long hair was a joke—another sixties drop-out in Bel Air. The movie, Wesley's scene aside, was a passable fair Western, for all she knew a hit. Wesley's scene was sexy.

He looked so broken down, beaten, and then there was this steady, slow attention coming out of him like the freshest thing in the world.

How was she supposed to sit through another evening like this?

"Oh," Gabby said, looking up at her young housekeeper in a Pierre Deux apron in the doorway. "Let's adjourn to the dining room."

"So what's the problem?" Wesley said to Janet that night sitting up in his double bed as she came out of the bathroom in an oversized peach colored tee-shirt.

"I told you I'm not crazy about Hollywood. That woman Hilary was the most pretentious little non-entity I've talked to since the last one of those parties I went to."

"What does she do again?"

"She sculpts. I mention Carl Andre and Donald Judd and Richard Serra, nothing. Then I say Giacometti, and her eyes light up. I think she thinks he's the special at Spago."

He watched her get into bed and sit up against the pillows.

She looked over at him. "I'm too old for this."

"Look, I told you, I'm here to do my job and we'll go back in a few more weeks. I don't love these people either."

"I may be too old for *you.*"

"What's that supposed to mean? This just reminds you of evenings you spent with Michael."

"Exactly. And you're going to be successful now and you want to enjoy it and not have a lady who's actually interested in Buddhism and Louise Nevelson gumming up your works."

"Jesus. Five-alarm fire. Listen, do you want me to heat up the Jacuzzi ..."

Wesley saw Janet's color deepen.

"Sorry," he said. "That sounded exactly like a member of the air head brigade. I was just trying to share my *equipment ...*"

She smiled and looked away.

"What will it take to convince you I just like the idea of getting some of the good parts?"

"I believe you, and you should."

"You just don't want to hang around for the dinner parties ..."

"I should go home..."

"Look, it's pretty much over out here. So many of the good people live on the East Coast now, or somewhere else, New Mexico, or Montana... This is just a part for me, OK? I really appreciate you coming out for a couple of days, OK?"

"Sure, OK. But you don't really expect me to believe that, do you?"

"Look," Wesley said, "it's fine. You get to go back to the Big Apple."

16

Wesley had only a day after Janet went back to New York before they started shooting the movie. He felt relaxed in the familiar rooms, walking in his bathing suit through the unlit house at sundown after a swim. He was glad to be getting back to a job after his hiatus. Sleep came over him easily that night, Rocky at the foot of one side of the bed.

He was up at four. The limo was waiting when Wesley stepped outside at five in the still dark, dew-shrouded dawn on his street. He was in his trailer a half-hour later, setting up a CD player he wanted in place for his waiting hours, getting settled in.

When Harold called him to the set and Wesley said hello to Isabel again, giving her a kiss on the cheek but feeling her waist and catching a whiff of some delicate scent she wore, the script they would film suddenly came alive for him. She certainly had something.

"How have you been?" he asked as they sat in the office furniture before the first take.

"Great," she said.

Everything in her seemed tuned to the slightest nuance, and when Wesley looked at her directly, her gaze was an avenue he couldn't see the end of. He made a sharp turn off it to keep himself oriented.

They spent most of the day working on a single office scene. Toward four, Harold collared Wesley and they walked out of the building containing the sound stage.

"You're scared," Sterns told Wesley.

"Of what?" he asked.

"I don't know–maybe it's having the lead–but it looks to me like it's the kid."

"I'm scared of Isabel?"

"Your eyes aren't there."

"OK. I'll work on that."

"Everything's fine. Slow and steady."

That meant he might have another day or two. Wesley went back to his trailer in alarm, discovering himself in a cold sweat. His Bud Powell CD looked like an antique from another epoch of his life. He had no right to listen to a man of the inventiveness and large emotion of Powell. He was an actor who had finally gotten a lead role and was scared to mix it up with his co-star.

Someone knocked and then Sterns called him from outside the trailer.

Wesley opened the door, and Harold looked up at him through glasses he wore on the set, smiling. "Easy does it, Ace. You're very close here, in a certain way."

"Sure I am." Wesley stepped down and began walking toward the set.

"I mean it." Sterns put his hand on Wesley's shoulder and walked with him. "The guy, Gold, is intrigued, of course, as who wouldn't be, but he's caught off guard. And you've got all that. What he's gonna do here, though, which maybe a lot of us wouldn't do, in his circumstances, or in our own, is, he's going to *let her* take him. He's going to let her walk away with him into the fantasy, OK?"

Wesley walked out into the lights and sat on the edge of a desk and looked at Isabel sitting behind it in her chair. Unsmiling, she looked at him.

"Is something I'm doing bothering you?" she said.

"No," he answered, relieved by her candor and too

exhausted to hide. "It's my problem. I don't do love scenes—or about-to-be love scenes—that easily."

"Oh, thank *God*," she said. "I thought it was me."

"It *is* you," Wesley said, smiling. He'd forgotten how young she was and how charming.

"What can I do?"

"Would you have dinner with me?"

"Tonight?"

"If you could."

"You think it will help?"

"Yes," he said.

"All right," she said, and looked at him with a little frown.

They re-shot the scene for the sixth time and, when Wesley arched his arm over a filing cabinet, instead of looking away from Isabel, he kept his eyes on hers, and she, sitting in her chair and then standing up and walking over to him, kept looking at him.

Harold called "Cut!" and walked onto the set.

"Good," he said to them both, and then added to Wesley, "Can you do it without the filing cabinet?"

Wesley picked Isabel up at her condominium on Franklin and drove with her in his old black BMW to Santa Monica, where they went to dinner at Louisa's on Montana. He ordered a bottle of wine and had more of it than Isabel, though she had more than he thought she might.

"So what's going on?" she asked him when they were almost finished eating.

"I guess I'm practicing looking at you."

She seemed incapable of a graceless gesture and only shrugged. "You didn't seem to have much trouble with Maria Fontes in *Wanted Man*. I went to a screening."

"I was just divorced, and I was fighting for my life, drowning, and I guess she was the oar in the water."

"I know you find me horrible."

"I don't believe that. You know exactly how beautiful you are." Saying that, Wesley could feel for the first time the possibility of a connection between them.

"I hate to have these conversations in..." She looked away.

"OK." He didn't want to fight, but had to get through her beauty, somehow, to her.

He paid, and they walked up Montana and looked at the stills at the Aero Theater. It was a balmy evening, with a little wind.

"I'm sorry to make it hard for you," he said.

"I've been having fun, actually," she said, and they walked from under the marquee and went on up the hill.

"Do you like L.A.?"

"I love L.A.," Isabel said.

"I live right near you. Would you like to see my house?"

"At least I can trust you."

"Absolutely," Wesley answered, noticing he was a little drunk.

But as they drove toward Hollywood he remembered they were each supposed to be up at four the next morning and said to Isabel they probably should save the house for another night.

"I knew we weren't going to have a mad, passionate affair," she said smiling.

"That would definitely cause major damage on my end," Wesley said, realizing almost gratefully that it was true.

"My boyfriend and I are having a fight."

"No kidding," he said. "It's perfect, I guess. But I'm pretty sure we're supposed to ignore that and just work very hard."

"Am I supposed to be impressed?... I'm impressed."

Wesley parked and walked with Isabel to the door of her condo.

"Doesn't your Mom live with you or something?"

"I'm too old. I have a housekeeper who comes in."

"Hey, thank you."

He kissed her on the cheek.

In the middle of the week Wesley called Janet in New York, where it was almost eleven.

"Do you think you could come out here again and visit the Getty and the Norton Simon and go to galleries?"

"What are you saying?"

"I need you right now. This girl is young and I need to stay centered."

"You're going to have an affair."

"No, I'm not... But..."

"Listen, I'm not a missionary. If you want to have an affair, have it, and just forget about us."

Wesley's bedroom was dark except for moonlight on one bright wall. He was lying in his clothes on his bed and now sat up.

"Oh, great. Look. This is about acting."

"Sure, it is. Wesley, I can't do this. I've got to go."

"Take it easy. I just wanted to say hello."

"Hello."

"Really. You've got to go."

"I told you. I don't like this."

"I get it."

He heard her hang up and put down the phone and got up off the bed and walked to the sliding door and looked at the garden and the pool in the moonlight. Rocky came from somewhere and stood beside him.

17

At odd hours of the day and night Wesley remembered a date he'd had many years before. He had taken out a young woman–Barbara? he no longer remembered her name–who was not only a great natural beauty, but one who commanded a repertory of expressions–from knowing smiles to bemused sympathy–that surely marked her as extraordinary. They sat at a table at a Third Avenue bar in the Eighties. It was a summer evening, just dark outside, and he watched her with growing restlessness.

She was beautiful and yet, Wesley was certain, tragically empty, and he began to pick on her, telling her she was vacuous, nothing but a face and a look that might fool someone, but wouldn't fool him. She was a young beauty trying on a style she thought might be workable in the world, and suddenly Wesley was sure that the most he could get out of the evening for himself was not to kiss her, to melt into her empathy and let that go wherever it might go—probably to one of their beds—but to surprise and hurt her, to put her down, let her know he didn't buy the act, well-practiced as it was, lovely though she might be. And in a few more minutes, he was pompously putting her into a cab, the date over before it began.

So, it came to him now, he had been cruel to a young woman who was still really a girl. He had done this big number on her—why? Because her beauty and poise echoed his mother's and that scared him? He waited in his trailer or between takes on the set, pierced with guilt but also, he knew, usefully bloodied and opened up for his scenes with Isabel.

Was it possible he both loved and hated women at the same time, the more the one the more the other? And had that been what had happened in his marriage with Annie, whom he fell in love with visually and felt an instant rapport with that quickly segued into lovemaking, but then seemed to spend the years of their marriage keeping his heart at a remove? He was cruel to her—to Annie, to the woman at the Third Avenue bar, to Trudy Winslow, most likely to all the nicest, kindest, prettiest women he'd known.

Now as he worked with Isabel through scenes Harold seemed to choose for their intimacy—keeping the set unusually subdued and using a skeleton crew—Wesley saw—as they sometimes repeated a scene for ten or more takes—that the young actress used her eyes with an exact, deliberate calibration tuned to the scene. Looking from inside his persona, Gold, he encountered in her both an enchantress and a co-worker with a real craft, and with nerves and kindness and her own vulnerability. If she was young, she was already a pro.

"This is really a funny business, isn't it?" Wesley said as they sat almost naked side by side in bed during a break.

Under the sheet he wore three pairs of underpants and she had on a flesh-colored body stocking.

"I hate it! It's embarrassing!" Isabel said and smiled broadly at him and they both burst out laughing.

In the end he saw them as two professionals plumbing their depths for the common denominator, the spark, that would light up the screen. Isabel seemed to know about it. As for him, he knew something about it from Janet, and maybe he'd glimpsed it–surely he had–with Annie too, but he'd been so shy of it, afraid of the feeling.

Harold seemed satisfied with his work. Wesley and Isabel moved carefully around one another not to upset the fragile trust that was catalyzing their scenes. Each night at home, Wesley watched a video–he was going through Pasolini–before going to bed. After a few days he called Janet again.

"I think it's working," Wesley said standing at the kitchen phone.

"Good."

"I miss you."

"What about the young lady?"

"She's a professional. I was nervous at the beginning. I'm doing the work now."

"I am too. It's hard, but I'm having fun."

Wesley could see himself in the dark glass of the sliding door. "I guess you just grow up."

"You sound funny... I've decided to make the look Italian lines with big colors and some other touches."

"That sounds great." He saw himself smiling in the black glass. More than once during the past several days he'd caught himself thinking about Janet, wanting to touch her delicate waist. He told her about Pasolini's *Arabian Nights,* which he'd just watched.

Wesley woke up in the early morning dark with his throat tight with sadness. He'd had a dream he could remember only vaguely. Back from the dead, John Lennon had been singing in it.

The night before he'd driven Stephen to the airport and had a brief conversation with Annie at the door of Bill Rogier's Santa Monica house before he picked up one of Stephen's suitcases just inside the door and took it to his car. Annie had regarded him with a combination of distance and good humor that stung him more than straight-forward hostility probably would have. She was inside another life.

But then, so was he.

Stephen had given him a warm hug at the airport after Wesley initiated it.

"Let me know if you need anything."

"OK, Dad, I will. Thanks for the car." He had bought him an older red Mustang for Christmas.

Dawn was barely in the room. Rocky's head was up and the dog seemed to be staring intently at him from the foot of the bed. The car that delivered the *Los Angeles Times* was going by outside, *Times*es slapping onto each successive driveway. It was almost time to get up.

Acting was the job he had found to do, and it was also a kind of mirror, showing him where he was virtually every time he went to work. Could there be something in the work too that propelled him forward in his life? Stirred by the thought, Wesley turned and sat up on the bed, his bare feet touching the floor, and switched off the clock-radio alarm before it came on.

Double Fries

AFTER A DISASTROUS series of financial set backs and delays, Ford obeys an irrational impulse and takes a position at the McDonalds in the local mall. "Would you like fries with that?" he asks a succession of antic or lugubrious teenagers. Ford is forty-five years old. His own teenagers stay away for several days by an unspoken understanding. Then he quits.

He takes a job driving an airport van. During a training period of an afternoon and evening, he is paired off with a young man who wears an earring and formerly worked as a bartender at a stylish Los Angeles restaurant where Ford has had dinner. Their trainer is a Vietnam veteran who's been with the company, Magic Van, for some time. "At least we'll see that you don't starve," he tells Ford and the young man in the darkness of the van as they study the airport routing system.

Driving the van, Ford worries that he will be spotted by an aquaintance at the airport, or worse, summoned to the house of people from his other life. One night after work–it's early spring–he attends a reading by a poet friend and leaves early, though normally he would visit with the friend afterwards, in order to be fresh for a job interview the next morning. Oliver Snow turns out to be an amiable giant of a man with an intricate beard and a part-time career as a television actor. He's jolted to learn how old Ford is. "It'll be nice to have someone my age around here," he says after hiring him.

Ford works on one side of a long room at the middle computer of five IBMs along the wall. On the other side is the same set up. Everybody but Ford and Oliver Snow, who works at a far corner, is in their twenties, all but one of them young men. Snow seems to hire them for his own reasons... looks, comedy, competence–probably in that order. It's a lively, sometimes raucous conglomeration, and in the middle of it sits the lone woman, a slim athletic red-head named Katrina–on certain days lovely indeed, Ford thinks–who is an outspoken feminist. She's two years older than Ford's older daughter, away at college in the East, and recently graduated from UC Santa Cruz.

Their job is to transcribe questionnaires filled out by the victims of job-related stress. Many of the victims are Latino: Salvadoran, Guatemalan, Honduran, or Mexican. Some answer the questions in an interview in their own language, and a translator writes down what they say in basic English. Ford finds some of the stories heartbreaking. A small woman who has a bad back tries impossibly to get her share of work done on a maintenance crew. Accidentally a beautiful sentence will be set down by someone with a meagre command of English. Ford sees lives in these documents: hopes, struggles, the generations, America, and disappointment.

The office is in a skyscraper in the mid-Wilshire area. Katrina seems to have fallen in love with Nathan, a good-looking aspiring screenwriter who was hired the same day as Ford. His deadpan style makes her more loquacious. A couple of times Ford catches her face flushed with a radiance that seems unmistakable. Nathan, hard at work in his off-hours on a screenplay, doesn't seem to notice.

Frequently Ford gets caught up in literary discussions with Raj, who sits to his immediate left. The son of a Hindu mother and an Irish father, Raj Haley is a poet who employs rhyme and meter but isn't aware that this is a current vogue. Ford sometimes joins him and Nathan for lunch. Mostly they eat at a nearby McDonalds.

"Have you noticed," Ford says to Nathan during one of their lunches, "that Katrina likes you?"

"My mother's a redhead," he answers grimly, and Raj starts to laugh. The two were roommates at UC Santa Barbara.

"Why are you here?" Nathan asks Ford at another lunch. He has a hard humorous side.

"I need a health plan."

"A major operation?" Raj asks.

"I want a designer brain."

"We are so silly," Raj says in his mock Indian accent.

Walking back to work in the summer heat, the three pass Katrina who smiles at each of them in turn.

"She is love," Raj says after they've passed.

"Why don't you ask her out?" Nathan asks him.

"You fool! She has no eyes for *me*."

Raj has a wonderful face where East and West seem to meet in humorous collusion.

One afternoon when Oliver Snow is out of the room, Katrina, who sits next to Nathan and becomes voluble at his side, tells a story about a friend of hers whose boy friend went away on a trip and left her with a vibrator. Slowly everyone in the room turns around in their chairs.

Katrina blushes. "But it wasn't the same as having Tom with her."

"I guess if I went to see her," Nathan says, "instead of flowers, I could bring her a pack of double-A batteries."

Ford enjoys the rush hour traffic home. It's an opportunity to unwind, to ruminate. But his nights are restless. He reads a self-help book about refocusing one's career in midlife and decides that public relations is a probable field. He starts making phone calls. Ford knows that he and Nathan will be fired soon. They're both too slow, though Ford is a little faster than Nathan. As it turns out, Nathan's script is suddenly optioned and, hired to re-write it, he quits before they fire him.

Late one night Ford takes a swim in the pool at the condominium complex where he lives with his wife and their two younger children. Lying on his back in the tepid water, he makes out one or two stars in the Los Angeles sky. His younger daughter and his son spend a lot of time away from home. Ford and his wife talk to one another only with great difficulty, and begin attending separate meetings of Codependents Anonymous.

In the middle of July, Ford is fired. Oliver Snow tells him he appreciates the effort he's made, but it's obvious this isn't the career for him. Career? Ford thinks. It isn't the career for anybody, except possibly Oliver Snow. But he takes the news coolly, secretly happy to have to get moving again. He goes back to his desk, gets his things together, and leaves. It's a stifling Friday lunch hour and he's been spared saying goodbyes.

The following week Ford makes a lot of telephone calls and, on Thursday afternoon, he gets a lead from a friend with show business connections. He's hired as the receptionist in an entertainment public relations office. It's a foot in the public relations door, Ford tells his wife. He handles twelve phone lines. Actors who make his weekly wage in an hour or two call up in various states of elation or euphoria, or occasional uncertainty.

"Remember," an older star tells Ford, "being 24 doesn't last forever."

"I know," he says into the receiver.

Ford's boss is a crisp Englishman in his sixties who can barely handle a press release. His resume says he was at Oxford but he must have been there boating. He hands Ford semi-literate first drafts on his way to long lunches at four star restaurants and asks him to tidy them up. The firm's other partner is a little Napoleon with a wig that sits on his head like a billboard. His rolodex is the central engine of the office, and the other publicists, all of them younger than Ford and each of them irritable in a different way, act as their boss's lieutenants. He micro-manages and refuses to throw Ford even a scrap. As fall begins Ford listens to a series of motivational tapes as he drives to work and starts to make calls again.

Surprisingly quickly, Ford finds a job as an account executive with a small firm specializing in corporate accounts, his boss a smart-looking woman in her fifties named Estelle. She works out of two rooms in her spare elegant hillside house. The rooms command a sweeping view of Hollywood. It's a new threshold, and Ford is heartened.

One cool October afternoon the other account executive, Anita, a single woman in her thirties, hangs up the phone and tells Ford a client's absurdly grandiose goal: an appearance on "Good Morning, America" the day of a fund raiser for a local women's organization.

"I always want to say," she says laughing, "'Would you like fries with that?' "

Traffic School

STEVENSON, A PAINTER, is at traffic school Tuesday evening in a well-lit room at the Adult Education Center in the town of Fairfax in Marin County. In trouble with his work, he's decided to break his rhythm by taking the class instead of paying an absurd speeding ticket. He was stopped in Mill Valley at 2:30 in the morning going 45 miles an hour in a 25-mile-an-hour speed zone.

The instructor, a thin man who looks to be around forty, Stevenson's age, has a pot belly. How could he allow himself such an indulgence, Stevenson wonders. Yet the man is charming and a good instructor.

There are four women and three other men. Stevenson immediately has identified the beauty of the group, a light-skinned black woman wearing a gray sweatshirt and jeans and a red flower in the back of her long black ponytail. He knows that he'll paint her, though he no longer employs models. He'll try to catch her somber gracefulness. She has a thick paperback novel with her.

The lights are switched off and the class watches a film about drunk versus sober driving. It's only mildly interesting, the point seems obvious. The trouble with being an artist, Stevenson muses as he watches, is that these dread days come up out of the routine of one's working life, and one is routinely expected to endure them.

The black woman sits three seats away, Stevenson is aware, already engaged in a mental triangle, or quadrangle, since the woman is surely involved too. It's a longstanding habit, eroticizing the tedious, keeping his senses alert. He worries that his work lacks a vital raison d'etre. Now that he's moved from minimalism to the psychological realism of Fischl, Clemente, and the German Expressionists, he's more exposed than ever. Sitting in the chair, he feels as thin as paper. The film ends and the lights come back on.

"I know that film by heart," the instructor tells them and there is light laughter in the room.

At the break Stevenson gets up and walks toward the door of the room and debates going outside. The black woman stands up and is as tall as he is.

"It makes you never want to get into a car again..." Stevenson says as she walks into his immediate vicinity.

"I've got a jeep," she answers mildly.

"That's different," Stevenson says and follows her outside into the July evening, which has a moist chill in it.

"My boyfriend and I are heading up to the Sierras in a week; I just wanted this off my record."

"Insurance," he adds, nodding, enjoying the night colors with the neighborhood's electric intervals. Cars are going by a few yards from where they stand.

"How about you?"

"I'm here to get out of my studio, make contact with the human race."

"You're an artist?"

"Yes." Stevenson feels pain that isn't quite physical. "I paint."

She smiles at him and exposes a discolored right front tooth. She's as beautiful as anyone Stevenson has seen in a long time. Lena, his wife, is beautiful, but they aren't as happy being married as they were being together unmarried. She's a computer astrologer and gets up every morning to go to work, which vaguely irritates Stevenson.

The canvases in his studio seem to Stevenson like fragments of his pain and inertia, like the cracked fragments of what was once a vase with a design on it, perhaps even a myth emblazoned in its colors. The night outside the room has turned suddenly quiet, the crickets have stopped. Stevenson carefully avoids his reflection in the picture window's black. His gallery has set back the date of his show and he can only agree. Or perhaps the myth of his life are these very fragments, accompanied by the smell of earth and moisture and the various fragrances of the flowers outside in Lena's garden, the heady night smell.

She isn't at home. Her career is going well and there isn't much use in her trying to pull herself down to his level. Stevenson has brought out a large canvas, mounted it on his easel, and now hesitates with his pencil, wanting to draw either the room at traffic school or the black woman with her high breasts and air of sad majesty. He hesitates to put a mark to the white gessoed surface.

For a moment he's aware of standing in a glass house, in the middle of the night, poised in a precipitous gesture which may not be important at all. Lena understands that he's lost touch with his work, that he's regularly in pain and panic, a knot of the two in his throat and neck, and it occurs to Stevenson that he's lived his whole adult life this way.

He is drawing her now, the woman in class, using that set of her lips, which was like the opening of a Mendelssohn symphony he heard on the radio that morning that somehow built a musical satisfaction. The woman's beauty held that same kind of satisfaction visually. Or similar satisfaction. The same could be said, maybe, of those cellophane packages of four rectangles of four different colors of clay that were given to Stevenson to play with as a child. The look of certain faces he studied in his school yearbooks. Those tiny wooden Quaker Oats boxes and other food items, miraculously reduced and rendered useless. What had it been, after all, that had charged him with the strange mission of his life? But as he works now, Stevenson is entirely, fatally absorbed, his pain vanquished by his activity, and, for the moment, perfectly happy.

The Genius

IT WAS ON AN EVENING in the early seventies, still light out, that I boarded the bus for Bolinas at Seventh and Market Streets in San Francisco. The driver was an African-American, tall and straight-backed in his seat, chewing gum, with a jaunty improvisatory quality about him. You sensed he was in a certain groove. The usual driver seemed to take the job as a routine diminution, a strictly mechanical operation, but this man was putting his personal, rhythmical stamp on it.

I was a new father and my whole idea was to become a dependable citizen. The sixties had been a kind of deconstruction for my generation—we had melted away our personalities, getting down to nothing at all—but now I wanted to feel something solid in myself. It wasn't an easy thing for me to feel, and paradoxically just then, with the sixties over, it probably got harder.

I took a window seat and looked out at the twilit streets with their after-work rush of pedestrians as we moved toward Lombard Street and the Golden Gate Bridge. The ride to Bolinas is fairly routine until you start up Mount Tamalpais in Mill Valley. From there it's a long climb with turn after turn, and then a long descent, with as many more turns, into Stinson Beach.

All of us, his passengers, knew immediately that we were in the hands of a special driver. We moved both faster and more decisively than normally. Then as we started the climb up Mount Tam and at the same time darkness began to settle in, it was as if we were inside something infinitely greater than a commuter bus on an evening run. The ride was like an enactment of an extraordinary, overseeing, protective power: it was like being a passenger inside cosmic grace.

In the darkness at the front, he sat erect but loose-limbed, turning the steering wheel–which lay just above his knees in a slightly pitched horizontal position–left and then right, right and then left again, as he negotiated turn after turn.

For a while the sixties had been a wrap-around, environmental reinforcement. Wearing long hair had been like being part of a ubiquitous and generally benevolent family. When we saw each other there was a sense of wearing our hearts on our sleeves. There was a lot of color on everybody. It was lovely in many ways.

These were dramatic, sometimes hairpin turns that required the greatest care and precision in a car, let alone a bus, and we were moving at an astonishing speed. Was it all right?

We stopped near the top of Mount Tamalpais. An old man moved to the front of the bus and before stepping down to the road he turned to the driver and said, "That was a beautiful ride. Thank you!"

Genius has the means to provide for what isn't as strong in others. Haydn seems to state something exactly right musically. D. H. Lawrence is sometimes the one writer of all of them to read. Black night now fallen outside, I realized what was happening was pure, unforetold wonder, and for a moment the tension in me broke.

The Musician

Visiting my dead father's house, I open a closet door and see boxes piled from floor to ceiling. It's a gray San Francisco morning and I'm wearied by the obsessiveness of his hoardings. My sister, Cici, is still asleep in an upstairs room of the house. She lives here now, perhaps permanently, depending on how the estate is handled, which is something neither of us has much say over. This is typical. He was a great cellist. He made the instrument resonate with Bach and Haydn and Ellington as if it were the speech of the soul, of the witness each of us carries inside. The witness was extremely strong in him. I close the closet door and walk upstairs to the kitchen where I start to do some of the enormous pile of dirty dishes Cici has accumulated.

There is a specific gravity known by the children of the famous that I'm certain is quite different from the gravity that holds most people to the planet. It is, I would say, a more horizontal force. Instead of being magnetized vertically, two polar forces seem to be at work from left and right. I step outside the front door. The house is up on a hill in the Sunset District. Everything here is inordinately quiet. A neighbor shutting the door of his house and going to his green Nissan and opening the driver's seat door is almost a pantomime.

The day is lovely, the air gentle and balmy. Cici wakes up around noon, early for her, and I tell her to get a move on, we'll drive over to Marin.

"Really?" Her eyes widen in mock-disbelief. She doesn't have a car here, but Cici's always been big on exaggerated reactions.

We drive down through the Sunset District, and through Golden Gate Park, and onto the Golden Gate Bridge. "Oh, this is exciting," Cici says coolly as we drive over the water.

Mill Valley around the Book Depot in the middle of the mild afternoon is the way I remember it from ten years ago, when I played with a trio at Jack's Pub. I park the car and we walk around window shopping for a while, and then go into a restaurant that's opened since I left, all light and air and nouvelle cuisine.

"Can you lend me $1,500?" Cici asks just after we sit down at a white table.

"No... I really can't."

She drops it immediately. I pay for lunch.

That night as I go to sleep in my father's downstairs bedroom, Cici's just getting rolling upstairs, with her television and books and marijuana and writing her novel. I wake up early, do my affirmations, and pray for Derek, my fifteen-year-old son who ran away nine weeks ago to follow The Grateful Dead. After a cup of coffee, I go to the badly tuned piano off the kitchen and begin to fool around with the chords of Miles Davis's "Nardis." The phone rings.

"I love you," my cousin Victor says. Victor is a Hollywood director.

"I love you too," I answer, looking at three old pocketknives my father had set out on the table beside the phone.

"We're a family," he says. "Cici's got to understand that too."

His son has just graduated from high school and Victor has been crying, he tells me, realizing the boy is leaving the single parent nest he's made for him. At noon—I've just opened a trunk in the basement and seen a pile of my father's old scores half-dematerialized with rot—Susan phones from L.A. and tells me she's gotten a call from the mother of a boy Derek is travelling with. The woman hears from her son by telephone regularly. The last time we heard directly from Derek was about three weeks ago. He called to say he'd been thinking about coming home in the fall and going back to school.

"She said they were in Wyoming hitchhiking to Humboldt County for a Dead concert."

"Hitchhiking?"

"Yeah, the person who was driving the van went on to Chicago, and they stayed in Colorado."

"Oh."

"Guess it's time to check in with your Higher Power," Susan says. "That's what I did."

After hanging up the phone, I go to the piano again. The sun is beginning to burn through. Cici comes into the room in her bathrobe.

"Hi, cruiser."

"You're up."

"You want some..." She holds out a joint.

"Cici, you and I don't ever talk."

"I guess not, Pete. Is it important?"

"I don't know. I think maybe it is."

"Do you ever see Roy Elvarez anymore?"

"Not since he went platinum."

"Roy was fun."

She walks out of the room. In a few minutes, I leave the house and drive over to Clement Street and walk around.

In bed downstairs that night I tune the clock-radio to the country station and remember Derek asking me to stay in his room to listen to different tracks on a Dead tape. Suddenly I'm crying.

"I'm sorry." I've woken Susan up.

"Are you sick?"

"No. It's like everything's getting small. I must be getting old."

"This is something I need to hear?"

"I don't know why I came up here."

"Because you don't have a gig for another four days and you love your sister."

"She barely knows I'm here."

"Don't be so co-dependent."

I wake from a fine dream of my father, and lie under the covers in his bed in the dank night chill of San Francisco that I remember from years ago when I was a child in this house. My father's face in the dream had a clear-eyed, open expression, a look that said he was *custodian* of his talent, charged with exercising it as fully as he could, and that this was an innocence in him. I make out electric noises above, Cici at her post-midnight mayhem. It's past three by the clock-radio. Derek is somewhere along the way to Humboldt County. He's got a concert on the horizon, a mandate to move through the world.

Just then a bird makes a single chirp outside, but it's the middle of the night and there's no follow-up.

Jobs

Through the blinds of the first floor office, David could see Gonzales Street, green and sunny with sporadic, silent traffic passing under the trees. Beside him, the two of them seated in front of Pepe's desk, was Francisco De La Cruz, and David noticed one of his pant-legs extended in front of him so that the sole of his shoe was against the front of Pepe's desk. It would be his good leg, David thought; the other leg probably wouldn't have been able to make that reach.

"You will never be able to admit this," Pepe said to De La Cruz. "Not in a million years. But I am the best friend you've ever had."

It was the kind of grandstanding Pepe liked to do when the door to the office was closed, which it was now. David had been to similar meetings, but under less stressful circumstances, and when Pepe was still the Vice Chair of the Board of Directors.

"I *know*, Pepe," De La Cruz said and giggled.

Pepe seized the moment, a softening in his friend that his broader behavior reliably brought on. "So don't try to bullshit me. Sanchez has been sitting in his office on Seventh Street running the Job Bank program between naps and getting a big check every two weeks. The only reason he wasn't given the ax is that Redman thinks he can still get out the vote."

"He runs the program," De La Cruz said weakly.

Pepe stood up in his black Gap jeans. His gut was getting bigger, David saw, but he was making a statement with the jeans and Reeboks.

"He runs the program, and a hundred other guys could do it better."

De La Cruz giggled again.

"Your instinct with the press," David interjected to him, like a small piano comp in Pepe's tenor solo, "is really impeccable. You never lose your cool."

Give the dysfunctional cripple a compliment, he thought. Of late, with his large head which always seemed to be peering up from behind his desk, he had taken on the look of the benighted Nixon during Watergate.

"But you talk to them first, David," De La Cruz said, and extended a diffident hand momentarily to his employee's shoulder, "and then tell me what I should say."

"Sure," David said.

Memo to the Executive Director: When the press call and ask what you think of the restructuring, let them know that you come from a poor farmworker family and had polio as a child, but that you indicated that you had a powerful memory and a nice feeling for the English language. Tell them that the fact that you are a micro-manager is the result of unhappy relationships with women and being the butt of cruel jokes since childhood. If you hadn't had Pepe and Sanchez as your protectors, you might never have taken the civil service exam and gotten into government service.

"That's right, use my main man David here," Pepe said, still standing and now lifting a white Reebok to the top of a two-drawer metal file cabinet. "Let David do some fronting for you."

At his desk at the Employment Development Department that afternoon, David listened to a vague message on his voice mail and returned the call.

After five rings, a female voice answered.

He said who he was and that he was returning her call.

After a pause, the woman said, "Yes. I called because I thought—maybe you could help me."

When she didn't continue, David said, "Are you out of work?"

"Yes. And I know what I'm interested in—either clerical or catering."

"How long has it been since you've had a job?"

"About two years."

"That would qualify you for our long-term unemployed classroom training program."

"Going to school?"

"Yes."

"I don't do well in school."

The voice had no obvious accent but continued to be weak and, David thought, young.

"Are you between 14 and 21? We have a new program..."

"I'm 25."

"I think the classroom training program is really the only opening that we have right now."

"But I don't do well in school. I'm not really able to concentrate. I think it has to do with depression."

"Are you on medication?" He wondered whether he was violating a regulation by asking the question.

"Yes."

He gave her the agency's Intake number, in case she decided to look into things further, and she thanked him. He said goodbye and put down the receiver.

"I'm a great story teller," Pepe said, and took a bite of a flauta. They were sitting at a table in a little Mexican restaurant in the Colonia. "Everybody says, write. I want to write. But I don't do it. How do you explain it?"

"I don't know," David said.

"David, my man, let me tell you why I don't write the great Mexican American novel."

It was another sunny cool spring Oxnard day. Two Mexican workers came in and placed an order at the counter.

They sat down at a table catty-corner from where David and Pepe sat.

"Go ahead, tell me. But actually I already know why."

"Why?" Pepe demanded, switching into his Mexican Godfather persona.

"You don't have time."

David knew this would defuse Pepe's fear that he was about to be unmasked.

"David, David, David..." Pepe said, his tone softening. "I'm scared I won't be any good."

"Hey, man, don't you Latinos have writers?"

"Of course we do. Great ones. Fuentes, for instance. Sandra Cisneros..."

A sudden breeze occurred when a customer left and Pepe seemed to lose the thread.

There was a big layoff at a water pump manufacturing firm. David met with the company's Human Resources manager, a handsome middle-aged Latino woman, and the Employment Development Department representative, a woman named Doris, a native of Brooklyn close to retirement. After twenty minutes, it emerged that 90 percent of the workers were monolingual Spanish-speaking, and that they generally would not be interested in training programs since they were likely to move quickly into other low paying production line jobs or become part of a team of farmworkers.

"They're very family oriented," the HR manager said, "and if something happens, they'll leave a job without notice and go home to Mexico. They have more money than I do. They keep their checks for a long time without cashing them. They'll pool their money and take a big house and rent out sleeping space to lots of people: someone under the stairway, another person under a table. And for each little spot, they'll get $100 a month."

"And these people," Doris said with a smile, "are actually the backbone of our economy, Pete Wilson to the contrary."

At the Monday morning staff meeting, on the other side of the table from David, Edward, a man in his seventies, a former employee who had been rehired on an interim basis to do monitoring, began to struggle not to fall over.

"Are you all right, Edward?" Blair, the assistant director, sprang to his feet on the other side of the table.

Edward normally spoke slowly but with intelligent emphasis. His face now seemed to be contracted in an effort to articulate words that had already arrived at his lips. At the same time his body was sliding sideways toward the end of the table, and he was trying to stop his fall with his thick peasant's hands at the table's edge. He looked like he was having a stroke.

Blair came around to his side and held the chair steady. Edward was able to move out of his posture and, eventually, to stand up. One of the chairs legs, it turned out, was broken and in the process of collapsing. Another chair was found and the meeting continued.

At a lull in his schedule, David dialed Pepe's number.

"Que paso?" Pepe said.

"Francisco told me today that he wasn't sure we should be having presentations from Consumer Credit Counseling Service for laid off workers because they were representing themselves as unbiased, whereas actually they're paid by the credit companies who don't want debtors to default on their loans and declare bankruptcy. He said there are times when people legitimately should declare bankruptcy."

"There are two things you need to understand about Francisco," Pepe said as David looked at a good-looking blond woman who had appeared at the front service window parallel to his desk. "Number one, he has always had, and always will have, the farmworker's perspective. Number two, he desperately needs to get laid."

At first David had believed that it was his job to make the organization work better. He had been a self-employed jazz pianist for most of his adult life and, after five years in and out of public relations jobs, was still getting used to regular, salaried employment. He was a little guilty about the biweekly pay check he received and eager to make his value to the organization known. After a few months, it became clear that although the organization was badly run, it wasn't his job to fix it, and if he continued to try, he could get fired.

David lent his son 16-year old son Stephen his car, and Stephen, who had recently quit his first job working after school at a drycleaners, knocked on the bedroom door on Saturday night and said he'd gotten rear-ended by his friend Jimmy. David got out of bed with Betty and put on his robe and went downstairs and out of their townhome to look at the damage. The right rear tail-light assembly had been shattered and pushed out of shape. He asked Stephen whether he'd been drinking and Stephen said no. Then he checked his son's breath, which was alcoholic. He asked Jimmy whether he'd been drinking, and he said no, but David didn't feel comfortable about giving his son's friend a breath test.

David and Betty took a walk in their hilly neighborhood in Thousand Oaks after dark.

"Let's do this every night," Betty said. "It's so good for us, and it helps me to unwind from Ethan Allen."

"Great," David said, inhaling as they walked uphill to a small park.

"God," Betty said, "when our kids are grown up, we'll be able to do things."

It was June but the weather was pleasantly cool and there were a lot of stars in the sky.

David and Betty's dreamy, creative younger daughter, Katie, who was 21, was going to take a course at bartending school. She didn't seem to be a natural fit with the job. She wasn't tough enough.

"What do you mean I'm not tough enough?" she screamed at Betty and David. "I can kick both of your asses. You don't know me. Because I don't associate with you. Dorks." She was sitting in the living room with the channel changer watching "Friends," and bits of other shows as she liked. She had embarked on a tirade, David knew, that could go on indefinitely. "You don't think I'm tough? You don't go out with me. People are afraid of me. When I tell them what I think, they just walk away."

"You shouldn't do that with guys," Betty said.

"I DON'T DO IT WITH GUYS!" Katie screamed.

She did it with her girlfriends. She also had engaged in physical skirmishes with her brother, Stephen. She was brave, it was true.

"I'm a lot tougher than you," she said again.

"What's with you and EDD?" Francisco asked David after a staff meeting in which the county's faster-than-anticipated timetable for their take-over of the agency was discussed.

"I wouldn't mind staying there, and it makes sense in terms of the work we do together."

"We'll have to see what the county says." He smiled. "So, David–how are you? What's going on?"

In spite of everything, David had found himself charmed by De La Cruz's demeanor at the staff meeting. He was, as ever, ready to talk exhaustively and, it seemed to David, quite uselessly on any subject that arose. At the same time, David worried that staff members would be misled that the company, stripped of its government funding, would survive under De La Cruz's leadership. The man actually belonged in Florence, in a Henry James novel.

"I'm all right," David answered. "A little uneasy with all these changes..."

"But David," De La Cruz coaxed, apparently delighted. "You have your music..."

"That, and some money, will get me a plane ticket to a small hotel in Vegas."

"You need to think of a good song, David. People make millions with a hit."

"You're right about that," he answered sheepishly. "What about you?" he said, hoping to turn the tables.

"Oh, I've been in this business a long time, and this is the way it goes. In a couple of years, I may be back at the county myself."

"Francisco's going to be opening a taco stand in the Colonia in a few months," Pepe told him that afternoon on the phone. "He's not a private sector competitor, and the county doesn't see him as a draft choice."

"So what are you going to tell him?" David asked. "He's still your friend, isn't he?"

"Francisco? Of course. But I've learned that he's only comfortable if he can give orders or receive them. If you want to be friends, it's impossible. That's why I behave the way I do around him. He loves it."

The take-over of the agency happened faster than anyone expected. All of the employees were summoned to a conference room at the Hilton across the parking lot one afternoon at 4:00. There was a vague expectation that this would be Francisco's swan song. Instead Pepe, who had been newly appointed Chair of the Board of Directors, appeared at the podium at the front of the room in a jacket and tie over his jeans and Reeboks and spoke to the employees about the change in a way David thought not unworthy of Ronald Reagan. By now David had received word that he would not be transferred to the county, that his job, after two years, was going to end.

As Pepe spoke, David found his heart beating faster. He needed to say something. He raised his hand when Pepe called again for questions, but Pepe continued to talk for quite a long time, and when he called on David, finally, he didn't use his name.

"Yes?" he said.

"Well," David said, "as this transition occurs, the Board of Directors will now be associated with the county, is that correct?"

Pepe said yes, and then talked about how the organization would also have a Board. David wanted to ask how it happened that Pepe could tell them of decisions that had already been made about the new organization they would become without input from front-line staff.

"Are you speaking, then, as the Chair of the Board for the county or the Board for the organization we are?"

"Both," Pepe said, and there was laughter from the back of the room.

David turned and saw that it was Sanchez, large and dyspeptic, standing beside the entrance.

Pepe described the organization that would remain after the county takeover. They would now compete for contracts, whereas before they had awarded them. But the same players who had brought the organization to this divestiture would still be in place: Sanchez, De La Cruz, Pepe himself, the old boy network, which didn't augur well for their ability to compete in the open marketplace.

David felt sorry for himself, and for the employees of the agency who might imagine that the organization would continue to thrive, and their jobs remain secure. But who could tell? Then too, the fact that Pepe should stand with De La Cruz and Sanchez didn't really surprise him. The worst thing about the agency was also what he most admired about it: These people were some kind of crazy family.

After the meeting, David ran into Pepe in the men's room. The loss of his job was getting to him, and he had trouble pissing at the urinal.

"I hope I didn't bug you with my questions," David said to Pepe, who was at the sinks in back of him.

"You goddam Communist," Pepe said.

David dreamed he was in an apartment on the corner of a city street. In the room with him were members of the mafia. He was concerned that they were all going to be shot at from the street, a story or two below. David asked the head figure if he was ready to have him play a gig in the city, which seemed of small importance at the time, given the threat of death.

In the dark before dawn lying in bed with Betty, David remembered Thelonious Monk nodding to him as the great man stood talking to Charlie Rouse at the bus stop across the street from the Five Spot on St. Mark's Place. Then he remembered Bill Evans opening for Herbie Mann at the YMHA. He sat down and hunched over the piano keys in that way that he had and launched into "Someone to Watch Over Me," and David felt a lump in his throat. Jazz was already his primary interest in high school, but he hadn't switched yet from guitar to piano. He should have stayed with guitar. In a few more years, everybody would be looking for guitarists and nobody but some worried lounge acts wanted a piano.

Bicoastal

I saw Lydia Sorenson again in New York last fall, after more than 30 years. I'd become famous–for fifteen minutes–for directing a commercial for the apple industry. It was strictly in the trade, my fame, but my stock rose in the Los Angeles firm I work for, and I was given a week of mostly vacation in New York. One night I went to a cocktail party at the Dakota, and there, sitting all by herself on one end of a red sofa, was Lydia. I couldn't have been more happy if I'd won a Peabody.

That night I realized the difference between us for the first time. She was *German* Jewish, hers among the families that had arrived here earlier in time and under less duress than my Russian Jewish ancestry. Lydia was beautiful, but when I saw her again, I saw that it was an evenness of temper in her, like a sort of pilot-light of the golden mean, that I'd loved most about her.

The next evening, sitting at a window table in a restaurant on Madison Avenue near the corner of 93rd Street, we talked about people we'd known and then about each other. She had been divorced for three years.

"For a while, you know," Lydia said, "I thought I needed–that I just *had* to be married again. Do you know what I mean?"

"Sure," I said. Over a decade ago, I'd been married for almost five years.

"But I discovered slowly that I had no desire *at all* to be married again." Her eyes twinkled mischieviously the way they had when she was sixteen.

After dinner, we took a walk down Madison Avenue.

"Remember doing this?" I said.

"Of course," she said and took my arm.

It was clear and cold. Suddenly I felt that old feeling of being almost a single organism, girded enough by one another's presence to weather anything.

"I'm almost fifty," I said.

"Getting older is terrible, isn't it?" Lydia said.

"You're still beautiful, Lydia."

"Yes," she said, "but there are all these little aches everywhere now."

We were passing the darkened Whitney Museum.

"I feel good with you," I said.

"Me too, Harry. But we shouldn't spoil it by being anything more than perfect friends."

"That's it?" In another lifetime we'd kissed for an hour but gone no further. "We might be ready now," I said, half-joking.

"Perfect friends," Lydia said solemnly.

At the entrance to her building, between Madison and Park on 71st Street, she didn't invite me up, and there was nothing left to do but say goodnight. I kissed her lightly. Cold with the weather, her lips lingered for a brief moment.

"Good to see you again, Harry," she said after the kiss.

"Good to see *you*, Lydia," I said. And then, "You're sure?"

"Yes, but we should talk more now."

"Maybe it's a control issue," I said. I knew I was pushing it, but why not? I thought. "Did you ever think of that, Lydia? But we owe it to ourselves to acknowledge that we care about each other. And it's perfectly all right to admit that and get completely run through the wringer, if necessary." Suddenly I was getting worked up.

"I do care about you, Harry," she said, giving me a

quick second kiss. "Call me." Then she disappeared into her building.

Not happening, as we say in California. I would return to my hotel room now and read the book I had waiting there. I'd brought it with me, not knowing I'd see Lydia again. Now I would read it secure in the knowledge that Lydia—was intact, I guess. Not everyone that I'd known from my Upper East Side days was, after all. She would return to her co-op, happy about ... knowing what she did and did not want to do, maybe. It wasn't Gershwinesque.

Back on Madison Avenue, I walked toward my downtown hotel. Why had her lips lingered like that? I wondered. Walking, I told myself that she might even be in the throws of a powerful attraction. I entertained this idea as if to see if it might take hold. Naturally, there was the potential of getting hurt. Was I hurt? I wasn't really hurt because it hadn't gone that far. I hadn't held her in my arms and wept. I could have done it with her, though. Not with my ex-wife, but with Lydia Sorenson, the first and perhaps the last love of my life. That I wanted to do this with somebody who, for whatever reason, didn't want to do it, probably indicated that I had an intimacy problem.

I walked across a deserted 62nd Street. Perhaps we were at our best just walking arm in arm, after all. However, I seemed at that moment to really *love* Lydia Sorenson, which was a breakthrough. Pure and simple. You didn't argue with love. I thought when I got back to my room, I might phone her. Then again, it was probably a bad idea. She might be upset and try to control the situation by pushing me away. Thank God I was getting a plane back to L.A. in the morning. I could avoid going to the telephone for the night, and then, when I got back, work would take over. So I walked and wondered, hearing my shoes on the deserted streets, in the perfect New York night.

My Literary Life

1

I was summoned to Los Angeles on the basis of interest in my first novel, a Hollywood satire I brashly titled *Sometimes a Moron*. It was the sixties. I remember the first phone call I got from Danny Laveggio. He told me he was in New York for only a day and wouldn't have time to see me but wanted to know what my favorite television show was. I was living with Beverly and our infant daughter, Lilac, at The Chelsea in a small suite next to Viva's larger one.

"Who are you?" I said into the old fashioned phone, surveying the low buildings on the downtown side of The Chelsea. It was a lovely spring afternoon.

"The head of Paramount," Danny answered, and added, "I hope not '*always* a moron.' "

I was silent.

"I'm joking with you," Danny said. "Loved the book, and I've got an idea for you, but I need to know, kid. I have to know about your favorite TV show"

"I'm a fan of *Mod Squad*," I said without emphasis. Then I heard a dial tone.

Literary politics is, of course, a gigantic tempest in the smallest imaginable tea-pot. People nurse grudges against each other that involve no remunerative dimension. My poet friends couldn't forgive me for writing a novel, even a postmodern comedy of manners like *SAM*. Simultaneously, I was being feted by the uptown crowd. My portrait with long hair and a torn shirt pocket was taken by Tim Zax and appeared in *Vogue*. Big deal. And yet it was.

On the other end of the literary spectrum, Orson Silo is a workaholic who likes to come on as a casual guy who hangs around street corners in Minneapolis/St. Paul. Hogwash, as he might say. In truth, Silo's *mother* didn't see him for two definitive years of his early adolescence when he was a contributing editor of a magazine called *Toys*. He spent all that time covering trade shows and conventions. The thing that fools people about him is his voice. He talks slowly so people think he just sits around. I met him at my editor's office and found his voice, which he's obviously over-fond of, a soporific. The man makes a bowl of cereal out of the most simple sentence.

I heard from Laveggio two weeks later via a telephone call at three in the morning.

"Hello," I said groggily after finding the receiver and bringing it to my face in bed. The baby woke up and started crying.

"Laveggio here."

"What time is it?" I asked.

"What time is it? If it's Tuesday, this must be Belgium, yadda yadda. Oh shit."

"Exactly."

"I'm jet-lagged. You're *later* there."

"Right."

"I've got a project for you. I need you to hop a plane. United. At noon."

"L.A.?"

"No, S.F. San Francisco. I'll meet you at the airport. Then we'll take the weekend in Bolinas."

"Bolinas?" I said incredulously. "That's where all my so-called friends live."

"So you'll feel right at home," Danny said, heedless to my situation.

He turned out to be this compact roly-poly–looking guy with tousled curly hair who actually had a strong physical presence, a vitality that seemed to strike sparks. All the legends, generally speaking, are like that, including Silo. The problem is what are the rest of us supposed to do if these guys don't hire us, or even if they do. (Write a book about it, I hear you saying, gentle reader. And, yes, why not write a book.)

The weekend in Bolinas was highlighted by an evening at the bar, Smiley's, and getting shanghaied over to Roy Parker's place in Paradise Valley with the poet Horton Dobbs periodically voluble. These two were native literary lights so I felt lucky. At least I didn't have to listen to Easton Forbes achieve torque through gibberish. It's enough to make one long for Silo's simple ways.

"I've got a movie for you," Roy told Danny when they were arm in arm in a room lit by two kerosene lamps.

I'd gotten comfortable with a pillow on the wood floor.

"Good, good," Laveggio said.

Roy went on to outline something about tree work in the depths of the Yucatan and then a peyote ritual that elevated him to an intergalactic parallel or some such.

"I hear you," Laveggio said from somewhere.

When I woke up it was day, and the tent was empty and smelled of recently split cypress, one of my favorite smells.

"This is where I want to live," I told Laveggio when I spied him off the porch, pissing into a dark spot of bushes.

We had breakfast at Scowleys, the restaurant across the street from Smiley's. Randy Fontaine served up fine omelettes and his brother Coon, sportswriter for the *Bolinas Hearsay News*, waited the tables. Easton Forbes peered in the window at one point but didn't come in.

The couple of days in Bolinas accomplished very little. Danny wanted a sixties black comedy and I couldn't interest him in a send-up like *Skidoo,* which in fact Preminger had just wrapped. My agent, Steve Huckle at United Lights, not wanting to waste the free round trip package to the coast, had me head down to Hollywood and set up a lunch appointment for me with the agent Samuel Zarem at the Polo Lounge to discuss working with him on his memoirs, a project that never happened. Now the place is wall-to-wall hookers, a silicone valley unto itself, but then it was still considered chic.

I had been warned that women in Hollywood could make a man an idiot but it was Orson Silo who did most of the warning and I had misinterpreted it as bragging. I see now that it's mostly youth itself that makes one ricochet like a pinball in an electrified maze. Women are everywhere in the business and they are often extraordinary looking, or acting, or both. Being married with a little daughter was gravity I needed, though I won't pretend I didn't stray in mind, and once, regrettably, in deed.

Women who are driven are only interesting to a certain point. Once you get past the drive, there's a darkness as big as the American heartland, and this is the inner personality, so to put it.

Laveggio suddenly had it in mind that I should write a picture for Trudy Winslow, who had a big series that year, and might be a big new star. She was a little like Streisand, although she came from as near as Pasadena, and a little like Lana Turner. They figured they had an opportunity.

The day after I met Sam Zarem, I took a story meeting with her.

"What's your name again, honey?" she said in her cottage in Malibu.

"Jamie," I said. "Jamie Read."

"Yeah," she said vaguely. "I might have heard of you."

It was obviously the Zax photograph.

"Well," I said, leaning back on the sofa. "I have a silly idea for a script."

She gave me a dark look and I hurried to amend any unintended slur. "I mean I think it might be fun."

"What's it about?" She sat down in a chair to one side of the sofa and gave me her undivided attention. She was wearing a dark silk blouse over a pair of jeans and was barefoot.

The night before it had come to me that I could do a sort of film version of my novel, do it all in a contracted time frame as a series of set pieces, and, I was fairly certain, an obligatory murder, but essentially maintaining a buoyancy that would be comic. A central character would be, as in Fitzgerald's narrative, the offspring of a studio executive, but the similarity would end there. It would be a guy and he would be the fulcrum for a series of scenes in which, while he remained unflappable, he routinely became the victim. I wanted to call it "Beverly Hills Moron."

"You sound real bitter, honey. What's the matter? Did someone fuck you? You want some coffee or something?"

"That's okay," I said. "Actually, I really do think it could be funny. You know these people who like, sculpt, these deals? I mean the writer gets routinely screwed, but this guy would be a producer. You know, he drives a Porsche, is seen with everybody who's hot, and has all the confidence in the world, but it's because he doesn't get it."

"That's sad, honey. Anyway, I don't want to play a moron. But it's the guy, right?"

"Right. No, it wouldn't be you. You'd be the heroine, who saves him. By sheer instinct and native smarts, you carry the day. You're this girl–woman–he meets on a plane."

"Like a stewardess or something?"

"Exactly. And he woos you so big time that you can't *not* go out with him, and each time you see how to turn around this mess he gets himself into."

"Who do you want for the guy?"

"Steve Stevens." He hadn't yet come off *Saturday Night Live* but was obviously slated for major stardom.

"I like it," she said.

That was my first meeting with Trudy, and it was one of the first times that as a writer my mind was set in motion by someone outside the circuits of what I innocently still thought of as normal life. I wouldn't have been likely to know her without the intervention of Laveggio. I called Orson Silo, who was at a theater in Atlanta with his one-man show for a week or two to get his input, and, also, I suppose, to let him know that I was now in the big time, too.

"Good for you, sport. Just keep your privates out of it. Take my word for it, it's bad for the life *and* the art."

"Just how far did you go with Esther Printemps, anyway?" I practiced such boldness with Silo strictly as a comic turn. He was no more likely to confide in me than in Richard Nixon–actually less likely. Nixon might have gotten him to open up. Silo's whole life was devoted to perfecting a persona that was a manufacturing phenomenon, a one man literary-commercial hydra, everything feeding into everything else, until he himself, Orson Silo, was nowhere to be found. Having glimpsed him unguarded once or twice, I believed he'd done us all a big favor, but I was fascinated by the drive behind his self-annihilation. He harked back to some pioneer instinct of self-obliteration. He seemed to be a verb.

"And if you do kiss, don't tell–anybody. But above all the wife," Silo confided.

Silo's wife was his childhood sweetheart, back in St. Paul. They saw each other for maybe sixty days out of the year. His marriage was a place for him to visit on the holidays. I knew of course that writers are not necessarily good people, as Plato explained. The personal volatility, which can contribute to the liveliness of a work, can also create interpersonal and domestic havoc.

"I'm getting a lot of mixed messages from you," I told Silo. "But I'm just trying to do my job."

"Good for you, sport," he said. "Write a monologue for me and I'll put it in the show."

I put down the phone and lay back on the bed and closed my eyes in the afternoon light that filtered through the hotel blinds. There are worse states in life for a writer than confusion, but it's not great to have too large a range of options except at the typewriter.

2

Beverly Hills Moron, while it made both Steve Stevens' movie career and *could have* made mine as a movie writer, wasn't an easy initiation. Trudy had certain standards as to what was acceptable in a script, Steve Stevens had more of them, and as the writer on the project, I was bounced back and forth between the two of them until I knew I had forfeited my compass. I forgot what time it was, what day it was, and enjoyed myself thoroughly, bought Beverly and Lilac nice gifts, and put a down payment on a little place on Outpost in the Hollywood Hills.

The problem was the compass. The compass was knowing who I was and knowing the things I liked to do when I was who I was. Los Angeles is quite beautiful, Beverly began to paint landscapes of the Hollywood hills, and I secretly envied her. She was being an artist and I had become a talent. There were certain things I knew I could do dependably well. I was good at dialogue. I had a good sense of humor. But my understanding, an overview, my writer's capital were all in hock. Or buried somewhere I no longer remembered. In place of it, though, I had a lot of money. I was a young guy. I was married to a lovely woman, I had a lovely little daughter. I was reasonably good-looking. After the picture was a hit, certain women let me know they were available.

At a cocktail party at my agent's I was introduced to a young New York actress who had just done her first film, and, as we stood idly chatting, she insinuated her leg between my two legs and we continued chatting. Beverly was standing maybe ten feet away and I was too callow: one, not to be duly titillated; and two, to go one step further. It was an odd short-lived tableau. If there had been a way to fuck her in this position I can't say I wouldn't have tried. I'd asked about her work on the picture and she was answering with a serious aspect while her leg stood, so to speak, against us. I never saw her again after the party. I heard she went on to marry an agent and gave up her career.

Trudy invited me over ostensibly for a meeting about another script. It was the following spring, the movie was just out, and she came to the door in a bright red bikini she was falling out of and kissed me wetly on the mouth.

"Hi, genius," she said.

In less than five minutes, I was out of my clothes and in her enormous bed. Beverly had taught me how to make love, but Trudy seemed to know every corner of my sexual psyche, and was ready to field even the slightest nuance of an idea. Then she popped an amyl nitrate inhaler in and out of my nose at the big moment and I'd never experienced *that* before.

When it was over, I gradually reassembled as a psychological and mental entity and realized I didn't have much in common with her, notwithstanding that she was a sexual special effects team in one person. With that kind of sexual radar, she was surely unique in the universe, and I think it must be hard for such a woman. Then over the years, I've wondered whether what we shared wasn't something between us that didn't occur between her and others.

After our liaison, I drove to the Chateau Marmont and phoned Beverly to say I had a late meeting at Universal and would be home after dinner. I figured I reeked of sex and needed to decompress and maybe shower again, too. I called up Orson Silo at the Sunset Marquis. He had left a message for me that morning, and it dawned on me that I might have gone over to Trudy's under Silo's psychic umbrella, so to speak.

"There's the boy," he said on the phone. "*Moron* does you proud."

I sensed ambiguity but let it ride. With Silo, it's all tease anyway so why get offended. I could tell him I thought his complete works were a load of shit, but why should he know that?

He had left the door open and when I peeked in he was sitting with a paperback edition of *The Gutenberg Galaxy* by McLuhan.

"Come in, come in," he said. "Take a load off. What will you have? Beer, wine, a Coke?"

"Have you got any coffee?"

Silo had stood up in his jeans and white tee shirt, a muscular ape-man with a large odd-shaped head and a little smile.

"I want you to try the house cappucino, so hold it." He picked up the phone and ordered two as I looked out his window on the eastern exposure, oddly green for being just a stone's throw below Sunset Boulevard.

"What I never realized about McLuhan before is what a great Shakespearean and Joycean scholar he is. Did you ever read *Finnegans Wake*?"

"A page or two," I said. "It's not my cup of tea."

"'Cup of *meat*'–to quote Bobby Dylan, who reminds me of Joyce."

"I hear he may move out here," I said.

"Dylan? But he's the very heraldic crest on the East Coast sensibility..."

"It just goes to show you, I guess."

"You can't second-guess poets."

"I guess not."

"All right, all right," said Silo. "What have you been up to?"

He looked pointedly at me. "Oh," he said, after a moment. "Well, now, no need to get *that* serious, is there?"

3

We rented a house on the mesa in Bolinas that spring. I needed to get out of town. If there was a lesson in the Trudy Winslow episode for me, it was that it would be possible for me to fall down the rabbit hole into a completely different life, ruin the one I had started, forget that I ever *had* a compass, and discover stuff that wouldn't have to do with anything I ever had it in mind to do. The silence, exile, and cunning Joyce advised *is* a survival kit for a writer. The problem was I didn't come by these qualities as a birthright, but was just a sociable fellow who happened to have grown up in an age when literature still mattered and Malamud and Salinger and Pasternak and Capote and McCullers and Kerouac and Mailer had opened me up and escorted me into a larger universe.

Then I got lucky and met Beverly, and then I started making money in Hollywood because the business loves someone in whom it assumes some kind of superiority, a novelist instantly qualifying, who can then be bought for relative peanuts.

I walked on the beach below the Mesa. Bolinas never has a summertime and I never went swimming there. It was said to be a healing place for the Miwok Indians, who would live there only temporarily. Now poets had moved in, as if they might heal the society by constantly healing themselves. But more likely you would find them in Smiley's Bar each night.

I was indulged as a mild curiosity for a while after having moved there.

"*Beverly Hills Moron* is a piece of shit!" a writer named Ray Brown shouted at me in Smiley's one night. But Joanne Abbott, the elegant poet from Vallejo, shouted back at him to shut up and he did, somewhat sheepishly.

"I liked the movie," she said to me at the bar. "I thought it was better than the book."

I didn't know how to take that and, as a stalling strategy, said, "You read the book?"

She laughed and so did Larry Anson, a red-faced expatriate from Brooklyn.

I laughed too. Then we stopped laughing.

"You did or didn't... read it?" I said after a while.

Joanne started laughing again and so did Larry Anson.

"Okay," I said, "I give up."

"We like you," Joanne said. Then she giggled again.

It was an interesting place to be at that moment and the fact that a lot of poets lived there was only a small part of it. The sixties were coming to an end slowly, and the sixties had given me a sense of belonging I'd never really had growing up. I was neither an athlete nor a scholar and my first forays into writing had gotten mixed and/or dubious results. Then I seemed to find my feet. I was living in a house in Cambridge, Massachusetts in Central Square that I shared with two other would-be artists, one a writer and the other an actor-director who was trying to get something going in Cambridge that he could then ride into New York.

One afternoon I started a play about the group of sixties drop-outs who frequented our rented house. I set it in the living room directly under my bedroom upstairs. Instead of spending a day trying to figure out how to splice a stanza of a poem that would be read by maybe a few hundred people, I suddenly had characters, action and drama.

It was retro I knew, of course, right away. This stuff wasn't going to mean a thing to Ted Theigs, the other writer in the house, but when I showed it instead to Ray Durand, the actor-director, he got excited.

"I'll run with this. I need it a little longer, like a full hour. Can you do that?"

"Sure," I said.

"Okay, we'll do a double bill with something by one of the new guys downtown."

"Great," I said. I didn't know any playwrights.

The theater was, and still is, for my money, the best party

of all. Nobody goes truly insane because the stakes aren't so phenomenal that you confuse yourself with a demigod.

I remember the night Easton Forbes came to see *Captain America* at the Cherry Lane, where it moved after a run at the Poets Theater in Cambridge. We went to the dairy restaurant Ratners on the Lower East Side.

"So, what did you think of it?" I asked him. He still hadn't told me.

"It's good," he said. "But, you know, I mean you have to ask yourself...The real point is, what?—that we don't see money because it's the coin of the realm, so it's invisible? So you have to ask yourself if the play is like the same thing. It's entertaining, you know, I mean I think you're talented, man."

Here I recognized that he was kicking in with an imitation of Ted Berrigan, the poet guru of the Lower East Side, who told me he loved the play. Berrigan was an anomaly on the scene since he had both generosity of spirit and social skills.

"Thanks, Easton," I said.

I knew I had talent and that his words were all hedges against something that had no relevance to me at all. I was making a small amount of money for the first time, too.

The novel happened after a first brief foray in Hollywood where nothing went right, and I went back to New York without an assignment. Beverly, whom I'd met in Cambridge, was pregnant. We got married at City Hall one afternoon with Ray Durand as best man and witness, and then left the city. We ended up renting a little apartment in Marblehead, which I'd visited once from Cambridge and Beverly knew from summer trips with her parents, who had lived in Boston and now lived in London. It was quiet and we waited for the baby and I wrote the book to have something negotiable before the little money I had ran out. Just before the baby was born Steve from United Lights came up to see me and I gave him the book.

"It's hilarious," he said over the phone three nights later. "I think I've got an editor for you."

"Great," I said.

The contractions started in the middle of the night and I drove Beverly through the dark deserted streets and over the almost empty freeway to the hospital in Stoneham. She was born around noon: Lilac, a little pink and white flower.

4

"Are you working on anything right now?" Steve asked me over the phone from L.A.

I was watching the rain fall on the houses out our living room window in Bolinas.

"Actually, I'm reading a lot and trying to plug myself in."

"What if I told you Danny Laveggio has an idea for you and is willing to tack down a deal right now."

"I can always use the money, but I really don't want to work down there right now."

"That's all right. He'll come up. He says he knows a lot of people up there from when you were there together."

"Yeah, is he going to bring up Heather Storm?"

"Nobody knows. Does it matter?"

So Danny came up again and made things quicken with his electric Hollywood vibe. And Heather Storm came up with him. They rented this big cubical house at the corner of Overlook and threw a big party the first weekend. Beverly decided to stay at home with Lilac, who had a cold, and I walked over there on a Friday night.

In the dark on Elm Road, I recognized Larry Anson walking toward the party too.

"How's it going, Larry?" I said.

"You want a hit?" he said.

He held out a paper bag, which I took, and, after a small swallow of whiskey, handed back.

"What's doing?" I said.

"Nothing much," Larry said. "Just trying to get along."

The place was literally pulsing in the night, every window

lit and the bass line of Jimmy Cliff's "The Harder They Come" seeming to animate the whole two story edifice.

"Jesus," Larry said as we approached the front door.

Everybody in Bolinas seemed to be there that night with their various, overlapping entourages. The attorney, Paul Razner, who was fighting the county sewer project which would open the peninsula to runaway development, was on the living room sofa with his girl friend, Sonia, an attractive divorcee with a perennially angry look. Razner, a big guy who stayed just shy of being fat, had a mild paternal demeanor, but was evidently a terror at meetings of the County Board of Supervisors.

Danny was talking with Joanne Abbott and Robert Squires, one of the poets who had made me want to write, who had recently moved to Bolinas with his wife Betty, with whom it was rumored he was breaking up. I got a beer in the kitchen and then came out and stood against the wall, trying to get my bearings. The mix of people, of worlds really, made me want to get out of the room.

"I love Hollywood," Squires was saying genially to Danny and eyeing him with a twinkle of kindness or contempt.

The great thing about Laveggio is that he would see the kindness and respond to it, and not consider if it was actually contempt. He told me the next day that he thought Bolinas had given him a broader horizon on our generation and that he wanted to do something relevant but not hysterical in the way of *Easy Rider.*

Larry Anson appeared beside me holding a drink. His friend Shadow came in, with his beautiful young wife. Heather Storm came from somewhere and took Danny's arm. Jimmy Cliff's "Many Rivers to Cross" came on, and Anson passed me a joint. I took a hit and passed it back to him. He took a hit and passed it back to me.

I had stopped smoking marijuana but Bolinas seemed to suspend the rules, at least at that moment. Sometimes when you are going forward into something, you know the momentum will carry you and old vices won't weigh you down as they would when you aren't in motion. I must have exchanged the cigarette once or twice more before I realized that it was some kind of homegrown grass that was far more powerful than the usual.

"That guy looks like a movie star," Danny said beside me sometime later.

"What guy?"

He indicated Shadow, standing with the beautiful Laurel Bay.

"Yeah, he's great. His father is the Director of the Winston Museum in Pasadena. He's a graduate of Princeton, and he and his wife live in a garage in back of a friend's house and cook meals on a Coleman stove."

"Jezus," Danny said. "I could take this kid and run with him. I see star power."

"Danny, wake up and smell the marijuana. This guy Shadow is like a self-styled poet slash paleontologist, okay. He doesn't want to do seven takes with Katherine Ross."

"God, you're witty. I won't ask you what paleontologist means. I once knew..."

"I read about it, okay? It's the study of prehistoric times... say, Mayan civilization. Charles Olson, who was one of the big poets for most of us, felt that the whole Western humanist Judeo-Christian tradition died in the gas showers at Dachau, that you couldn't go on after that with the anthropocentric heritage passed down to us from Socrates. That it failed us with literally industrialized, mechanized murder... So he ended up hunting among stones..."

"Gotcha! This place is exciting," Danny said. "I want you to tell this to Heather, too, or put it in a memo to me so I can tell her. We all need intellectual stimulation."

Heather, the big crossover movie star from England, came and took Danny's arm. "Where's Beverly?" she said.

"At home with Lilac, who's out of sorts tonight."

"I want to come over and see her new paintings..."

"That would be great," I said.

"Who is Laura Santz? She says she writes for *The Village Voice* and she offered me Owsley acid."

"Oh, Laura," I said. "She's a writer, but she's pretty

heavily into this new vision thing..."

"See," Danny said. "Look at this mix..." He was addressing Heather now. "This is a new society... This is the promise of the sixties actually taking shape as a new society..."

"Yeah," Heather said. "But a lot of these people have private money... It's like some kind of downward mobility thing."

Just then someone put on The Stones' "Brown Sugar" and Laura Santz, as I found out she was famous for doing, took off her clothes–she had a kind of classic Maillol body and actually looked better naked–and danced with a jazz flautist named Sammy O, who looked like a refugee from The Fabulous Freak Brothers comic strip.

5

I didn't mind getting high again that night, but noticed that the next several days involved realigning my brains so that I could approach work with a normal reserve of reliable identity. Marijuana tended to turn me into a psychologically cubist version of myself, all attitudes, but lacking Picasso's central passion. I was too aerial not to be blown off my center by marijuana, and this created a fissure in my social fluency in Bolinas. Everybody else liked to get high.

But you couldn't help being swept up in the transforming vision that seemed, for a moment, to take hold there. There had recently been a successful recall election, orchestrated by newcomers to the town like Paul Razner, which had replaced the old timers on the Utility Board, the town's only governing body since it was an unincorporated municipality, with newcomers who were around my age, under 30. I guess we only had a little while before we became untrustworthy, according to our leaders, and here we were the new town officialdom.

Imagine being young and living in a town in which the town fathers, the political powers-that-be, were your own age, many soon actually friends of yours. It was a beautiful moment, and of course the place itself was beautiful. Being a bicoastal child of a broken marriage, all the years had gone by without my understanding the reality of the moon waxing and waning, which I now observed first hand from the darkness that engulfed the mesa each night, deeper dark than I'd ever known in Los Angeles or New York.

Beverly was at the opposite end of the spectrum from the women I'd met professionally in both publishing and Hollywood. She was a painter who viewed the world with a sense of its deeper nuances of color and feeling, someone who shared with me a slower sense of time, and while she was otherwise quite different from me, this allowed us to engage a kind of short-hand with each other, not having to tack every comment down.

"Was it fun last night?" she asked after I'd finished some new pages to discuss with Danny that afternoon.

"Laura Santz took off her clothes and danced with Sammy O. Danny was in heaven."

"How did Heather take it?"

"Well, she said a lot of these people have private money, and they're doing this as a Bohemian trip not because they have to ..."

"That's true, isn't it? She's smart, Heather."

"I know. Is Danny, though?"

"Danny's a force of nature. So I guess it doesn't matter ..."

The other thing that Beverly had, which seeing different types of the women of my generation helped me to appreciate, was a natural interest and aptitude for domestic arts. She would pick a bouquet of wild flowers if we went for a walk and come home to our house and put them in a vase on the kitchen table where we ate. Or she would cook a certain dish that she liked in a restaurant or read about in a cookbook or the newspaper. This, while we went through the first year and a half with Lilac. It was, after all, that critical moment in one's life when one relinquishes being the center and pivot of the universe. Once you have a helpless creature in your midst, your ears and eyes do double duty, which is maybe why marijuana seemed so arduous to me now, as if I were already tuned to a higher frequency.

Danny reviewed my pages that afternoon at the house on Overlook and then came into the room and fell down on the sofa. I was sitting in a black leather chair beside it.

"I don't know," he said.

That was bad news, but the fact of the matter was I didn't care. I'd saved enough money to be free for a while.

"Okay," I said.

"Don't get me wrong. You're working. I see that. But I don't know what we should be working on, if you want to know the truth. I'm thinking about quitting the business."

This was new, although Danny was a grandstander if he was anything.

"What do you mean by quitting the business," I said.

"Jesus. Quit." There was a big, muscular dark and light cloud formation out the living room window that seemed to begin right over the tops of the cypress trees but there was no rain yet. "Do something else. These people seem to be on to something. So, you're reading tonight? What are you going to read, *Moron* or something."

"I don't know," I said. I'd been invited by Joanne Abbott to read in the series she was doing at the Public Utilities Building main room on Monday nights, but still hadn't figured out what I was supposed to read. "I don't want to sound too..."

"... Hollywood. Too Hollywood. I mean *I* know you're not, but do they know it?"

"I don't know. How does Heather feel about it?"

"Your reading? Nothing..."

"No. About you're quitting the business."

"Listen. Heather's a friend, but don't think for one minute I delude myself that she's really into me. She's great, believe me. I don't want to talk about that part."

Danny actually didn't brag about his conquests, Hollywood-style. There was an endearing and reassuring modesty in this. He took his success with gratitude, with no ingrained sense of entitlement.

Almost everybody who attended the reading was a friend or acquaintance. Joanne Abbott introduced me as "a writer we all could learn from," at which point Ray Brown shouted "but not about writing!" Joanne shushed him, giggled, and continued. "His early poetry had a fluency that many of us noticed, but I don't know if anyone could have predicted what came next. He's proven himself to be a contemporary master of dialogue." Somebody then yelled, "Copout!"

I wondered as I read a scene out of *SAM* that I thought was funny whether it wasn't time that I said something to Ray Brown. All I could think of was, "Fuck you." Then Easton Forbes laughed at something, and a couple of people laughed at something else, and in the next thirty seconds everything turned around. The scene I read started striking them as funny.

It was about taking a meeting with a very young studio executive who was a street smart babe who makes the writer, director, and producer squirm with artistic frustration and bemused libido.

Beverly held Lilac sleeping in her arms and I went to her directly from the podium.

"Who is that guy?"

"Ray Brown. I guess I'm supposed to punch him or something."

"Please don't," Beverly said. "He's mentally ill, and when did you start punching people?"

"Never. I'm just wondering when I should start."

"Don't," Larry Anson said and smiled. "If he gets out of line again, I'll knock his lights out." Anson didn't strike me as particularly formidable.

Ray Brown came over wearing a battered baseball cap, decades before it was chic. "I apologize," he said. "Please accept my apology."

He had a sort of half-assed grin and I couldn't tell whether he was kidding or not.

"Sure," I said.

Joanne Abbott came up behind Brown and said they were all going to go down to Smileys. After driving Beverly and Lilac home, I joined them there. That night Brown told me he was going to punch me unless I gave him a good reason not to: we were both standing at the bar and I couldn't think of anything to say so I shoved him as hard as I could. My father had once told me that if you're going to fight someone put everything you have into the first move and you may cut it short. Ray Brown stumbled and then fell down on the floor. Then he looked up at me and smiled crookedly.

"You stupid fuck," he said.

Larry Anson grabbed me hard around the shoulder and said, "Don't do anything else, okay? Ray's a sick guy. This was your initiation."

"Did you punch Ray Brown?" Danny asked me the next day in his living room. It was raining.

"No, I pushed him. He told me he was going to punch me."

"What is he, sick or something?"

"I guess it has something to do with integrity. That's why I came up here, to get away from Hollywood. Only you follow me up here and confuse everybody."

"Yeah, well, Ray Brown doesn't want to punch me."

"Are you still thinking about quitting the business?"

"If I did I'd have nothing to do ... I'm thinking of trying to do a documentary about this place, though, you know. Bring the Maysles brothers up here, and do something. Do you realize the women here have a regular peyote meeting?"

"How'd you find that out?"

"Heather. Joanne Abbott invited her to eat some buttons on the beach on Wednesday night."

"So far they haven't asked Beverly."

"She's taking care of a baby. They're not going to ask her. That's why it's good that Heather and I can scout some of these other scenes out. I don't know, it's like a weird matriarchy, you know. Is that what was at the bottom of the sixties?"

"You got me. But maybe that's good. Anyway, I don't want to just cover this as a story; I'm sort of *inside* the story. Larry Anson told me last night that it was an initiation, what Ray Brown did to me."

"Look, let's not lose our marbles, okay. By the way, where are Roy and Horton?"

"They're around, but I gather they hate the poets. You know these guys are friends from before the influx of East Coast savvy, Harvard and all. They see some of these people as interlopers, but some of the others they like and get along with."

6

I walked home. Beverly had gotten a phone call from my mother in Los Angeles. It wasn't often that she called, and I tried to stay in touch but had a hard time thinking of things to say on the phone. She had married an ophthalmologist after my father and since I'd dropped out of UCLA and moved to the East Coast our relationship had never really found its ground.

"She sounded worse," Beverly said.

"Like what? She's dying?"

"I don't know. There's no particular direction to the call anymore, like she just happened to dial here and have my voice come on the phone out of a bunch of choices..."

I dialed the house in Pacific Palisades, and Janey, the black maid, answered.

"Hi, it's Jamie. Is Mom around?"

"Jamie, listen to me," Janey said. "Don't you know your Mama's dying? When are you coming down here?"

"I didn't realize that, Janey. When should I?"

"That's for you to decide, honey. Don't you love your Mama?"

Things had gotten confused around the time of the divorce, and my mother, a good-looking young woman suddenly thrown on the high-seas of the reality principle with an eight-year-old boy, hadn't been up to the shift. I'd had an idyllic time with her the first year and a half of my life when my Dad had been overseas in the army during the Second World

War. But at eight I'd begun to perceive her not just as an individual but as one with an obdurate self-absorption that was stronger than I was. In other words, she wasn't great as a Mom. She had been struggling with some kind of malabsorption syndrome for several years, but when she wasn't suffering pain because of it, she exulted in her weight loss. My step-dad, Harry, was on perennial call and the two of them, while operating from the same address, seemed to have drifted apart.

Beverly and I decided to go down with Lilac for a visit. Lilac had said her first word–"Ball!"–and had been walking for a few weeks. We drove over to the house in the Palisades in a rented Corolla. Janey, a large black woman who was forthright and sometimes seemed to be in charge of the family, let us in.

"Who's this?" she said, smiling at Lilac. "Who's this *big* person? Hunh? I don't know who this one is, do I?"

"Ball!" Lilac said.

"Ball?" Janey said. "What 'ball' she talking about, Jamie? She want a ball or something?"

"It's her first word," Beverly said.

"Well, ain't that something," Janey said, and we stepped into the kitchen and hugged her.

My mother was upstairs in her bed, Janey told us, and we could go up there. She was expecting us. When I got upstairs and walked into her rose-wall papered cornucopia of a room, riddled with small expensive accessories but with no photographs of her granddaughter let alone her son and daughter-in-law, I was surprised at her weight loss. She looked drawn, although she was fully made-up.

"How are you, Mom?" I said smiling and went to kiss her.

"How are you, darling," she said. "Beverly, darling..." Beverly followed me, holding Lilac down to her grandmother. "Oh, my God!" she said. "Oh, my God, who's this beautiful girl?"

She focused directly on Lilac and the baby seemed to respond.

"Ball!" she said.

"Ball!" my mother echoed. "She said 'ball.' Oh my God! That's the best thing I've heard in ten years. She said *ball,* didn't she?" My mother looked at me, smiling, old, but suddenly infused with interest.

"It's her first word," I said while Beverly sat down with Lilac.

"She's a little divinity," my mother said. "Beverly, how are you, darling? It's hard work, isn't it?"

"I'm fine, Amy... We like it in Bolinas, and Lilac's sleeping more..."

"Good, darling. And how's my darling boy?"

"I'm good, Mom. What about you?"

"Sweetheart, your Mom's dying," she said and made no obvious attempt to underscore or undercut the words.

I sat down and nodded. "Really, Mom," I said.

"Your old Mom's dying," she said again and shrugged.

"What is it?" I said.

"Darling, I haven't got a clue. I've got the body of a fifteen year old. I haven't looked this good in years. But it's because I'm not digesting anything. Finally I can eat as much as I want and I'm dying. Well, fuck it! Oh my God, how could I talk like that in front of this beautiful, beautiful little girl."

In our room at the Westwood Holiday Inn, the message light was on, and I got Silo on my Voice Mail. "Hi, old timer. How's the boy. I called Steve and he told me you'd chucked in the towel and become one of the Bolinas lames and mutes. Jesus, grow up. If we don't do it, who will? That question worries me a lot because I know I don't want it to be Gordon Lish or Harold Brodkey or the rest of that high-strung stable who don't know how to put one foot in front of the other."

He left his number at the Sunset Marquis. Maybe he secretly lived there. Beverly was nursing Lilac to sleep on her side of the big king-size bed in the middle of our room. I took my shoes off and lay down on the bed.

"Where's my step-father?" I said looking up at the ceiling.

"Oh, I don't think they're together, really, are they?" Beverly whispered.

"She's dying, though," I said.

"So what do we do?"

Beverly sat up on the bed and buttoned her dress. Then she took a small blanket out of our suitcase and put it over Lilac.

"I don't seem to be able to feel anything. I remembered that when they got divorced, when I was eight, for some reason she bought me this expensive blue suede jacket, and I was really proud of it and loved it. But she couldn't really pay attention to me. The jacket was in lieu of that, I guess. I remember I once opened a door to the bedroom of this little apartment she had on Olympic and McCarty Drive in Beverly Hills and she was lying naked face down across the bed, with her head away from me, and just as the door opened she farted."

"What did you do?"

"Closed the door. She was this beautiful young woman then, completely lost I guess."

"She doesn't seem to care about dying. It's strange."

"She's only in her sixties."

"I guess her whole life has been about being beautiful..."

"Let me ask you something," I said.

"What?"

"Will we ever make love again?"

"Once I recover my energy and identity maybe," Beverly said. "You don't know what it's like to be tied to this little engine all day. She's tiny but she's the locomotive and all I do is just follow her around, while you get to go off and talk to Orson Silo."

"Consider yourself lucky. Can you get a sitter? Maybe we can have dinner. He's probably dating somebody famous."

"I thought he was married."

"He is."

"How hideous," she said.

"Power is the ultimate aphrodisiac."

"Maybe in Hollywood. Love is actually more exciting."

"Anyway, I'll call him. Let's get a sitter."

"Dinner," Silo said on the phone. "Wonderful... Have you been to L'Orangerie yet? I'll take you. I'll bring my friend."

"Fine," I said.

The friend turned out to be Trudy Winslow, which was a dirty trick. But Trudy behaved with impeccable cool that had me wondering if I'd misjudged her. Was she really that woman I'd known?

"You two don't belong in Bolinas," Silo said. He turned to Beverly. "This boy needs to get his incredible reserve busted by the unplugged dams of furious ambition, vanity and commerce flooding over him so he has to swim for his life. Otherwise, he's too goddam contemplative."

"Bolinas is quite exciting, actually," Beverly said.

"It's very new agey, right?" Trudy said.

"Well, yes, but it's much more than that," my wife, an Aquarian, answered. "You really have these people thinking they're going to create, or already have created, a new society. They're political."

"Yeah, politicians of marijuana. That's a dead issue," Silo decreed.

"I agree," I said. "That's not what's exciting. It's that they have this egalitarian model of a society that's also ecological. It's like the sixties model of the communal in the personal, and the political in the communal. I mean it's funny sometimes. You get this old timer telling some dewy-eyed Harvard boy trying to learn carpentry to go get him 'a left-handed screw-driver.' But they actually like each other."

"None of them can write like shit."

I restrained myself from telling him that neither could he. He had released an album of stories from some archive, "Tales of the Cigar Store Indian," that was a spoken word phenomenon. It was the voice. I guess it's the voice of someone who will never change: that's what it sounds like, which helped to ground us in the middle of ongoing cataclysm. Here he was sitting with Trudy Winslow. I looked over at her.

"I liked 'Silver Lake,' " I said.

"Thanks," she said not unbashfully.

"What are you doing now?"

"This lady," said Silo, "is going to be my new leading lady. We're doing a sitcom pilot. Trudy plays my business partner."

"What business?" Beverly asked.

"A small town newspaper... We're on different sides of the political fence."

"Let me guess. You want me to write it."

"Frankly, my boy... if I allowed you in on this—even the thirteen weeks we're guaranteed—you'd make so much money you'd be insufferable. However, I am considering it."

I looked at Beverly and she smiled. Then I looked at Trudy.

"We watched *Beverly Hills Moron* last night. It's really not a bad picture," she said smiling.

I was unschooled enough to imagine that writing for a sitcom would approximate what I had done as a screenwriter. But writing for a weekly television show is the literary equivalent of midget wrestling. Bring four or five desperate and funny people into a room with some sort of basic story line for the week and have them tie each other in knots of comic ingenuity. I met some of the people who would dominate the coming decades with their powerful dramatic instincts. These weren't exactly writers but they weren't dumb. It's tag-team writing.

Since our place on Outpost was rented, we got a little apartment in Santa Monica and I burnt the midnight oil at Studio City with the gang and *Print It!* was born. Silo was actually a better actor than I would have thought. His physical stolidity came out in the same way his voice played, the "just folks" thing he had going. Then we got Jimmy Coco to do an inspired turn as the leader of a new age cult who moves into the little town in Humboldt County, and the show started to take off.

The problem was I missed Bolinas in Studio City, and, to be honest, Studio City in Bolinas. Steve at United Lights was practically turning cartwheels every time I got him on the phone because television is where the real money is. He wanted to get me writer-producer status.

"You'll never have to work again! I swear to you! You'll never have to work again!"

"Steve, I'm twenty-nine. What am I supposed to do with the rest of my life."

"You're right. I hear you, buddy."

I don't think he heard me, but he said there was nothing wrong with building the nest egg so that the next big project that I generated could be done, and that that's what I needed to think about...

I walked below the mesa on the beach in Bolinas in a raw wind and a bright raw light. Beverly and I recovered our equilibrium with Lilac now in tow. One night we got a baby sitter, had dinner at The Station House Cafe in Point Reyes and as we were driving back toward the house, I pulled over on Route 1 and stopped the car for a while.

"Jesus," I said.

"What," she said, smiling.

"Well, I mean you never do that kind of thing. What happened?"

"I know that's what Trudy Winslow does..."

"How do you know that?"

"I can just tell."

"So," I said. "What do you think about it?"

"It's okay, if I'm in the mood."

What I counted on in her was that her mood was based on her own self-generated interests and not tied to me. It was reassuring to me because if I was uncertain about who I was, if that seemed to be an occupational hazard of my working life at the moment, I could trust that she was in her own state less conditionally. Not that Beverly wasn't sometimes hard to fathom, and sometimes hard to be around, but that in itself testified to an integrity that reassured me. I kept selling myself, and if I actually wasn't sure if that in itself was good or bad, sometimes thinking of it as a kind of literary-spiritual calisthenic, not to mention the fact that I was making a living, still I needed something more certain, something I could count on when I came home.

The sexually protean Trudy Winslow was like a mirror of my own capacity to transfigure at will—not necessarily my will at that. Beverly, like a priestess of domestic tranquility, was absorbed in questions of curtains, flowers for the garden she quickly planted in Bolinas, recipes, Lilac's schedule and her own painting. If she was unfathomable to me in her depths that also made her dependable. I knew I couldn't blow her away.

7

Growing up in Manhattan and Los Angeles, I had the mistaken assumption that a small town like Bolinas would be a simpler way of life. The fact is, aside from whatever business one has to do, cities for all their numbers are isolation chambers. Whereas a small town, and this was a town of under 2,000 people, is a place where you are soon operating under the only partial delusion that you know everybody. I got mad at my neighbor's son because he was playing his guitar too loudly early in the morning and late at night, and the kid, who was bigger than me, threatened to push my face in. I could have stood my ground and taken a big punch in the mouth or maybe delivered one, but standing in my neighbor's living room–the step-father of this boy who looked like Peter Frampton and probably dreamed of being him–I had no stiff-backed resolve to get my point across. I didn't even feel like a coward.

"I'm sorry you're taking it this way," I said, with some inner benignity I didn't want to disturb.

"I can't believe how mellow you are," the kid said.

I walked out of the house and back to our house up the hill. I wasn't a fighter, but I'd gotten in a few fights and this was a different reaction than I could have anticipated and, after the initial impulse waned, it scared me.

"What did he say?" Beverly said.

"He threatened to push my face in," I said.

"What did you do?"

"I said I was sorry he was taking it that way..."

"That's all?"

"Yeah, I should have knocked his lights out."

"No, you shouldn't," Beverly said. "You're not a teenager. Anyway, how do you know he wouldn't have knocked *your* lights out."

"Because I'm Ernest Hemingway."

"Right. Do you want some soup?"

"I guess so. If that music starts in again, I'm going to kill him. I don't know what happened to me."

"Just stop it. If it really is a bother, we'll call the police. This isn't *Gunsmoke.*"

"Don't tell Roy or Horton or Larry Anson."

"Ever since you pushed Ray Brown, you think you're a fighter."

"Look," I said, sitting down to a bowl of miso soup in the dark of the living room with a single candle on the table for light. "I didn't fight. I backed down. I don't want to fight some teenager. I'm too old or something."

"Good. You have a wife and child. You can't afford that nonsense."

So I went from being the guy that pushed Ray Brown to the guy that backed down from the fight with young Peter Frampton in a brief time frame, and this is where the whole crucible aspect of the place began to kick in. Both stories circulated like wildfire but the latest story was the one that cut through my own circuitry. A slow-burning sadness seemed to take possession of me.

"What the fuck has happened to you?" Silo said over the phone. "Look, I read the new pages. What is this shit about the priesthood?"

"Yeah," I said. "I know it's over the top. Maybe we could have him visit the Zen Center, you know, make it nontheistic."

"Something seems to be happening to us. Is it Watergate?"

"One thing about Nixon," I said. "He won't be rushed. There's a lesson in that for a writer."

"Nixon is a fucking criminal," Silo said. "I think you've got to stay in L.A. while we wrap this. That place is killing you."

But I wasn't dying. My youth was dying and, I think, for the first time I was starting to accept myself for who I actually was. When I look back at it now, I see that this was the real healing I found in Bolinas. I'd made a couple of passes as a writer but maybe violated my writer's capital and needed to plug in again and that involved not insisting I be somebody I never was. Youth is interesting because you have enough energy not to be yourself; as you grow older, though, either the pose stiffens into your actual identity or you transmute.

There was a tree in our meadow and for a while I imagined being buried under it. I kept confusing what I was going through with dying. All I was doing was accepting myself but actually I was having to buck the tide of the weight of received opinion that doing that was a cowardly thing to do. In fact bucking such a tide was, I think now, from the advanced perspective of my fifties, not unbrave.

I walked with my daughter to the cliff overlooking the ocean. I held her hand and listened to her language, as if she were scanning meaning.

"The bottle lost me," she said.

And: "Don't laugh without smiling."

I may have been laughing without smiling for a while. When I got home Beverly said Silo had phoned again.

"He thinks something's wrong with you."

"Yeah, he wants to fire me. I'm not in L.A. to do lunch and polish the magic."

Then we got the call that my mother had died.

My mother's funeral was at the little church at the end of Las Pulgas in the Palisades where one idle summer I had dug a cave with two or three neighbor kids and we'd spent time under the earth. It was dark down there, but we liked the cosy effect. Since I'd identified my own character as too aerial I had my own ideas of being buried, but my mother surprised me by leaving the same sort of instructions, having purchased a plot at a burial ground in the Santa Monica mountains, flying in the face of the vogue in cremation. Our kind seemed in need of gravity, a place to touch down.

Before we left Bolinas, I got a call from my father in Princeton.

"So," he said, "the old gal moved on."

"Yeah, Pop," I said. "She did."

"Well, I'll tell you one thing," he said.

"What's that?" I said, watching Lilac on the living room floor do a crayon drawing of a big red bird.

"It's a complete mystery to me, Jamie," he said. "I used to think it all made sense and maybe it does but I don't know what the sense is anymore."

"I know what you mean," I said, surprised at what he was saying.

"What do you think I should do?" he said. "I can't come out there; I just can't do it and Ellen wouldn't like it anyway, but I was thinking of sending a wreath."

"That sounds good, Pop," I said.

"I'll tell you one thing, Jamie."

"What Pop?"

"When I met your mother, she was the most beautiful thing I ever saw on this earth, to this day."

"No, kidding." He'd never said anything like that to me before.

"Oh, yeah," he said, "your mother as a young woman was like an accident that put heaven on the earth. Well, that's what she *looked* like, anyway."

"Wow, Pop."

"Well, then it was impossible, as you know, so—end of story," he said, pulling himself up short.

"I'm glad you called."

"How are you, my boy? Making big bucks..."

"Oh, we're getting by,"

"That's the guy," he said.

I had entertained saying something about my mother that would lend an overview to the proceedings, something about Jewish immigration and the push to assimilate at all costs, and the price attached to that, and how her native smarts and ability with language had guided me to my own career, but when I got to the funeral there were mainly her old girl friends, and my step-father, looking upset.

"Hello, Jamie," he said. "Well, I guess we all knew it was coming."

"Right," I said. I couldn't believe his dissociation, but we'd never been close and it was too late to start.

When I stood up, instead of an overview I found myself talking about some of the nice memories I had of her.

"Before she met Harry," I said, glancing at him, "my mother went through some difficult times, which some of you remember because I know you helped her during those times. She always liked having her friends close by, and she had wonderful loyal friends. When I was a big baseball fan and *Damn Yankees* came to town she somehow managed to get me into a sixth-row orchestra seat and it was one of the great experiences of my life. I remember she loved Ethel Merman, and when I heard Ethel Merman singing that song from *Gypsy* on the radio the other day I realized how right she was. It's funny..." For a moment, I stopped. I'd forgotten where I was going. Then I started again.

"Life is short, maybe just because it doesn't go on forever. The thing I've learned from my mother, though, is that if you do something nice for someone, the way she did for me many times over the years, that gets remembered. I can remember it right now and the gift is right there again, and the good feeling it made in me... never goes away. Thanks, Mom."

Overcrowded with unresolved emotion, I sat down. An old girlfriend of my mother's, April Norton, stood up with a bouquet of daisies in her hand and talked about how much fun it was to spend time with Mom because she wasn't afraid to enjoy herself.

"Amy was fun," April said. "And nobody seems to have fun but the hippies anymore, and I can't remember whether there are still hippies or not, after all that horrible stuff. There was no horrible stuff with her, though. Just fun. She liked the cherries jubilee at Bullocks Wilshire with a cappucino and she used to have it every time we went there. She always looked great. She looked great the day she died. And she's gonna knock 'em dead in heaven..."

We were laughing.

"I'm serious," she said.

Afterwards Harry came over and shook hands with me and Beverly on the sidewalk.

"Thanks for coming," he said. "Your Mom has some stuff she wanted me to give you. If you're not doing anything tomorrow or the next day, stop by and I'll give it to you."

"You mean big stuff?" I said.

"A few things," Harry said. He was a small, compact man who seemed preternaturally clean and always smelled of Yardley's lavender. "An envelope and a box of stuff."

"I'll come by," I said.

8

"I honestly believe you're losing touch with the seventies," Danny said over the phone from L.A. when we'd gotten back to the Bolinas house. "There's some interesting stuff happening right now, but I don't think you're interested."

"What did you think of my idea?" I said. Silo had gotten other writers and I wanted to do a multi-generational story. My mother's envelope had pictures of her family in it. A young woman in ancient sari-like clothing smiling giddily. My great grandmother in Kiev, I thought. There was no identification, just the photograph, obviously laboriously doctored when the invention was in its infancy.

"Look, I've got to sell some tickets. If you write something funny, it'll pay for a novel of your idea."

"Got anything in mind."

"Why would I be calling?"

"I thought you and I were friends."

"First I want to hear your answer. Then we'll decide."

"What's the question."

"I spoke to Steve Stevens. He thinks you're terrific."

"I like Steve a lot, although he can be a hard taskmaster."

There was a knock on the door. Beverly went to answer it and Roy and Horton walked in, looking like real men of the West in dirty work clothes with their faces smeared with grime, smiling.

"Well, we got to talking and he's ready for the next one."

"What next one?" I said, signalling Roy and Horton that it would be a quick minute.

"*Beverly Hills Moron 2,*" Danny said.

"Danny," I said, "let me get back to you. I've got some people here."

I spent a morning or an afternoon with Roy and Horton once or twice a month. We would drive around in Roy's pick-up truck between his tree-work jobs. He employed Horton as an assistant, holding the rope when he climbed a tree, making sure a branch made a safe landing and then cutting and clearing it. I assisted too sometimes, indulging Roy his legend as the man among men. He was a handsome guy a year or two younger than I who had gone to Vietnam, and would later survive a bout of cancer contracted from Agent Orange. At night in the house he built in Paradise Valley, with his girl friend Kathy and their young son asleep, he liked to read the *Federalist Papers* by kerosene lamp. He looked you directly in the eye, man to man, and yet the macho was undercut, as it often is, with a self-deprecating sense of humor, a corollary of which was his liking for the epic stories he retailed of near-fatal calamities high above the earth. He was a shy man under it all. He explained to me once that he had known guys like me in Vietnam who were good under siege. I considered it sheer luck that such a comparison would occur to him, but nonetheless got caught up in the sense that maybe I *would* have been able to come through under pressure. It was a flattering idea. I'd gotten a psychiatric 4-F at my draft board physical, having come to it with a note from a psychiatrist that stated, honestly so far as I could tell, that I had trouble with authority structures.

Horton was from the northwest and had the deep voice of a cowboy bard, a genre in which he was becoming outstanding. He was also known as a barfighter and evidently had almost come to blows with Robert Squires, who could be a mean drunk. But then he'd balked in deference to Squires's work. After that Squires became his official sponsor to the poetry community at large. It was great to be able to have coffee with these two and be seen in the town with someone other than my fellow Eastern seaboard aesthetes.

"What's up?" Roy said when I put down the phone. "Hollywood calling?"

"How'd you guess," I said. "You gentlemen want some coffee?"

"Yes, but we don't need to trouble the Mrs.," Roy said with a gallant half-bow to Beverly who was sewing a shirt for Lilac, who sat on the floor by Beverly's feet watching *Sesame Street.* "We'll drive you down to Scowley's. I have some business. You feel like working?"

"Now?"

Roy gave me an indulgent smile. "Take it easy," he said. "We'll get you properly caffeinated."

"Fine," I said.

We drove down in the truck, and on our way passed the Peter Frampton kid who looked directly at me in the cab and smiled.

"What's his problem?" Horton said.

"Nothing. He likes me, I guess."

"We already know he told you he was going to tear you limb from limb and you folded."

"I'm too old."

"So why'd you hit Ray Brown?"

"I didn't. I pushed him. And I guess he made me see red. This kid made me see I was older than him."

"I'm worried about this dude," Roy said to Horton, indicating me.

"I'm worried about him, too."

"I'm thirty," I said. "You guys are younger..."

"I'm thirty-three," said Horton.

"Yeah, but for you fighting's a sport, right?"

"Not necessarily, my friend. Not at all—unless of course I'm feeling no pain..."

Both of them laughed.

Later that afternoon I ended up holding one end of a rope in the chilly sunshine while Horton held another and Roy high in a tree cut branches. Later we cut and cleared the branches that had been felled. I loved the cypress smell and was sure it did me good. I was depressed about not being more of a fighter. At the same time I was nurturing the sadness because it was making me think in a different way that, it seemed to me, might deepen my writing.

"You read any James Dickey?" Horton asked.

"Not a lot," I said. "I read *Deliverance*. I liked it."

"Well, it's great, but I meant the poetry. See, he talks about the power of iambic pentameter, when it's used right. And you can find that power sometimes even in Robert W. Service. It's the heartbeat behind it. That's what makes it powerful."

"That's interesting," I said.

We were sitting on a log together. Roy had come down from the tree and was divesting himself of his belts and tools. It would be dark soon.

When I was with Roy and Horton I took on a troubled, reluctant persona in their macho hierarchy, and that was secretly my stubborn and perhaps lazy way of being even tougher. Wasn't it tough to buck the tide of the tough guys by keeping one's softer side in the picture?

And then when I was with Joanne Abbott or Larry Anson or some of the others, I could play the role that I was much closer to the rough and ready crowd than I in fact was. And when I was with Danny I would invoke the nobility of the solitary artistic life. And when I was in Bolinas I also had the option of playing the worldly sharper with my literary friends.

With Beverly, I dropped most of the routines and tried to get into my work. A lot of artists together can be an oxymoron because in the end, I think, artists need a lot of solitude to get any work done. They lone it to hang out with their creations.

We had sold our Outpost place and gotten ourselves a house on Hawthorn on the mesa, and actual ownership of a house, plus being inside a community in which I was recognized, had thrown me into an unanticipated panic. I began attending Public Utilities District meetings and writing the Bolinas Hearsay News on the issues of the day. I was no more a politician than I was a fighter but I didn't know that, and the fact that it was our house, and that we were parents now, made me more nervous than I could admit to myself.

It was as if in staking a claim within a community of some kind, I got panicky about how everything worked. Where did the water come from? Was it clean water? What about the asbestos shingles on the outside of the house? Didn't asbestos cause cancer? The place would look better and most likely feel better without them. While wood breathed, asbestos seemed to encase the place, so that nothing penetrated or escaped.

Joe Alsted built us a beautiful wrought-iron wood stove, with a butterfly-shaped flute. I discussed the shingle removal project with Dick Herald, a slight amiable man of around forty who lived, it seemed not unhappily, in his car. I knew I needed physical exercise each day and thought the project would be something worthwhile that I could do myself with Dick's help.

There was something about the personal economy of such a man that engaged me, as if in living closer to the bone without panicking, he offered an example that might help me to lighten up. These were the years when I was stepping into the actual life I would lead and Dick was an unexpected benefactor. Beverly would serve him lunch each day and he would eat it slowly, savoring it, but clearly directing the food to the front part of his mouth because there were teeth available there and not elsewhere. He had a young son by his marriage to a woman who had lived for a while with Shadow, the guy Danny wanted to make a star whose father ran the Winston Museum and who was still with Laurel Bay, both of them now doing Biofeedback together.

"I should have been a tailor," Dick told me one afternoon as we paused in the sunlight from stripping the tattered sheets of shingles from the house. "That's what my father did, and he could have trained me." A tailor, I thought. That was the disposition he seemed to bring to things. Quiet, unhurried attention.

When the shingles were gone, the wood under it needed to be repainted and Beverly came up with the colors: yellow, with red and blue window trim, inspired by Karl Larsen's paintings. The house became a kind of fairy tale cottage set in the middle of a hilly knoll.

We got rid of our television and for a week or two went through something that might be called withdrawal. Then it was as if the world opened out in the evening. We took walks or read books that otherwise would have sat on the shelves as mere promises. I had recently come across an old paperback of *Pride and Prejudice* and was reading it for the first time. Nothing could have been more remote from our lives than the courting rites of eighteenth-century England. I was in thrall to the diamond clarity and felicity of the twenty-one-year-old Jane Austen's prose.

A resident of downtown, Liz Childress, explained to me that the big 19th-century novels were wonderful over the winter months, allowing you to settle down into them and get to know the characters like friends. When Lilac began nursery school we got to know the parents of some of her friends. Her friend Lizzie's mother, Mary Webster, from one of the richest families in America, was living with her husband Orin and their two daughters in a cable car, while Orin, also from a very wealthy family, built a house for them. They owned prime agricultural land at the entrance to the town and Orin was farming it by himself with an old-fashioned plow.

Many of the people of Bolinas, the newcomers, were similarly disposed to rethink business as usual in America. Although neither I nor Beverly discussed it at the time, in retrospect I see now that we were in essence trying to see our work as a part of a larger life from which it flowed, rather than making it the central mechanism, the career determining the shape of one's whole life.

As my distance from Hollywood grew, I was forgotten. Knowing that I'd exhausted my own resources in work I'd already done, I began reading more, casting around for what might help to shepherd me into the next phase of work.

I began to see Arthur Slocum, an older Bolinas neighbor, the editor of the poetry anthology *The New Generatio*n that had defined the post-war counter-establishment in poetry, including Robert Squires, Charles Olson, Robert Duncan, Allen Ginsberg and the rest, which had given me my first understanding of writing as a kind of action, rather than something that only described something else.

I'd known about Dave Wain since high school when I'd read his poems in the Slocum anthology. I liked his poetry but didn't get involved with it in the same way that I had with Ginsberg's, for instance, or Robert Squire's. He was right there in the pantheon, but he wasn't the brightest figure for me. I heard about him in Bolinas again because just the year before we moved there he'd disappeared with a gun into the foothills of the Sierras where he'd been staying in a trailer on Japhy Ryder's land. He just walked away, leaving a note appointing Slocum his literary executor.

Known to have struggled with alcoholism, he was presumed to be a suicide, another poet suicide. Years ago I'd come across a line in Andre Gide: "In sympathy lies contagion," and it used to come up regularly for me in those days. In other words, don't be too interested in or sympathetic to a suicide, or a drug addict, or an alcoholic, or the next thing you knew you'd be picking up the tendencies that drove him yourself. Dave Wain I'd mentally tucked away with others under that warning label.

One afternoon I was in Berkeley at the KPFK offices with Slocum and they played a tape of Wain and Ryder and Ben Holden talking about a big reading they were going to do in

1964 in San Francisco. Slocum I imagine had been told that there was some archive tape he might want to listen to. I periodically drove him into San Francisco or Berkeley and we had lunch together. He told me he'd enjoyed my novel, which was nice to hear from a Bolinas neighbor, a simple unequivocal compliment, and we began to be casual once or twice a month friends.

I'd heard both Ben Holden and Japhy Ryder before, but not Dave Wain, and in spite of the mind set about him that I carried in, something started to happen as I listened to the tape. It really didn't have that much to do with writing, per se, although a lot of the tape was about poetry, the breakthrough into the idiomatic language and musical structure that had set *The New Generation* apart from the one that had come to light before and during the war: Lowell, Delmore Schwartz, Berryman, Jarrell et al. The new poets were tremendously influenced by jazz, pioneering an improvisatory emphasis that was also highly attuned to the melodic play in the syllables.

But listening to Wain circa 1964 was like listening to a psychic twin who was a little older than I was and had already weathered the storm I seemed to be going through. He had a kind of boyish enthusiasm, tempered but not squelched by having traveled the hard road of an American poet without any university affiliation. He was appreciative of the little niceties in his social circuit. He praised a girl who danced atop an aquarium at a big San Francisco eatery as a wonderful contribution to the night life.

"I certainly think she has given me as much pleasure as any recent periodical," he stated with boyish ingenuousness.

What was unmistakable about him was that he'd dissolved in himself any notion of us and them. If something was good he heralded it enthusiastically. On the 1964 radio show, he spoke of the recent death of President Kennedy with sadness, saying that he along with most people loved the man, while Ben Holden had no interest in Kennedy whatsoever. I understood Holden, but was taken by the slightly out-of-focus generosity in Wain. As generic as some of his responses were, they were voiced in an unmistakable way, comprising a self-portrait of a writer in mid-life who was nakedly present in a way that the other two, tougher perhaps, genuine survivors, were not.

Wain spoke of being an advertising man in Chicago for a while, living the American dream of marriage with a pretty woman and a nice Chicago apartment, and losing touch with himself. He had returned to the West Coast with the advent of the Beat Generation, finding his college pals Holden and Ryder in *Time* magazine, and soon got a divorce. He ended up driving a cab for a living in San Francisco. Then he spoke of a recent sojourn in Forks-of-Salmon, a small river town in Northern California, where he'd lived like a hermit. He had spent the summer and fall there and written many new poems. Hearing what he had to say somehow reassured me, as if I were getting guidelines for the passage I was still negotiating.

At the same time, there was no mistaking the harsh reality that lay under Wain's ardent avowal of the role of poet, no matter how far afield it took him. Later that afternoon Slocum stopped at a San Francisco rug emporium and looked at several for his living room. He was a deeply civilized older citizen of the poetry world but evidently abashed that I'd see him in such bourgeois environs.

"Please don't mention this to anyone," he said softly as he signed his credit card slip for the purchase of a plush white and blue Empire design.

9

Beverly told me she was pregnant again and I got the idea to write a biography of Dave Wain the same week. In retrospect, this was probably the pivotal moment in the turn of our life away from the possibilities of mainstream American success that Hollywood had held out to me.

Arthur Slocum said he would share Wain's papers with

me, and I set out to discover what had created the voice I'd heard that provided a companionship and solace I didn't find among my immediate fellows, and that I'd probably missed in my father.

Steve Huckle at United Lights wasn't calling anymore, but I called him to tell him about the book idea.

"Is there a movie in it?" he said. "Can you put it into treatment form?"

"I don't know yet," I said. "Maybe."

"Well, other than that," Steve said, "you'll probably just have to write it and then I can sell it."

"What about my track record as a writer?" I said.

"Well, you've got to realize it's been a few years. Plus this guy isn't known, really, is he?"

"Well, not to everybody, but it's a great story, an American Everyman."

"Lemme think about it," Steve said, which I knew somehow was a sign-off. He was polite but I had by his lights willfully put myself out of the loop and he had other priorities.

We were as deluded as anyone we knew in making the choices we made, and yet... I was in *my life* again, the whole spectrum from bright to dark over each day. It was as if Hollywood exchanged the money for an amputated experiential palette and everybody conspired not to mention it. It was Dave Wain who somehow brooked the missing colors.

Joanne Abbott invited me to a party at her house. I stood with the first guests, fellow writers, nervous before the party actually found its rhythm. A poet named Louis Adrian passed a joint around. I took it and passed it on to Larry Anson without taking a toke, since Bolinas had long since stopped being a threshold to me and I depended on my normal mind.

In a moment, the party had found its rhythm. Adrian put some Hamza El Din music on the phonograph. Larry Anson lay down on the floor, his whole length across a Mexican rug and stared at the ceiling. Joanne danced for a moment with her boyfriend, the Harvard ecologist Mandy Reichert. More people gradually arrived, but it seemed to me that the social threshold the party might have represented had been effectively detoured. Everybody got stoned instead.

"Is Beverly pregnant?" Joanne asked me a little later.

"Yes," I said.

"Well," she said and laughed. "Well, well, well..."

Around the corner lived a couple who had become friends, Kerry and Enzo DeGuzman. Enzo was a Philippine painter, and Kerry, who was from the East Bay, had become a potter. They already had three sons of their own, and an older child, a lovely teenage girl named Elaine by Kerry's previous marriage. Enzo was a small dark man with a handlebar mustache and seemed on first glance an exemplar of old-fashioned machismo, but instead proved to be a gentle and well-educated man whose sister was an M.D. in Philadelphia. Kerry was a voluptuous blond who spoke softly and exuded an overripe sensuality and sweetness. Finding a kindred female spirit in Beverly, she asked her to be the mid-wife at her birth, a trust Beverly accepted with excited anticipation.

The day Kerry's contractions began, Beverly, who was close to term herself, was away most of the day at the DeGuzman house and I looked after Lilac after her morning at nursery school. Beverly came back at around four, took a shower, and told us we could all go over now and see the baby, a little girl they had named Mutia, "black pearl" in Tagalog.

"How was it?" I said.

"It was hard," she said. "She had twelve hours of contractions. She's really exhausted. But the baby's healthy."

"Let's go," Lilac said, pulling my hand.

There were no lights on in the house and the front room, furnished with mats and candles, was filled with neighbors and family. Judy and Steve, the couple from across the street, Ibou and Princeton from the little guest house Judy rented out, as well as the three boys, and Elaine, who was looking after them.

Dr. Elson Haas, the local new age doctor, was also there. Kerry was sitting on a mat in the corner and Enzo held the little girl beside her. The baby let out a wail and I saw Enzo wince in the half-light. I heard later that Elson had just then cut the cord.

Two weeks later, our daughter Lara was born in the back bedroom at twilight. When the contractions began, it was as if we were in the presence of, and effectively subsumed by, the force that gets the baby born. While Beverly had practiced for the moment, the contractions themselves were involuntary. It was fierce–with blood an integral part of the process–and at the same time there was a dimension that was other worldly. Beverly began to hold a single note as a contraction played itself through her, singing it through her body. Then the baby was born: the result of the ferocity an infinitely gentle, permeable being, dependent on her mother day and night for a long time to come.

We named her Lara, after Beverly's maternal grandmother, a stylish old lady I'd met once when we passed through Tulsa during the sixties. She owned a dress shop and was very religious and it seemed to me Beverly resembled her.

The difference among children is surely a great adventure of a family, and Lara was startling in this way. While Lilac was self-possessed, articulate and outgoing; Lara operated on another frequency, sometimes it seemed at the mercy of moods and idle whims that would overtake her.

When she was two, for example, we went as a family down to the beach and she began picking up rocks to take them home, but couldn't understand that she could only physically handle so many. She became angry and frustrated and it was impossible to explain what was going on rationally to her because she wasn't rational yet. At the same time, she was very kind and loving and possessed of a raucous sense of humor that sometimes reminded me of my mother.

Apart from the reading I did, I initiated my research for my book on Dave Wain with a visit to Ben Holden in his apartment on Page Street, just around the corner from the Zen Center in San Francisco. Holden answered the door barefoot in white pants and a green tee-shirt and invited me into a one-bedroom apartment that had a bare minimum of furniture. His books stood on the floor upright against the wall and ran around the circumference of each room. I had seen him a few years earlier just after he'd joined the Zen Center to become a Zen monk. He was in his mid-fifties now and recently had been ordained a Zen priest. He had lost a lot of weight since I'd last seen him.

"Would you like some tea," he called from the little kitchenette while I stood in the virtually empty living room looking out at the San Francisco cloudy light of day.

"Great. How've you been?" I said, walking over to the kitchen.

"Just fine," Ben said. "I don't know how much help I can be to you."

"Well," I said, "you and Japhy knew him as well as anyone, I guess."

He handed me a big mug of tea.

"Here," he said, and took hold of a couple of padded mats and put them on the floor. "Let's sit down."

We sat down on the mats together, the two of us in a room in which, aside from the books that ran along the floor too far away for me to read the titles, there seemed to be none of the accoutrements of normal life.

"Do you write here?" I asked.

"I have a notebook by my bed."

I took notes but Holden wasn't interested in saying much of his old friend short of expressing his admiration for his writing. His hermetic tendencies–he was one of the informal but deeply learned scholars of the Beat Generation–seemed enforced by his circumstance now as a Zen priest, a man who in earlier days had written rueful and funny love poems to a blond named Sally.

"How are you finding life these days?" I asked.

"Well," he said, "for a writer, this is the perfect

circumstance. Nothing to do but sitting meditation for a few hours each day. So it's perfect, but I'm not writing much. So go figure."

Taking the temperature of my precursors twenty years ahead of me down the line, I no doubt had the idea of learning something more about the journey ahead. Japhy Ryder had in the meantime become a genuine eminence, a Pulitzer Prize winner. I met him one afternoon at the Mill Valley home of Jack Fielding, an old friend from Ryder's days in Marin County before it became the capital of the Me Decade and was still undeveloped with horse pastures where there was now expensive Mill Valley real estate. Fielding was an ex-longshoreman who had built a fishing business and obviously loved and admired Japhy, who proved to be more accessible about Wain than Ben Holden had been. We sat side by side on a sofa in Fielding's living room. I had set my tape recorder between us.

"Dave wasn't a scholar," he told me. "He was a poet: he believed in the direct path. And his mind could cut directly through most things. He was incisive. But he understood in the way of the poet. He only..." He hesitated.

"What?" I said and then smiled. I was learning the non-fiction ropes, so to speak.

Ryder smiled. "Dave had this erratic strain that would sometimes keep him from doing the best work that he could do," he said. "It all goes back to his mother, I think, whom he loved and hated, because his father wasn't around much. He craved stability. He'd get involved with Scientology, or psychoanalysis, or Zen Buddhism, or being a successful advertising man. Did you know that he wrote 'Raid Kills Bugs Dead'?"

"He actually wrote that? That's a classic, isn't it?"

"Yes," Ryder said laughing. "But he'd take umbrage at you pointing that out."

"Of course," I said. "He's written some classic poems too."

"But that really was Dave, too," Ryder said. "See, a line that emphasizes consonants like his favorite Jacobean poets.

In other words, gigantic life-determining enterprises: analysis, Buddhism, marriage to the American Dream, but he wouldn't buy in all the way, because his ultimate real work, as he eventually understood it, was being a poet. Now he and I might have arguments, in fact we still do..."

"You still do?" I said.

"Oh, sure," Japhy said. "Dave's someone I talk to most days." He chuckled.

Though he was older than the wild man depicted in Kerouac's books, in his smile you could still read the keen woodsman and Zen adept. He was easy to talk with, a genial man, and yet there was a pronounced sense of his aloneness even in the geniality. It was as if he were on another wavelength, one that he may have found and cultivated in the long sitting meditations he'd done during his studies in Japan, and still practiced.

"So let me sum up," I said. "There was a kind of neurasthenic streak in Dave?"

"Oh, I don't know that I'd go that far," Japhy said. "But something along those lines."

In the late sixties, Arlen Thule, the San Francisco poet, had interviewed Wain for a book, and he gave me the tapes upon which he'd based the interview. In the middle of the interview, a part of it not utilized in Thule's printed piece, speaking of his mother, Wain erupted in rage and tears.

"I HATE that STUPID CUNT!" he yelled into Thule's machine. "I HATE her! I HATE her more than anything or anyone else in the world!...Y'see?" he said, as if remembering poor Thule in the room with him.

There was some sort of mumbled assent in the background. Thule was a nice guy, married, a father, and obviously unprepared for such a scene. This was close to the time Wain would disappear, at the age of forty four. It was embarrassing but it was also riveting and completely deconstructed the interview format in the way that Kerouac had in his Paris Review interview.

That was surely a big part of what held me. He would go

for broke, as he did with his life, and his death too, but it would be on his own terms. At a low ebb, in the midst of a nervous breakdown at the cabin of Lorenzo Monsanto at Big Sur, he had written a long letter to Robert Duncan, the great poet of the San Francisco Renaissance, who was homosexual. It was about being an artist, about keeping "the mess of doors a human being is open." So far as I knew he wasn't close to Duncan, but honored him, the fact that he had kept at it and explored poetry as a vocation as exhaustively as anyone in Wain's orbit. He never sent the letter. Perhaps I was reading it before Duncan had.

After a laborious first draft that comprised the working notes I made as I did my reading and interviews, I began the real writing on a perfect blue day in Bolinas, thinking I wanted to get that color into the book, and *Traveling Light* was done in thirty days, as if I were Kerouac writing a beat saga without thinking beyond the next thing to be said. It accomplished something I only recognized later. It broke my prose out of the first person. I switched to third and had multiple protagonists: Wain, Kerouac, Ginsberg, Burroughs et al. They were all in some way exemplary to me and so to write of them sprang me out of a single voice, which can get to be a trap.

Steve Huckle thought it was for a little press, not a mainstream publishing house. Samuel Zarem, whom I'd met years ago to discuss his autobiography, took it on mainly out of courtesy, I think. He was now genuine Beverly Hills royalty with his beautiful porcelain doll of a wife, Jean Zarem, the two of them in every issue of *W*, to which Beverly had subscribed.

"I don't know what it's about," Zarem shouted on the phone, "but I believe in your talent."

"Thank you," I said.

I wasn't sure he even remembered who I was. Maybe it was the Zax photograph. Zarem sent the manuscript out personally to—it seemed to me—the heads of the multinationals who owned the publishing houses these days, and they in turn farmed it out to their chiefs of staff, who must have been bewildered. A short, "poetic" book about a Beat poet nobody had ever heard of, along with some of the other, better known figures. General bemusement. All manuscripts returned. We'll pass on this one, but Sam, I understand Brando may be considering breaking his silence. Please keep us apprised.

I had made a terrible faux pas and would pay for it the rest of my life. Hollywood had forgotten me and my book wasn't publishable. I had a wife and two children and no prospects. The book had to be published. I phoned editors and agents and mailed out manuscripts but nothing panned out.

One afternoon, driving on the Bolinas-Olema road, to avoid a motorcyclist who was coming at me in my lane at the top of a hill, passing a van on a blind hill, I swerved across the lane and the car went into an grassy embankment and I fractured my ankle. Lying on the pavement outside the car, I could smell the day, feel the breeze, and hear the birds for the first time in recent memory and realized I was alive again after being virtually dead with the cyclopean pursuit of publication.

I was in the hospital for a few days, came home, and called an agent in New York I'd known years before, Jason Lines. He sold the book in a week. Not a lot of money but it would be seen and I'd be back in the arena.

When the book came out it was surprisingly widely reviewed, but the most important reviews were attacks by writers only a decade older than I was, who had missed the sixties: Tony Forrest in *Esquire* and David Walker in *The New York Times Book Review*.

The reviews made me physically sick. I had a cough I couldn't shake. Forrest and Walker were angry about stuff that had nothing to do with me—maybe it was residual anger at the Beats who had stolen their thunder when they weren't young enough to catch the wave of the sixties, which continued what the Beats had started. At the same time, they were part of the palace guard for the literary establishment and seemed to loathe at a visceral level the idea that someone of a younger generation wasn't particularly interested in the doors where they were posted.

These two, whose own work I'd never read because it had nothing to do with anything I was interested in, were incensed perhaps without actually knowing they were. What it boiled down to was Hemingway. Forrest and Walker were both in the manly tradition and, again perhaps without actually consciously comprehending it, were fighting for the waning archetype in the face of a defection by Kerouac that actually hurt because he was an ex-football hero. Kerouac, a literary genius, seemed to understand intuitively that the literary palette of the fifties was as wan and joyless as it was because men were stuck with a hard guy persona that, Hemingway aside, didn't make the colors flow.

Over the years, I discovered that my own personal best as a writer wasn't the same as the Kerouac archtype I espoused for the book, but for me he was perhaps *the* writer, of all immediate precursors, that I had to come to terms with to take the next step in my own development.

Beverly and I both had deep tissue massage sessions with a man named Allen May and this was both powerful and confusing. The idea was that the tension pockets in one's body—the shoulders, the neck, the waist, wherever there was stiffness—tended to hold unresolved emotional and psychological conflicts. Allen worked these areas hard as you lay on his massage table virtually naked.

There was an immediate increase in physical energy. The pockets seemed to lock away vitality that now came into play. But more than that, the range of emotion one knew opened out precipitously. Beverly seemed to fall in love with Allen. I got very jealous and fell deeper in love with her. Allen meanwhile was in love with a woman named Jennifer, who was getting together with him, or all hell might have broken loose.

The problem seemed to be that the deep tissue massage was extremely strong medicine, but lacking was a necessary psychological component that would allow one to recognize and sort out whatever it was that had originally led to the holding back of the energy.

Many nights I held Beverly as she lay crying in bed until she decided not to go on with the treatments. Allen could do the massage but had no particular knowledge or instinct for dealing with what might come up psychologically. With Beverly it had to do with her father ignoring her as a little girl and the pain of that situation, which seemed to duplicate itself in her falling in love with Allen.

It was the Me Decade, of course, and all sorts of important cynics in New York and London were laughing at such ingenuousness.

10

"My doctor tells me I've got to take heroic measures," my Dad told me on the phone three months after the book had come out. "But I don't feel heroic."

"What are you saying, Pop?"

"I've got prostate cancer is what I'm saying. Important safety tip: don't drink too much coffee. It's bad for the lower part of the body."

"How do you feel?"

"Not good. Ellen wants me to go in for this, of course. But there's another opinion that I could last just as long without the whole rigamarole. I feel bad: I haven't seen enough of my grandchildren."

"I'll be there," I said, "but I have to figure out about the kids."

"No, don't bring them," he said with sudden force. "I can't take it. It was my mistake not to see them when there was time."

"Let me call you back, Pop," I said.

"Sure," he said. "Take your time. You've got to realize something, Jamie. It happens to everyone. How bad can it be?"

"What–cancer?"

"No, my boy," he said in his archer tone. "The other thing."

"I'll call you in a little while, Pop."

Beverly was painting in Audubon Canyon Ranch. Lilac was at pre-school, and Lara was taking a nap. The house was quiet, with the mid-day sun just beginning to burn through. He had paid us a quick visit in Bolinas shortly after Lara's birth. There was a possibility of a development in Marin that he would invest in, but then he'd kept out of it. What was he telling me? That he wanted to pack it in? He was just 70, which made it demographically okay, I supposed. Ellen was in her fifties, a handsome divorcee with two grown-up children of her own. The two had taken cruises together, done the New York theater seasons, taken walks through Manhattan when my Dad gave himself a day off.

It surprised me that he had had enough. In my fifties now, I have glimmers of what he was going through. Every morning I wonder if there will be an obituary in the *Times* of someone who touched my life.

"Do you want to come to New York?" I said to Beverly later that afternoon on my way out for a walk. "He mentioned not seeing enough of the kids."

"First you go; then if you think we should, we'll come."

I went along Hawthorn Road straight to Elm and then all the way to the end of it, and down to Agate Beach. Agate Beach, so named because it's nothing but rocks, hard little syllables of time, thousands and thousands of tiny black rocks, with the water lapping down at the shore line. Suddenly there was a fighter plane roaring by overhead, quite close to the ground, a frightening apparition, made to wreak havoc and destruction, colorfully painted. I never saw one again.

I took a room at The Geary and met my father on a bright Saturday morning in front of the Metropolitan Museum. It was October, somewhere in the fifties.

He came jauntily across the street to where I stood. But I

could see something different in his eyes, as if to say,"Take a look what I've got inside me. How about this?"

"Are you ready to walk?" he said.

"Yeah," I said. "But don't try to break any records, okay?"

"It'll do you good," he said, suddenly a coach. "I'm just kidding. I'll take it easy because I *have* to."

"Good."

We took up a leisurely pace.

"You should have been a doctor, my boy. You've got a healing pace."

"I'm going to take that as a compliment."

"What's wrong with the fucking critics?" he said as we crossed 79th Street.

So he'd read my reviews. Those who write reviews forget that parents and relatives read them. Children may read them. I personally never forget.

"You don't want to know," I said.

"But I'll tell you what," he said.

"What, Pop?"

"I'll be happy if you tell me you know and it doesn't matter."

"I can say that, Pop," I said, "but I'm honestly not sure."

"Good," he said.

"Good?" I stopped. We were surrounded by sidewalk displays of paintings and photographs.

"Yes. Because that means you're in the real world."

At one display I looked at a photograph of a snow storm in Central Park. Then one of a man sitting a table in an apartment. Then one of some ornate grill work in front of a building.

"Come on," he said. "You gotta keep the rhythm."

"Art is hypnotic," I said.

"So you got hypnotized," he said. "The same thing happened to me with real estate."

"You always loved making money," I said.

"You see, you never 'got' your Dad, even though your Dad probably understood *you* better than you think."

"The next thing you're gonna tell me it wasn't about money..."

"It wasn't."

Now he stopped on the wide cobbled sidewalk with people coming and going beside us. "Only partly... One morning when you lived with me I took you to breakfast at the Brasserie in midtown. Maybe you were ten. We had eggs benedict, before I had any idea how bad all that stuff is for you unless you work out all the time, and who has the time for that."

"Pop?" I said. "Let's walk."

"Sure," he said, walking again. "Sure, making money is good, because it affirms value. Someone or something out there pays you because you make sense. You fit the world. See what I mean, my boy. But what it's about is breakfast at a nice place with your boy—forget the marriage problem—because you made the cut. You fit."

"Being an artist is a little like that, but you fit in another way."

"What way is that?"

"I don't really know, Pop."

"You've said that twice now. I'm surprised at you."

"Well, really, everything went great for a while in one way, and not so great in another way; and those two ways have traded places."

"You're learning then."

"Yeah, probably. What about you, Pop?"

"My learning's done."

"You walk pretty well," I said.

"We're gonna cut over to Madison in a minute, so I can sit down and have a good hamburger at Three Guys. You know those guys who yell 'Cheeseburger!... Cheeseburger!...' on *Saturday Night Live* got it from those guys when they were at the corner of 80th and Madison at a place called The French Coffee Shop."

"No kidding..."

"Yeah, they used to yell that all the time exactly the way Belushi did. I don't know why they called it the French Coffee Shop. It was all Greeks."

"Belushi..." He had only recently died.

"See, that's something I never had to deal with, except for

booze and it never interested me so much."

We moved over to the edge of the sidewalk and the 75th Street crosswalk and then out into the street, jaywalking New Yorker style.

When we got into the restaurant, the guy at the cash register smiled hello to my father, and indicated we could have our choice of available booths. Pop slid into the seat opposite me in a booth about midway down the aisle. We both ordered cheeseburgers, mine with coffee, his with just water.

"Coffee, when you get to be me, isn't good. But you've got plenty of time for all that. You can drink all you want and it won't hurt you in the least. Come to think of it, so can I now. So maybe I'll join you later."

We ate the cheeseburgers and then he had some coffee, too.

"What next?" I said.

"Nothing," he said. "Just sit a while. You look healthy. That country life is good for you."

"It's a lesson in love thy neighbor, Pop."

"Now, look. I don't want to be overly dramatic about this but I feel myself getting helpless. It's interesting you know, you've got this thing inside you, and it's not you, but it *is* you..."

"What?" I said. "Exactly?"

"I don't know," he said. "Death, I guess."

"You can feel it?"

"Sure, I can," he said. "I can see it, too. So can you, can't you?"

I looked at him and he had that look I'd seen when I met him.

"You want to go to the Whitney?"

"Yeah, I'll look at some art. Then I go home. What are you doing tomorrow?"

"Nothing much," I said.

"Good," he said. "You can out come for lunch."

The latest Biennial was on. There was a certain amount of ugliness in the work this year. I reminded him that he'd taken me as a kid one year to the Museum of Modern Art and I'd seen a Franz Kline.

"I thought it was ugly," I said.

"So what?" he said. "You were dead right."

"Yeah, Pop, but now for some reason it seems beautiful."

We were standing in front of a monochromatic painting by Eric Fischl of some naked people lolling on a boat.

"Don't tell me that's what's going to happen with this," he said.

I took a bus down Third Avenue later that afternoon. New York is an odd state of animated nostalgia for me. I usually have more time on my hands than I would at home and take the opportunity to commune with the place and its echoes of my long gone past.

The bus surprised me even so because the mix of passengers brought back the sense of equilibrium I'd found in such heterogeneity. A metropolitan bus line is a small hub of democracy.

Oddly, I was able to read better in transit, especially if I found a window seat off the fray of the aisle, than anywhere else. Then there was the stopping and starting, the loading and unloading of people of every variety, a constantly changing showcase of visages and lineages. Once I had shared an afternoon ride with the young Edward Albee, just making his mark with *The Zoo Story*, and, consumed with admiration and jealousy, I couldn't manage even the courtesy of a respectful nod.

But it was anonymity that was the first principle of this charter soul-making experience, each of us filaments of the ongoing American experiment. The last minute plunge of a passenger to the back exit after pulling the cord to alert the driver, the mute cooperation of the other passengers to allow the laggard exiter his wish.

It was like sitting in the bosom of a large family, given a place to plot and figure one's own progress surrounded by the human temperatures of parents and siblings of infinite variety. My Dad had given me that.

Less than two months later, a little past noon, Ellen found him slouched over in the bathtub filled with still-warm water.

She'd been out on her morning errands. The autopsy showed that he'd taken a lethal dose of seconal.

11

A year after *Traveling Light,* came out, Delia Rogers, an old friend of my mother's, the same Delia Rogers who inherited millions of dollars when she was twenty-one and had been a lot of trouble before and since, oddly and magnanimously decided that I was the person to write her autobiography. A few years earlier, I wouldn't have taken the offer seriously, but now I'd burned too many bridges. Copies of *Traveling Light* hadn't sold as briskly as they might have if those reviews hadn't been virtually libelous, and the money I'd saved from work in Hollywood was all but gone.

I took a plane to New York and checked into The Geary again. Delia had invited me to dinner that night with Timothy Zax. I hadn't seen her for a dozen years or so, and wasn't certain what to expect. The apartment was the penthouse in a Sutton Place building and it was a rainy winter night when a taxi drove me through streets full of reflections to the building, which had a drive-in entrance.

Instead of the young writer of yesteryear, living at The Chelsea Hotel and inhaling the heady orgone of youth, my mind-set was now effectively that of a spy. What was I doing at this building, in this elevator, and soon at the entrance of Delia Rogers' home? She answered the door, a woman a year or two younger than my late mother, but she appeared as sleek and honed as a well-taken-care-of forty-year-old. Still, there was something about the mouth one didn't trust. Not so much that it could take a bite; there was an intimation in the extraordinary elasticity of the smile that it could swallow you whole.

Men and women are more delicate than we give ourselves credit for being. We are sculpted psychologically by circumstances we have no control over. Delia had been in a media spotlight since birth and she had taken all the varieties of heat and was still in the kitchen, in the strictly figurative sense.

"Darling," she said. "It's so good to see you. I miss Amy so much. I loved her, darling. Well, you know that. Come in."

Her maid took my raincoat, a Burberry, a present from my mother ten years ago, and Delia and I hugged and then she took my arm.

"Oh, my God," she said. "You're so firm. Do you work out?"

"I saw a lot of wood," I said. I was a little proud about developing muscles in my thirties after the move to Bolinas. At the same time, there was well-nigh sexual insistence in Delia's hand, squeezing, unsqueezing.

"You know Tim," she said.

Here was Tim Zax.

"Jamie," he said, smiling with that elphin delight he brought to most everything.

"Of course," I said. "Great to see you." We hugged.

"And this," Delia said, with a kind of laughing delight in her own social conjuring, "this is Pamela Stevens."

Pamela Stevens was everything you ever wanted in a woman in one look. She was like the young Susan Sontag, but one who wasn't necessarily your intellectual superior. You could imagine lying in her arms while a boat sailed down the Nile at midnight. Or perhaps there was somewhere closer by.

"Hi," I said, and shook her hand smiling. She returned the smile and had a hand that was small boned and soft.

"Hello," she said.

And then something my Dad used to say came to mind, stemming the tide. "All in a day's work, Jamie."

It was probably the best advice I ever got. Take it slow and easy, but take it, and try to deliver on time. He didn't mean it sexually, of course. But when you enter the arena of non-fiction, you use yourself physically in a way the novelist isn't required to do.

We brought our wine glasses into Delia's dining room, which was exquisitely laid out with long thin white candles–giving Pamela's features a delectably edible essence, like human marzipan. She was a writer and a decorator.

"She helped me get the portrait," Delia said, alluding to the famous Sargent of her mother, Baby Rogers, an international beauty who had almost married the Duke of Windsor. It flanked the table, a life-size full length portrait, full of Sargent's high contrast palette of dark blue and black, white flesh and red lipstick.

"It's great," I said. "He was sort of the Timothy Zax of his day."

"I want you to see my new series, Jamie," Tim said with uncharacteristic solemnity.

"I'd love to," I said.

"And Pamela, you too," he said.

It was like being set up, I thought for a moment. Still, the evening kept unfolding, and as a writer I'd now developed a strongly incremental sense of things. The evening wouldn't last forever. I would take my leave. Jason would write a deal for me and I would be able to feed, cloth and shelter my family for another year or so.

After dinner–a nouvelle chicken dish with old fashioned mashed potatoes and fresh string beans; fresh strawberries for desert, and coffee–we adjourned to the living room. It seemed as if Tim was Delia's date. I recalled that years ago she had sent my mother a photograph of herself in a silver frame inscribed with love and that that photograph had been taken by Tim.

"Can you imagine the ego," my mother had fumed about it after they'd had one of their fights.

Delia and Tim were two natives who had never left New York: they had each staked claims at the top of their respective heaps and battled off the *arrivistes* of successive decades with a dedication and tenacity that baffled me. How could anyone believe it was worth it? But that was my problem. The very fulcrum of the cultural life of the great metropolis and by extension the world depended on such people with their significant gifts who also had a capacity for boundless enthusiasm often in the face of mediocrity. Zax was a professional enthusiast. Still, Delia was something else. She lacked a defining talent, unless it was an ability to blithely stare down the media medusa that had stalked her from birth.

When we resettled in the spectacular living room, with its big window looking north over the East River, the subject of the book came up. Pamela and I sat at a respectable distance on a big sofa upholstered in white and green English chintz while Tim and Delia had big red baronial chairs, like thrones.

"I'm so glad you're back," Tim said. "You're so good, I felt bad when you moved to Bolinas."

"Well, I didn't retire," I said and then remembered to smile. I had to forget about defending myself. "I think it could be a fascinating book," I added.

"That cunt Barbara Orchard actually phoned me this week about doing an interview on *Prime Time,*" Delia said.

"Oh," I said, "that might be good, but when the book is done, of course."

"Oh my God," Delia said. "Do you know what I'd do if I had that woman beside me?" She looked directly at me.

"What?" I said.

"I'd take a knife." She gripped an imaginary dagger. "... and shove it right into that bitch." She executed Barbara Orchard with a murderous thrust to the right of her chair.

I had glanced at Tim, who wore a half-smile, as if he were observing Delia with dispassionate curiosity, a distant phenomenon. Now I looked over at Pamela who was looking at the big window hung with red curtains.

"... Y'see?" Delia said.

"I didn't realize you felt that way," I said.

Just then, Delia's 17-year-old son by her last marriage, Justin Briley, came into the room.

"Hi, Mom," he said and leaned down and kissed her directly on the mouth.

"How are you, darling?" she said.

"I'm okay," he said. "Hello, everybody. Hi, Tim. Hi, Pammy."

I was introduced. He was a good-looking blond young man, elegant in his blazer and jeans and loafers.

"She's a great subject," he said to me, apropos of his mother. "Really the best."

"Oh, I know," I said.

"How was the party?" Delia said, beaming at her son.

"The usual," he said. "Well, I'm off to dreamland... Nice seeing you all. And nice to meet you," he said to me.

"Nice meeting *you*," I said.

"Goodnight, darling," Delia said.

"It's going to be a great book," he said to me.

I smiled and nodded.

This seemed unusually supportive behavior on the part of an adolescent with his mother, but as the hired scribe, it was useful to know the lay of the land.

I shared a cab with Pamela downtown. It had stopped raining but the streets were still shining under the now clear sky.

"That was a little scary... about Barbara Orchard," I said.

"How well do you know her?" she said.

"Well, not that well, I guess. I mean is she usually like this?"

"Only at night," she said. "She drinks at night."

"Oh," I said. "So it could get a little crazy. I guess I should talk with her during the day?"

"If she'll agree," Pamela said.

"How do you know her?" I said.

"I went out with Lionel, her son by Arnold Reichman."

She had been married to Reichman, the congressman, for a decade. "I once visited them with my mother," I said. "What's Lionel doing?"

"He's living on The Farm in Tennessee, you know with that guy Stephen?"

"Oh yeah," I said. "The Farm. We got a natural childbirth book they published."

I had already alluded to my wife during the evening, as my own sort of emotional-psychological ballast. Beverly and I were going through a hard time and a lot hinged on a successful outcome of this business meeting. Susceptible to Pamela Stevens charms as I was, I was also wary of getting thrown off my mark. In the taxi, I talked to hear her responses, but scarcely looked at her, which was probably wise.

"He doesn't talk to his mother at all," Pamela said. "He married a Southern girl, I think."

Another Upper East Side drop out, I thought. Once you knew what it amounted to, you had to light out for the territory.

The cab pulled up to The Geary on West 47th Street. I told Pamela we could talk in the morning about getting together at Tim's to see his photographs.

"Or we can just meet there," she said.

"Sure," I said.

I supposed she might have been insulted that I didn't press some advantage in the matter of sleeping with her. It wasn't that things didn't make me nervous enough, or that she wasn't beautiful enough, to make me want to distract myself, but I was in no position for a romp in the wrong meadow.

There is a garden variety Bohemian artist who sleeps with everybody and sometimes, especially if it's a young poet, it can't be said to do much harm. By one's late thirties, however, it gets to be a way of *being* an artist, the vocation can become sleeping with various people *in lieu of* working. Or maybe I'm justifying my own incomprehensible reticence in the face of such a perfect flower of a woman.

12

Tim was the photographer of the thoroughbred at its athletic breaking edge. Everyone he captured looked to be at the finish line of a winning race. Exhilaration chased by adrenalin chased by pride, with barely the suggestion of a price in exhaustion, and barely in the frame—because the race was still ending—the potential of human discourse of any variety.

Then he decided to do the biggest project of his life, the American Failure series, which, as culminating pieces sometimes do, reversed the circuitry. At the age of 57 he took off across the country in a series of RV's for himself and his crew and photographed the flotsam and jetsam on and off the road of the perennially forgotten America, or at least forgotten in New York.

When I got up to his apartment over his studio the next morning at a little after eleven, Pamela was already there, wearing jeans and a pretty pink tank top without a bra. Tim was his perennial alert self but with his hair a little more tousled than on a work day.

"Jamie," he said, smiling. "A little coffee?"

"Great," I said.

Pamela had seriously upped the ante. She looked ready to rock and roll with a mere lift of the tank top. I tried to be focused and contained, sipping coffee at Tim's circular wood coffee table where Pamela also sat beside the kitchen area in one corner of the big room.

Maybe the two of them had already taken a tumble, I thought. My mind routinely scouted out sexual configurations, especially when I was unsure where I was.

"She's very excited about working with you," Tim told me apropos Delia.

"Well, I'm excited too," I said.

"This could be very good for you right now," he said with a look that seemed inquisitive as well as friendly, as if to say, are we on the same page here.

"Oh, I know... it really could."

I had small interest in writing Delia Rogers' autobiography, I knew now. I thought of her as a one-of-a-kind sport of our republic, a mega-crone of the *W* crowd who had seemed, the night before, dangerously unencumbered by the normal restraints of the social contract.

Still, part of a writer's job is to know a bit about the actual monsters of the day. They are likely to be signature statements of what we are, at any given moment, by virtue of their very exaggerations. Well, so I write from this distance. Part of the job actually seemed to be to be confused. At this late date, I woke up this morning remembering the smell of the new linoleum in a new school I went to when my mother rented a little beach house in Malibu after the divorce. It was all new: the rooms, the black board, the chalk, the faces of the kids. Everything was confused in me and yet my senses were keen enough to take a kind of deep if unwitting delight in such things.

I looked over at Tim's huge macho prints of American failure. The photographs were like images of human whiplash from the collision of the psyche with the national machine. Drifters, bums, psychos, and then, in the midst of these psychic disasters, prim waitresses, stolid factory workers, a circus performer in reverie.

"This series is your masterpiece," I said.

"Do you really think so?" he said. He was the richest and most famous photographer of his day but he was insecure about his standing in the art world. Diane Arbus, a slip of a girl who had done fashion work with her husband Alan in the fifties when Tim had already assumed his ascendancy as a fashion photographer, had emerged in the interim as the legend of their generation by photographing people he wouldn't have known were there. But Arbus died in the late sixties having progressively been drawn into the lives and problems of her subjects, as overwhelmed as any of them.

"Who's this?" I said, standing and indicating a snake-like half-naked torso of a Latino man with a comb stuck in his hair, a veritable fire-breathing dragon.

"Oh, just some guy we found," Tim said.

He wasn't corresponding with the man and sending him checks for his ill mother, no matter that he had been vouchsafed this masterpiece by him. Arbus was known to have done the equivalent for her midgets, giants, and twins.

"Did you read Susan Sontag on Arbus?" I asked him.

"Of course," he said.

"So what did you think?"

"Interesting," he said.

"I didn't think she got it," I said. "Arbus's photographs aren't about freaks, really. She'll photograph a midget, but also twins. It's like a way to register the mystery of the universe–through the cosmic sport, you know, which allows you to see that it's this big mysterious generative process..."

"Well, but..." Pamela said, coming abreast of me in front of the big print Tim had just put in front of us, a blonde waitress who was as elegant as any model, but full of true grit. "How about the sequence at the end, of the crazy people."

"What about it?"

"How is that cosmic?"

"I guess I'd have to look at them again," I said, wondering if they weren't the same order of vision.

"What you have to realize about Diane," Tim said, "is that she uses the picture frame with tremendous authority. I use it well, but she'll do it better. With that picture of the crying child, for instance. It's like it's the whole universe. Do you guys want to take a walk?"

He had a kind of proprietary, semi-acquisitive sense of the people of the planet at large–from movie stars to athletes to dancers and now to drifters–and his technique was to set them in front of a drop sheet and look at them closely. He didn't truly understand narrative, I didn't think, the unfolding of life and meaning in increments. But being in the middle of Manhattan with him and Pamela was like being momentarily inside a Fred Astaire tableau.

He and his wife Rene, although still married, were no longer together. She had been a beauty I remembered from photographs of the two of them.

"So Diane Arbus probably learned about the picture frame from you," I said as we crossed Park Avenue and 62nd Street, muted on a midday Saturday.

"Well, that's very nice of you," he said.

Pamela walked between us, and at a certain point in the walk, a little after we got to the zoo, it dawned on me that she was into him, and they may indeed have been sleeping together.

I felt relieved by this and enjoyed the afternoon. He had been a friend and that was about as much or as little as I could understand, a simple fact, like the clouds over the grass and rocks of Central Park.

13

A few weeks later, just as Jason was about to close what he called a "healthy six-figure" deal with Simon and Schuster with me as the writer attached for 40 cents on the dollar, Delia went mad and decided she was going to do her own multi-volumed autobiography and had no need of me. I already suspected that we wouldn't get along. She was a power person with a lot of transparent veils. The most interesting thing about her was how little she was willing to disguise herself.

"What do you mean multi-volume?" I said to Lines in New York, standing in our living room in Bolinas. It was overcast outside, the colors of the eucalyptus trees like wet clay.

"I don't know," he said. "But Joni Evans is going to buy it."

"So I'm out?"

"Unless you can think of something else, and make it very fast."

"Like what?"

"I don't know," he said. "Do you know her well enough to do a *roman à clef*?"

"About Delia? Wouldn't it be libelous?"

"Only if you call her Delia Rogers."

"Let me call you back."

"I'll keep your buzz alive for two more days and then we're dead. It's all about timing."

"Have we betrayed the spirit of the sixties?" I said, smiling at nobody.

"Fuck you," he said and hung up.

I talked to Beverly about it but even as I did I could feel the challenge stirring. The big canvas of Delia's life, from the thirties into the present day, was filled with deeper reverberations of our republic in its power epoch. She was a wealthy beauty of her time with a wayward, spoiled, entitled personality, mostly having a ball.

"One caution," Jason advised the next day.

"Yes, sir."

"Don't get too radical. It's got to be a beautiful painting, remember, a Milton Avery or a Marie Laurencin for the reading public to buy into it. This can't be an Izzy Stone piece. Okay?"

"Okay. So I'm just supposed to do it practically as if she had hired me."

"There you go."

It isn't as if a novelist can work like Izzy Stone, anyway. The trick, after all, is to suspend judgments and let a character come to life. I had my eponymous model for *Betty*, which some people think is my best book. Gide's line "In sympathy lies contagion" actually comprises an antidote to any viable creative impulse, at least in my case. Even if one is writing about a spoiled brat, one needs to lighten up and realize, for instance, just how much she enjoys ice cream.

I worked hard on *Betty*. It was published well and became a best seller and I was back in currency. But Lines didn't sell it to the movies–they ran scared of Delia–and while promising me a good advance on a novel with a few chapters, couldn't make that deal either.

In the mid-1980s we sold our house and moved from Bolinas to Thousand Oaks, just north of Los Angeles, where the public schools were said to be decent. Still nothing broke for me beyond a few small jobs.

Eventually both Beverly and I went out and got jobs.

It had been some time ago, in fact, that I'd started to carry around the knowledge, with a kind of subterranean but obdurate constancy, that what I really needed to do was to get into the mainstream of American life, to plug into the real world, as they say. After several months of hit or miss jobs just getting the lay of the land in Los Angeles, I found work in a small public relations firm and set up a home office too. It was while I was at my job in Universal City that the next writing job came my way.

One night I took home a couple of grocery cartons of material from a woman I'd met named Esther Soloman, whose father had been murdered and who was interested in having a book written about the case. We had moved to an apartment on the third and top floor of a building set high on a hill with a commanding view of Thousand Oaks. Lilac was ending high school and applying to college, Lara was deep into the dark of adolescence, and Beverly and I were under the obvious strain of starting new careers. But the money from the sale of the house allowed us to pay off our accumulated debts and, for the moment, clear our financial decks. The girls shared a bedroom and I had made the smallest bedroom into the home office. I went in there with the boxes that night and sat looking at them for a moment, the lights in the distance outside twinkling, the rest of the household asleep.

This was a new threshold. Somewhere in the two boxes, full of trial transcripts, photographs of the crime scene and related ephemera, was, I knew, the murder weapon–a small knife with which Mr. Solomon, a big man who had lost the ability to walk from M.S., had been stabbed over fifty times. I knew nothing of these people and was now committed to writing a book about them. I fixed on the murder weapon and decided I needed to get it out and see what it looked like rather than be spooked by having it hidden somewhere in one or the other box. It turned out to be in a small paper bag, which had been folded around it, a small kitchen knife of the sort that would be used to cut scallions for an omelette. The tip of it was slightly bent.

Beverly got a part-time job at the Ventura Museum as an assistant to the curator, and one evening we attended an opening there. All of us were asked to wear stick-on labels that said "Hello. My name is..."

"Jamie Read," a compact Latino man about my age standing nearby said, reading my label. "Like the writer."

"Yes," I said.

"But you're not the writer, are you?" he said.

"Of what?" I said.

"*Sometimes a Moron*?"

"Yes," I said. "That's mine."

"No, kidding, brother," he said smiling and shaking my hand. "I read that last year."

"Last year," I said. The sun was going down and the stone patio in the museum's courtyard where we stood was starting to darken under the heat lamps. Beverly was working the crowd with the curator, a younger woman. "Where did you find it?"

"I don't know. I got a paperback. I gave myself an assignment to read only novels that were less than two hundred pages. That way I'd learn something and not waste too much time."

"Learn something about what?"

"Writing, my man. I want to write."

"Well," I said, "did you learn anything?"

"From *Sometimes a Moron*?" He smiled. "Plenty, man. You had me laughing, my man."

I'd turned in the first hundred pages of my murder book, which I'd sold myself to Jules Carson at Flashpoint Books in New York, and gotten a cool reception. He told me it took too long to get started and he couldn't figure out who was who. I knew I needed to cut it and reassured him that I was a professional and knew where I was going. Carson had made his deal with me with much preamble about giving a small advance but doing superb marketing that guaranteed me money on the other end of publication. I was waiting to hear back from him again with the second installment of the advance when I got a call at my home office, Writing Inc., from Arturo Sandoval, the man I'd met at the Ventura Museum.

"You say you do brochures?" he said.

"Yes," I said. "Brochures, press kits, press releases. I can provide complete public relations services."

"That's good to know. When can you be here?"

"When–today?"

"Yes, brother. I have a job I'd like to discuss."

I drove the Conejo Grade downhill from Thousand Oaks into Camarillo and then into Oxnard and found the office in a two story commercial building on Gonzalez Street.

Sandoval, like me approaching fifty, turned out to be one of the best connected political players in what is affectionately known in Oxnard as the Mexican mafia. He introduced me to his pretty daughter, Martha, who was a college student and answered the phone in the front room of the office Sandoval shared with Pepe Ayala, a tax man. Then he ushered me into his office, on the left, which fronted, like Ayala's on the right, on Gonzalez street.

"Sit down, brother," he said.

He pointed to a small bookcase behind his desk.

"See, here are my books. *Of Mice and Men, The Stranger, Notes of a Native Son, The Grass Harp, My Name Is Aram, Notes from the Underground...*" He laughed gutturally and fell into a chair. "Good reading, my friend."

"Very good," I said with a slight smile, not quite knowing what my demeanor should be.

"And...," he said, opening a desk drawer, and putting the Ballantine edition of 1972 down on the table, "... *Sometimes a Moron*... It sounds like a song, doesn't it? 'When the moon hits your eye/Like a big pizza pie/That's a moron...' "

I laughed. "Amore," I said.

"Well, my man, same thing, eh? This is marriage number three for me, but you know something, I'm still friends with my ex-wives."

The job turned out to be a brochure for a company that didn't currently exist but was seeking a major client in Mexico. The company would provide parts and repair services for oil drilling machinery. The principals were wealthy players in the Oxnard plains.

"What we need here is something that looks like old money. Do you follow me?" Arturo said.

"Understated elegance..." I said.

Sandoval collapsed back in his swivel top chair, laughing.

"Understated elegance ... I knew I had my man when I saw you at that museum. So your wife works there?"

"Well, it's more of a part-time job. She's a painter."

"Two artists, hunh?"

I nodded. Cars were going by silently outside the office window under the trees lining Gonzalez Street. I told him I would need to interview the principals in order to get my language down for the brochure copy, and then I thought maybe there should be a photograph of the company officers.

"Who'll the photographer be? You got someone?"

"Sure," I said.

I drove around with Sandoval that afternoon meeting the other officers of the The Ventura Company, Arturo himself being a Vice President. The others were all Wasp types, taller than Arturo and paler, and that made me feel like a co-conspirator in his company.

He soon called with another job, the text for an annual report on a non-profit group that provided cultural and educational opportunities for gifted Latino students in Ventura County. The founder and chairman, Steve Flores, was a junior high school guidance counselor who had worked with very little money to establish his program and now wanted to take a quantum leap in funding it. He had made Arturo chair of his advisory board with that in mind.

I interviewed Flores, a roly-poly middle-aged man, in the room he used as an office at his tract house in Oxnard one October evening when it was still light out and his wife was preparing dinner.

"You see," he said, smiling and pronouncing each word carefully. "The young Hispanic who comes up with his family from Mexico—this is not a person with a refined sense of the principles of Jeffersonian democracy. And this young man or young woman is going to quickly find that the neighborhood is teeming with gangs, and in order to get along, in many cases, he or she will be recruited into those gangs.

"Now, from there you need to look at demographics: the non-white population of America is in a growth surge that by the millennium is going to seriously challenge and eventually overturn the majority status of the white population. I have these kids, who are the best and the brightest we have, studying parliamentary procedure and putting into practice *Roberts Rules of Order* at our debates.

"You might say the graffiti is on the wall. If too many grow up to be gang bangers, we may have not only the demographic tipping of the scale, but an ideological one, too. Who's to say that Jeffersonian democracy is the government of choice for this citizenry? You see what I mean?"

"It's very clear," I said.

Flores leaned back in his chair. It was the end of a long day for him, I knew, since he went to work at the high school each morning. His wife called him into dinner, and had set a place for me as well. I protested but she insisted, and I ended up sitting down in the little dining room with religious prints on the wall to a fine Mexican meal of enchiladas, rice and beans.

One evening Beverly and I went to dinner with Arturo and his wife Eleanor at the Founders Club at the top of one of the two Oxnard financial towers. That night Arturo talked about drinking himself to insensibility in the days before he had met Eleanor. She was a Scottish Irish woman who worked as the public relations director of the Oxnard transit district. One night after midnight, she told us, Arturo called her and asked if she would come over to his apartment. She debated with herself whether she should or not, but ended up going. She threw a coat over her nightgown and drove to his apartment.

With that, the relationship took the turn toward marriage, Arturo's third, her first.

He was a strange character, with a combination of bravado and self-deprecation that was a variation on the macho posturing of Roy Parker, tangled among his support lines high in the trees of Bolinas or the Yucatan.

Arturo had quit alcohol cold, he told us.

"Now," he said to me. "You've got to help me with something."

"My pleasure, sir."

"I want you to teach me how to write."

"You should take my course at UCLA Extension," I said. I had taught there on and off, one evening a week, since we'd moved to Thousand Oaks.

"No, man," he said. "I haven't been over the Conejo Grade in over a year and a half, and I'm not ruining my record—even for you."

"Okay," I said.

"But I know you can give me the keys to the kingdom, brother."

What kingdom was that, I wondered silently. I suppose he reminded me of my father: the breakfast club, or the Founders Club, up in the morning to meet the world with sustained interest in its ends and means.

I met him at eight one morning at the Coco's on Vineyard in Oxnard and he introduced me to Francisco Draga, the head of the local arm of the Job Training Partnership Act, a federal program that provided job training and job placement services for laid off workers and others in Ventura County.

Draga had an interesting face in the mode of a medieval prelate in a Spanish court, full of strong lines but fluid in its moment-to-moment play, especially around Arturo, who, while he held no comparable position to Draga's, was a greater power behind the scenes.

"We want you to do a little PR for the agency," Arturo said.

"Great," I said. "What specifically have you got in mind?" I turned to Draga.

"Well," he said smiling. "We would like people to know more about our programs and what we can provide in the community." He looked over at Arturo.

"What you need to understand about Francisco," he said, looking at me, "is that he is a consummate politician who will give an answer like that, 100% generic bullshit, you know, and never for a moment be tempted to break out of it into saying anything more interesting, which is why he's the important player that he is."

Draga's face imploded slowly into deep smiling. "But Arturo," he said. "I thought you..."

"What?" Arturo shouted. "What?—you son-of-a-bitch, say something for yourself..."

An older gentleman at a corner table turned in our direction. Arturo nodded politely.

"I'm just getting on his case," Arturo said to the man. "It's the only way to deal with him."

The gentleman smiled and turned away.

"See, look at me," he said to us *sotto voce*. "Scraping and bowing to the white man, and we Latinos own this town. So why do I do that?"

"You're making at least *one* whitey do some scraping and bowing," I said.

"What whitey?"

"I'm not at liberty to say."

I woke up this morning after a dream in which I saw Roy Parker again for the first time in years. I was on a flight of stairs and passed the open door of an apartment and glimpsed a man brushing his teeth. He seemed to recognize me, I paused on the stairs, waiting for him to finish brushing his teeth, so he would take the toothbrush out of his mouth and I could tell whether or not it was really him, but it went on for quite a long time. Roy Parker? I thought. And then he took the brush out and rinsed his mouth and looked back at me and I saw that it *was* him, but instead of the lean youth I'd known, he had filled out into a mountain man.

"You're so big," I said stepping into his apartment. Beside him stood his wife—his former girlfriend?—who looked comparable in size though sweet and pretty, and his son, also big, though half as tall as Roy.

Do we, then, assume the shape required of us by what we do?

A week later I met Draga by himself at Baker's Square, the restaurant on the corner of the financial towers plaza on

Esplanade Drive. I had been put on a monthly retainer to do Public Relations for the company and was putting together the press kit. The newly elected President Clinton was proposing an economic stimulus package that would double the local Summer Youth Employment Program for "at risk youth" in the county.

Speaking of the young to be employed by the program, Draga said: "This is the segment of society most likely to part with its money in the shortest time frame. He or she gets a paycheck for doing work in the public sector, filing stuff in a government office or erasing grafitti in the park. The weekend comes and they go to the mall and buy things. The stores make money, and the upsurge in business may involve hiring a new clerk. For each federal dollar, they estimate there is three dollars worth of benefit to the economy. It's known as the multiplier effect."

As I took notes, a press release took shape: the new President was initiating legislation that would directly benefit the County–and I had an intimation of headlines in the local newspapers and the front page of the newly born Ventura County section of the *Los Angeles Times*.

I worked on the press release, "New President Doubles Ventura County Summer Youth Program," and phoned and then faxed it from my home office to all the local city editors.

The next morning just before nine my business phone rang. It was Arturo.

"Whatever you did, my man, never tell them your secrets."

"What're you saying?"

"You got headlines across the board, my man." I had only seen the *Times,* which featured the story on the front page of the Ventura section.

The other headlines proved to be even bolder. "$$$ ON THE WAY" ran the banner headline in the Oxnard *Star-Free Press.*

14

Six months later I mentioned to Draga that I could use the agency's benefits if he had an in-house position, and he hired me the following week as the Rapid Response Manager. The position involved making presentations about the services offered by the agency and other county agencies to workers let go in a plant closing or a mass lay off. I would also handle the agency's public relations. The multiple ironies of finding this particular full-time position after spending my adult life outside the job market barely grazed my consciousness. I was too happy to be a full-time employee.

One afternoon Alan Winterbourne, a thirty-seven-year-old laid-off aerospace engineer who hadn't gotten another job in seven years, entered the Employment Development Department office off of Oxnard Boulevard and opened fire on the staff there, killing three people, including a policeman, and wounding three others. He was chased by Oxnard police to the Ventura branch of the EDD office, where he got out of his car and was shot and killed by police.

The man was well-known to many of the case workers in our office. With shoulder length hair, he had been regarded as eccentric but harmless. Rupert, a courtly Portuguese-American originally from Massachusetts who was the Intake Manager, stopped by my office and sat down in one of my two visitors' chairs.

"You heard about the EDD incident?" he said.

"Yes."

"I knew him well. Alan Winterbourne... Crazy Alan." He shook his head.

"Why do you think it happened?" I said.

"Why? I haven't got a clue. He got fed up. He wasn't a stupid man. But there were psychological problems. I mean, have you seen what he looked like?"

"I saw his picture."

"I said to him, 'Alan, let's lose the hair.' I mean, you do a ponytail or something, you know. You don't walk into an interview like an emaciated Ozzy Osbourne. It's not going to reassure an employer."

County Supervisor Gilbert Frym wasn't happy with the reports circulating that the agency wasn't responding to the needs of the larger community and wanted to see new faces. The County Board of Supervisors were the directors of the Agency, the counsel, of which Arturo was the Vice Chair, their instrument.

One of our training providers was Orlando Gorre, a compact sturdy Filipino man with a benevolent look who had once played the role of the cop in a Northern California production of *Captain America.*

He mentioned this to me one day, sitting in my office.

"I said to myself, can this be the man who wrote that play? I doubt it, but still, I thought it worth putting the question."

"How did it do?" I said.

"The local critic loved it."

"Really," I said.

"The audiences were divided, but you know what they say. If everybody loves it, you must be doing something wrong..." I nodded. He waited a moment. "Well," Orlando said, "I'll say what I have to say. Rupert, as you may know, is being shunted around by Francisco on an almost daily basis. They have stripped him of his rights after ten years as a loyal employee..."

"I didn't know. I thought he was Intake Manager..."

"Yes, but as an interim position with no benefits, and they may demote him to team leader. He is no longer being invited to the Monday managers' meeting..."

"I noticed that, actually."

"Can you call the *Los Angeles Times*?" he said in a whisper.

"About what?"

"What we are speaking about. A reporter there, Dave Surry, wants to run with the story, but he needs an inside source."

"They'd fire me in a minute."

Orlando sighed. "Rupert won't tell his story, of course," he said.

"I want a press conference about NAFTA," Arturo told me one morning over the phone. "Tell Francisco."

"Tell Francisco?" I said. "He's my boss."

"Yes, and I'm his boss." He sighed. "Who is Jamie Read? Who the hell is Jamie Read? When you know, will you please phone."

"Absolutely," I said.

"Thank you," he said and hung up.

I was a Jew, among other things, but I saw the writing on the wall. These people didn't have any particular interest in the finer points of Jeffersonian democracy. My job was to keep my job. My press conference on NAFTA, involving an Under Secretary of Commerce from Mexico Arturo hoped to do business with, was a great success. Nobody seemed to get it that an item like this in Oxnard brought the press out in force. It wasn't as if we had heady competition. The predominant news out of Oxnard was of small armed robberies and murders in the Colonia, the Mexican old town, which seemed to happen at least weekly.

The *Los Angeles Times* Ventura section ran a front page story on the agency funding questions–one of our training school providers was complaining of favoritism–and went on to quote Orlando Gorre sounding off about an old boy network that had the whole thing tied up. Dave Surry, a respected investigative reporter, wasn't the writer, but I knew that he had to have okayed it and I phoned him.

"How can you run this story as if it's hard news?" I said. "The Gorre part is nothing but speculation on his part and yet it besmirches the agency..."

"Look," Surry said. "Everybody knows what's going on. The homeboys own the agency. You yourself know that."

"Dave," I said, "we all respect you as a reporter with the

highest ethical standards. This just surprises me."

"I repeat: You yourself know better. Or I hope you do."

Arturo was suddenly standing beside my desk.

"I want to talk to you," he said when I hung up. "Come back here."

We walked down the corridor to an empty office he used periodically. He closed the door and sat down behind his desk.

"I have one question for you," he said.

"What?" I took a seat opposite him at his desk.

"Should I resign?"

"As what?"

"*Chingada,*" he said. "As Vice Chair of the council. My question is, how much trouble is all this going to be? What's Orlando so upset about?"

"Orlando is upset about being treated like riff-raff, the same as his friend Rupert."

"What should I do?" Arturo suddenly looked drained and frightened. "You were just talking with the *Times,* right?"

"Right. I don't think they have anything. I don't know what there is to have. Is there something?"

"You never know," he said.

The agency had been investigated ten years earlier when it was run by a white career bureaucrat who had funded his own service operation out of the agency budget. He was now periodically seen entering and exiting a liquor store in Port Hueneme with a beard and the rolled-up pant legs of an old and poverty-stricken Prufrock.

"Why don't you call Orlando?" I said.

"What, you mean just call him?"

"He's saying there's no real give in the procurement process, that the fix is in before anybody even submits bids. If you phone him, and say you're surprised or upset by the story..."

"Okay."

He picked up the phone and dialed. Orlando was out and he left a message.

Over the weekend I got two calls from Arturo, whom I hadn't heard from at home since I'd gotten the in-house job. He was in a panic about his future as a player and whether the best he could do now was to get out and put the agency behind him before it led to some sort of public exposure that would hurt his standing. He depended on being perceived positively in the larger political and business communities.

At the Monday morning managers' meeting Francisco continued to conduct business as usual although it did seem to me he was hunched further down on his shoulders.

When I got to my desk after the meeting, my phone was ringing.

"Jamie Read, Job Training."

"What's going on?" Arturo said.

"Whataya mean?"

"What happened at the meeting?"

"Nothing. Business as usual."

"Francisco didn't resign?"

"No."

"All right, brother. We'll talk soon. I'm out, you know."

"You resigned?"

"He didn't mention it."

"No, not so far."

"Fine," he said.

My murder book, *Heart of Glass*, was going to be published soon. Jules Carson had had it line edited and sent out advanced galleys to the trades. The reviews in *Publishers Weekly* and *Kirkus* were both good, and I was suddenly getting calls from production companies about the book as a film project. I also got a call from the *L.A. Times* new *Ventura Life* magazine section, who wanted to run an article on me and the book.

Arturo wasn't a man to brush off a perceived slight, at least not one from Francisco Draga. Since Francisco was still coming to the office and no other shoe had dropped, Arturo may have jumped the gun in leaving his position–because he got no clear mandate from Francisco, as he saw it. It seemed to me that Francisco had no instinct for giving advice. He reminded me more and more of Nixon hunkering down during Watergate. Removing him easily from office looked for a while like expecting a painless dental extraction. If Arturo wanted to revenge himself on his friend, his trump card was Supervisor Frym who was upset enough with the agency to clean house.

"This is my job," I said on the phone when he'd demanded I meet him for an update at his office.

"Excuse me, Mr. Read. Do you recall who introduced you to Francisco and set the whole thing up?"

"Fine. I'll be over there in a few minutes. But I have a presentation at Dole today after lunch."

"Don't worry about it. You'll be there."

The *Los Angeles Times Ventura Life* section put me on the cover and, along with discussing the new book, told the story of a writer at 50 joining the ranks of the mainstream as an employee of the county job training agency.

While I had sold the book myself, I had to have an agent to deal with the interest in Hollywood and arranged with Johnny Orton of the Sartoris Group to represent me.

"I remember you from the *Moron* days," he said with a New York accent on the phone. "That was a fine piece of work."

Francisco summoned the entire staff to a four o'clock meeting across the parking lot at the Oxnard Hilton and announced that the Personnel Director for the County of Ventura, Ron Borden, would soon become the Director of our agency, too, and that he, Francisco, was stepping down.

Shock hit the whole agency. Would we still have our jobs, several people shouted.

"Mr. Borden," Francisco said from the podium, "will be calling a meeting of everyone on staff in the very near future.

I called this meeting to let you know what was happening first."

"Why is it happening?" someone asked.

"I wish I knew," Francisco said. "Some of you know that not everybody approves of us, but still..."

When I got back to my office I called Arturo but got his machine. Two days later, he hadn't returned my call but I ran into him at the elevator when I was going down for lunch. He signalled me to follow him into his sometime office, the unoccupied room next to Draga's office, and shut the door.

"I told you something was going to happen," he said, sitting down.

"Do I still have a job?" I asked.

"With me or with the county?"

"Well, for the moment, with the county," I said.

"Time will tell, Mr. Read," he said.

The wheels had begun to turn but I had no contact anymore with the power centers. A woman named Sarah Tyne, a career county employee who had been briefly employed by the agency and left for another position, was brought in as Interim Director. I was moved from my office to a cubicle at the Employment Development Department, which turned out to be a blessing in disguise. Since the Rapid Response presentation I coordinated was given jointly with an EDD representative, who spoke about Unemployment Insurance, it made sense that we would work out of the same office.

Crucially, being at the Employment Development Department allowed me to escape direct monitoring by my own agency. My partitioned cubicle contained a desk, a telephone, and a computer that wasn't on a network. One afternoon I began to write a play–the first time I'd ventured into that form in years–and it exploded in my monitor like nothing I'd written for years.

If I'd known viscerally that I'd needed to get out of the literary life and into mainstream America some years back, it seemed that I had now made that passage and that new writing was on the other side of it.

15

Lilac graduated with honors from Barnard in New York—Beverly, Lara and I spent a weekend in May in New York for the ceremony—and now had a job as an assistant editor at *Vogue*. Lara, having graduated from high school, tended to spend days on end in her room. Desultorily she took courses at Moorpark Junior College and had a succession of desultory jobs. She was the artist type in a family of artists who had paid a heavy price for that choice or destiny, and I found her alternately lovable and exasperating.

When I came home from work, I often found her in front of the television and would tell her to turn it off, that I needed peace and quiet. I was losing my job again after a period of relative calm in our lives, and the good news of writing a play aside, I was upset. Over the years I had attended various 12 Step meetings and now found an Al-Anon meeting in Thousand Oaks to attend each week. If I didn't fit the addict-alcoholic profile, I wasn't quite a codependent either, though I had been to Coda meetings. Al-Anon from the beginning sounded like my meeting. These people, it was clear to me, were, like me, control freaks. We believed that we could take care of any situation that might come up.

"Turn that goddam thing off!" I yelled at Lara, who would click the remote and disappear into her room.

Sometimes when I stepped into the apartment after a day at work, it was simply that I didn't want a household with bad television blasting into it. At the same time, I noticed an involuntary, visceral level to my anger when I saw my daughter shipwrecked on the tides of a bankrupt culture. Compulsive as I was, I still had to wonder at this reaction.

"You're always in a rage," Beverly said, "and we can't live like this."

The meetings were the usual revelation of other selves, each holding up at least a sliver of oneself in corroboration. A community of souls. There was a huge aging surfer with a deep and sorrowful voice named Pete. He was married to an alcoholic who periodically went on binges and maxed out his credit card. An engineer, he liked to get up early in the morning and head out for Zuma or Trancas for a few hours of surfing and solitude before work.

There was a tall man named Marvin, who designed sound systems. He constantly extolled the benefits of the program. He was frequently asked to lead a meeting and we became familiar with his story.

"A year ago," he told us more than once, "when you asked my name, it was dishonest when I answered Marv. Oh, that's what I said, but it wasn't true. A more honest answer would have been, 'My name is Sharon.' "

Sharon, a charismatic alcoholic, had stolen his heart, his billfold, and finally his identity. It is a corollary of our steady-as-she-goes, controlling personalities, that we like to get blown away.

When I entered the house now, I monitored the involuntary, visceral tide of my anger and repaired to the office and lay down there, rather than rousting Lara from her television. I said a quick prayer, thanking God for my blessings, and asked for help to live God's will for my life, and then said the same prayer for Beverly, Lilac and Lara. I had prayed as a child, notably when I went to the race track with my father—prayed that my horse would win. I remember standing at the railing at Yonkers Raceway and giving, at twelve or thirteen, my entire body weight to the enterprise. The horse was named "Prince Albert." I prayed as hard as I could for that horse and, as I remember, he came in third.

What the Program did was to detach the notion of a Higher Power from the idea of one's individual will: in fact, the first step was an admission of powerlessness in the matter that brought one to the Twelve Step meeting: alcoholism, codependency, or in the case of the Al-Anon meeting, an addiction to turbulence as opposed to serenity. The powerlessness of the individual became the catalyzing agency of the Higher Power, by the same principle perhaps that declares that nature abhors a vacuum. The relief of prayer, in turn, wasn't that one stood a better chance of achieving a specific goal but rather that of consciously placing one's life in God's hands, letting go. It occurred to me that by not believing in God, I had been assigning to myself all of the duties assumed by the deity.

It depended on faith, faith that the Higher Power—or the Universe, as I often thought of it—had a design. The strongest recent manifestation of this, as I saw it, was in my writing a new play for the first time in decades. It was elemental:

1. I was a writer who wasn't making money and needed to get a job. I sensed too that it would be salutary for my work to touch down in the mainstream of American life.
2. I got a job and brought home a paycheck and learned more about the larger world.
3. At my job, I was eventually assigned to a desk and a computer and given free time in which to write.

If I'd sat up night after night trying to conceive of such a work situation for myself, I could never have come up with such fortuitous symmetries.

My last name was the answer in the *Los Angeles Times* crossword puzzle one Sunday, clue being "*Betty* author," and the following morning I was coordinating the filming of interviews with the various members of the County Board of Supervisors at their offices in the County Building on Victoria Street in Ventura.

"I just wrote your name down in the crossword yesterday," Supervisor Judy Mikels told me.

"No kidding," I said, though someone else had mentioned it that morning at EDD. I was in the crossword. That and a dollar would buy me an old-style cup of coffee.

I prompted each Supervisor with a series of questions from off camera, and they responded with the generic volubility of politicians. Supervisor Frym, a small, wizened old warhorse who had been in local politics for decades, enunciated with great relish, taking credit for the restructuring of the agency and its new responsiveness to the needs of the community. By then I'd been given my two weeks notice.

I had been getting up each weekday morning for going-on three years to be at work by eight or a little after. The first week or so of unemployment was delightful. I slept in. Fortuitously I was hired by the Graduate Writing Program at USC to teach a class or two that fall. I began to answer ads in the *Los Angeles Times* and fax my resume. In the meantime, I was finishing a second play.

Beverly wanted to get out of the branch of Ethan Allen where she had been working as a designer and possibly to transfer to the outlet in Santa Monica. Since I now had work in L.A. I began to answer employment ads there, and we started looking for an apartment in Santa Monica. Living near Los Angeles and having often visited friends there, we knew it was the area we liked best, although apartments were scarce.

While looking at a two-bedroom apartment one morning, we realized that if we took it, Lara would move in and that the most important thing for her now was to get into her own life without her parents in the immediate vicinity. A week later we found a lovely one bedroom north of Wilshire and began packing up for the move. At the same time, Lara found a room to rent in a home in Thousand Oaks. She was making money baby-sitting and off-and-on telemarketing.

The theater was a very different game than it had been during the sixties. Virtually everybody but the playwright seemed to have a handle on what needed to be done with a play. The playwright, of course, believed that the play ought to be produced. With our move into Santa Monica, I started to get my plays around and several staged readings were done with actors generously lending their time and skills.

After writing the first act of a third play, before my Cobra health insurance ran out, I checked myself into Midway Hospital one morning for the long overdue hernia operation, and Beverly picked me up that afternoon and drove me home.

I was told to get out of bed as soon as I could or it would take longer to recover so I began to hobble around almost immediately and in a few weeks was getting around fairly easily. After I felt I had recovered most of my normal energy, I wrote the second half of the play. Then I wrote a fourth play. And finally a fifth. It was a late efflorescence.

Walking around our neighborhood in Santa Monica, I was surprised that other pedestrians frequently said hi, good morning, smiled and nodded. During the years we'd spent in Thousand Oaks, nobody had done that. The mindset of exurbia is a strange one, or one into which Beverly and I never quite fit. Santa Monica gave me the sense that I had at last found a place that made sense to me, and at the same time come full circle back to where I'd spent years of my boyhood. In my fifties, such a place was full of echoes and colors that brought back the past in a gentle enlivening way.

At USC I was treated as a small-scale eminence and realized with some surprise that my years as a writer had given me experience that might prove useful to my students. I had found a job tutoring Korean students for their SATs in Torrance and saw the first wave of emigration among these people with particular piquancy. When the Korean financial crisis occurred, the tutoring center was forced to let most of us go, and I started private workshops in Santa Monica, where recruitment was far easier than it would have been in Thousand Oaks.

The fourth play I wrote took off on the speech rhythms and provocative manner of an actress who had worked on the staged reading of my first play, and I had an interesting revelation. As a writer, I was constantly fielding impressions of people, places and things in my environment, and these comprised a virtually infinite resource for the writing I did. As a young man, I'd been disoriented by the power of the impression made on me by various women, and wondered what it meant in terms of my life in the world. Significantly, though, after my initial foray in Hollywood, I kept a guarded distance from that world and managed to go on working.

I fielded the nervous system of the actress to write a play, but not to write a new and disruptive chapter of my life, because that part had nothing to do with being a writer, and perhaps it ran against the grain of my character. I hadn't pressed any opportunity with Pamela Stevens in New York, and there had been other instances. I had remained married to the same woman and lost touch with celebrated colleagues like Orson Silo and Danny Laveggio who had lived vastly different lives in and out of the headlines.

It occurred to me that I said no almost reflexively because early on my mother and my father had each in their own way blown me away, before, during and after their divorce. I'd live with my mother, and then go with my father, and my own sense of things would mutate in the process. My mother had been an especially vivid and, I would venture, precipitately erotic presence to me as a child, and this may have made me more diffident in my love life than I otherwise might have been. At the same time, my mother, I think, made me an artist by opening up my senses to the colors and textures and the swoon of eros in the sight of a blue sky on a certain spring day, for example. Then my Dad gave me an example of being in the world and making ends meet and fitting in that might be salutary, and might, in other circumstances, close down the shop of colors where the artist works. Not to mention an animosity toward my mother in the years after the divorce. They took each other so hard that neither of them really recovered.

My strategy then was to be in some sense out of the loop, never quite the snug fit that someone else might have exulted in being. It made me an artist, I suppose, in imposing a distance from any scene in which I found myself.

In my mid-fifties, I know I'm going through a change of life similar to what women go through, to what Beverly is going through these days herself. In the evening we walk over to Montana Avenue and stop at the library for a while or just walk down to 10th Street on one side and back up to 16th Street on the other side and then walk back home. She has started painting again. Beautiful scenes of the light here, the streets with palm trees. No longer at Ethan Allen, she takes freelance work now when it comes and we watch our budget, but there is a sense of having passed a threshold. I live the life I want to live, with all its oddities, and will go on living it. Beverly is in touch with her parents in London and we may visit them there when summer comes. She's been over there with the girls from time to time over the years, but I realized I haven't left America in 25 years.

M

KLEIN HAD BEGUN TO SUSPECT that he was losing his mind–this on the heels of an intimation that he had unearthed an extraordinary secret of worldly existence.

"Tell it to me," said Mathias, his friend from their New York days of 35 years ago, at lunch at Dupars at the Farmers' Market in Hollywood.

"I believe I know what death is," Klein answered.

Mathias cast his eyes down into his mushroom barley soup and it was a moment before Klein realized that his friend was crying with silent hilarity.

"What?" said Klein.

Mathias, who clearly would not be able to speak, waved him away, hardly daring to look him in the face.

"I know," Klein said. "I'm a goddam crank. But bear in mind I've been a crank–a benevolent one, I hope–from the beginning, and it's served me if not well, not badly either."

Mathias was trying to pull himself together. He was a man who was often struck by absurdity so forcefully that it more or less dismantled him, but he remained politely circumspect about it. Klein enjoyed this politeness in his friend. He wasn't a grandstander–as were, for instance, many members of Klein's immediate family. His sister, for instance, would mount an invisible soapbox at the drop of a political nuance.

"You aren't allowed to say that you've figured that out," Mathias finally iterated with a studied flatness, as if any inflection would reignite his hilarity, glancing briefly in his direction and away.

"I understand your saying that," he said, "but my thesis isn't speculative, it's experiential."

"What?" Mathias said. "You had a near-death experience?"

As his friend said this, Klein's mind had hit a snag. He was trying to remember the name of that photographer who had taken all those dirty pictures and created havoc with the National Endowment for the Arts. He had an intuition that the name began with an M. He pushed a little bit of mashed potatoes onto his fork with meatloaf on it and the first name Robert occurred to him but the last name continued to elude him.

"Not near death, no," he said. And then, breaking stride: "Sometimes my mind shuts down. Like the hard drive goes down, you know?"

Mathias began the silent laughter again, again looking down at his soup. "We're fallin' apart, sonny," he said in a Yiddish accent.

In the middle of the night, Klein woke up with the image of bubbles in the water. Bubbles—like lives, so to speak. When a bubble burst, when it arrived at the surface of the water, it became the water, or the air, or both at once. Instead of being a bubble, that is, a finite enclosure in the midst of the water, it turned into the water, or the air, or both: it became everything, as it were. If this were the case, why would one fear death?

"So what, sonny?" he could hear Mathias say with his Yiddish accent. "I ain't dead yet."

A college teacher by profession, Klein longed for a larger bully pulpit from which to discourse on such insights. His current graduate seminar included a handsome young mulatto woman whose sporadic attendance had become a problem. She had been dating a famous athlete—Klein hadn't been able to find out who it was—but had broken up with him when she discovered his multiple unprotected infidelities. Klein had been apprised of this by his student via e-mail. The girl was obviously having a hard time and he tried to be understanding. These lives would intersect for fourteen weeks with his life—like a school of fish at the center of which he sat at his desk—and then they would be gone. The young woman was full of innocence and bravado, longing and powerful energy—and it was anyone's bet how things would turn out for her. Life was short, as they said, and now Klein himself knew for a fact. He was happy to be married to a woman his own age with whom he could share the intimation—unlike his colleague and boss, Czerny, who was forever scouting the horizon for sexual distraction. Czerny was a man without insight but one who seemed perpetually delighted by variety in the world.

For a moment, lying in bed, Klein wondered if he should initiate lovemaking with Sheila. They hadn't for so long, and it seemed to be some sort of passage for them both to leave one another alone benevolently, as it were. Something was changing under them—tectonic plates were shifting beneath their lives. Their children had moved out and their only household conversations now were with one another. It was earth-shaking. Sheila was sleeping soundly, and he let it go; let her re-gather her forces for day, he thought. He got up out of bed and went downstairs to read in the living room of their new townhome in Baldwin Hills's Village Green, with the big greensward out their front windows.

It was the dead of night and he was reading a primer on Carl Jung, who also had come to a reckoning with death. Indeed Jung had constellated the universe so that a single life was a signature of everything: a unique fingerprint or grain of sand, a snowflake or a star, that bore the stamp of it all.

There was no noise in the place, Klein noticed again. What a relief to have quiet in these times so roisterous with irrelevance, the daily paper now like a massive deposit of immediate obsolescence. Or was it he himself, rather, that was obsolete? Then again, what did it matter? Either you were yourself, or you were everything, and surely either possibility was okay. Jung was saying the same thing, it seemed to Klein, and this was a deep concurrence, even a Jungian synchronicity. In his happiness at this thought, like a small cosmic bonus, the name Mapplethorpe slipped into his consciousness.

Hollywood Lessons

THE BEST STORY I EVER HEARD about Hollywood came from a black novelist who was flown out from an east coast college where he was a professor to discuss writing a script for a movie about the life of Malcolm X. This was several years before Spike Lee made the movie.

The novelist was at lunch at L'Orangerie with the producer. He didn't know what was what yet–he'd been flown out because he was black and had written a novel that had been reviewed in the daily *New York Times* where his photograph had accompanied the review. He got the call the day the review appeared.

The producer looked like a well-preserved seventy-something and wore English Yardley lavender. The writer had been rereading *The Autobiography of Malcolm X* on the plane and it seemed to him more than ever one of the great American books. Quite apart from the money, he was interested in the possibility of being a part of something that would honor Malcolm.

He and the producer ordered lunch and then, without any preliminary discussion, the producer smiled and winked at him and told him he'd woken up in the middle of the night with the answer to the central question of who would play

Malcolm. Denzel Washington wasn't a big star yet but there were a lot of possibilities.

"I'm not sure if I dreamed it," the producer said, "or thought of it after I'd just woken up."

"Who is it?" the writer asked.

The producer paused for a moment and said, "Neil Diamond."

The black writer never told me how he reacted but I gathered he got an early plane back to the college. I've been here so long that the producer's answer makes a certain sense to me. Neil Diamond had recently done the remake of *The Jazz Singer*, the story of Al Jolson, in which he appeared in blackface, playing a fake black man. Sure, it was a little out of left field, but it was original in that way too. I don't mean to sound perverse; it's only that after you've been out here a while you understand this species of thinking, or, more accurately, you are familiar with the type of producer who thinks that way.

Elson Capps is, of course, not that Hollywood, the Hollywood of that story, but more of the new Hollywood—new Hollywood being a designation that occurs with each decade, and in fact Capps has been part of the new scene so long he may have passed off the radar screen. But that's never going to matter to Capps. He's an East Coast rich boy who originally was an actor, but had, and has today, a quirky, querulous New York Jewish look and style that could only take him so far. Eventually, like Mazursky who also began as an actor, he became a writer-director. The thing that set him apart from the beginning was that he could make a movie with his own money. People like Mazursky are scrappers, street-wise fast-talking showmen who schmooze and flatter and cajole their way into position, and then, when the pieces are all in place, make a film.

I once told Mazursky that he seemed to me like a cinematic heir of the great Jewish novelists of the 1930s, Nathanael West, Daniel Fuchs and Henry Roth, and he nodded and smiled and didn't say very much—and it dawned on me that he probably had only a hazy sense of those writers. I was at his house because PEN, the writers and human rights organization, was having a fund raiser to sponsor an initiative on behalf of a political prisoner, a female writer in Salvador. Mazursky's wife was on the action committee and had volunteered their Hollywood home for the meeting.

That was the year just after I'd gotten divorced. I was the President of PEN, taught a writing class at UCLA Extension, did freelance public relations work, and, three hours a night, Monday through Thursday, was a telemarketer for We-Tip, a telephone hotline to report child molesters.

Two brothers from a ranch family in Arizona had rented a room in an office building on Ventura Boulevard just off of the Topanga exit of the 101 freeway. They were easy-going young dudes, and they'd hired a mother and daughter team, Donna and Paula, who were actually more like just a mother team, since Donna was the only one who ever closed a We-Tip pledge. Paula was long-legged pretty, though, and Tony, the older brother and the manager, obviously had a crush on her.

Paula would get on the phone, dial a number, and go through the opening salvo: "Hi, this is Paula from We-Tip..." —and then get shot down by somebody, and, without skipping a beat, completely fold, and close with a very polite, and even slightly shocked: "Oh, I'm sorry, sir, I promise never to phone again"—like she'd just been accused of stalking the guy and wanted to avoid a follow up by law enforcement and/or she was a person of rare refinement and whoever it was had completely misjudged her and she couldn't get off the phone fast enough. It was the wrong tone, the wrong approach, and as time went by, and she was shot to pieces over and over again, she seemed to grow listless with the routine and actually made calls less and less.

Every "no" is just a request for more information, as the old telemarketing adage goes, so when you got shot down, you started talking: "Really? I'm sorry to hear that. I'll tell you why I'm calling. I myself wouldn't even be here unless I really believed in this. Are you voting for Clinton. Four more years of Bush, and the whole house goes up in smoke, I fear. Did I catch you at a bad time. A lot of us have this in our families, and we have to protect our own, first of all..."—Not that any of it led to a pledge necessarily, but it was more or less the nature of the gig to go this route, to try to locate a door in the wall, so to speak. It wasn't like anybody picked up the phone and called out to husband or wife: "Honey, it's We-Tip. How much money have we got—because I want to pledge it all except for next week's food budget, although God knows we're both overweight..."

But Donna was pretty good, although I think I had a slight edge on her. And while Tony was taken up with Paula, every so often I'd get what seemed like a little buzz from Donna, who wasn't bad looking in a weathered forty something way. Once when I stepped out onto the dark patio balcony, she was there smoking a cigarette and I had the feeling she was marinated in sex, if you can say that about someone you barely know.

Capps invited me to a private screening of his latest film and I invited Donna to come with me. It was a Saturday afternoon and when the lights went down in the little screening room on the Sunset Strip her hand started moving lightly on my pants along my thigh and eventually over my groin. By now we'd spent one fairly lively night together, and I was worried she was going to do something embarrassing in the midst of these Hollywood players, including a couple of bantam to middleweight stars. I put my hand on her hand and moved it just to the side of my dick, which pissed her off so that she moved away from me in her seat.

Driving to her place after the screening, she wouldn't talk to me.

"Look, I'm sorry," I said. "I got a little embarrassed."

She didn't say anything as we drove between Tampa and Topanga on Ventura Boulevard in the late afternoon. The San Fernando Valley just isn't a Saturday afternoon type of place. I was figuring I'd drop her off at her two-bedroom apartment, which was a few blocks from the We-Tip office, and then pick up a sandwich somewhere and take in a 7:30 Al Anon meeting on Laurel.

"You think I'm beneath you," she said out of the blue.

"What the hell gave you that idea," I said, surprised.

"Any man I play with his dick better be ready to kiss the earth I walk on and you're pushing my hand away?"

"I *am* grateful. I told you, I got a little uptight. I'm not really comfortable at those scenes."

"Why?"

She looked over at me at the wheel and then back at Ventura Boulevard.

I'd become a regular at this stag meeting. It took place in a first floor room off the courtyard of a church. We'd pull our metal folding chairs into a circle and talk about what was going on in our lives.

I had had a dream about encountering an attractive, straightforward woman with dark hair (Donna was red-haired) and it had somehow come to me that the woman was myself.

The guys not only put up with something like this—they applauded it. It was the period of *Iron John* and retreats where men played drums together for hours and this was an interesting turn in the proceedings: Jamie Redding was a sincere, nice-looking woman.

A guy named Harold, short, intense, maybe thirty-five, ten years younger than I, seemed to look up to me.

"I've been reading Jung," he said during the break while we stood outside in the courtyard. "And that dream is great, man. You can be proud of that dream."

I thought it probably had something to do with my mother but didn't feel like delving into it at that moment.

"Thanks, man," I said.

It was beginning to go dark in the courtyard, the end of another summer day. We went back inside, and a guy named Jim, who was some kind of major telemarketer, pulling down big commissions selling time shares in Cabo San Lucas or some place, talked about growing up in the cheapest and worst kept up house in a rich neighborhood on the other side of Ventura Boulevard in Sherman Oaks. There were weeds in the front yard instead of the manicured lawn everyone else had.

The guy periodically buried himself alive in the telemarketing job—he made big bucks, but there was a workaholic and rage-a-holic aspect to it that he recognized and was trying to mitigate. It was all a matter of self-esteem, but it seemed as if the only way you could make a decent living these days was to crucify yourself working 15 hours a day under insane pressure—or get hired to write a sitcom because you were young and nice looking and carried no baggage at all.

Being a writer wasn't necessarily a plus for that end of the business. After all, writing is about fine decisions, relatively minute distinctions, and what I saw on the other side of town, so to speak, were people who were ready, willing and able to put all that aside, if they'd ever taken it up in the first place, and make a nice living.

A year before Al Fontaine, a writer-producer on *Public Law* who had been interested in adapting a book of mine, threw me a bone—he hired me to write an episode. More specifically, I would write the dialogue that would advance the "beats" they would give me, in essence a story they'd already concocted.

It was an hour drama, and I took the beats home to the Thousand Oaks house my ex-wife Cynthia and I lived in, and wrote the script, all stops out, in two weeks. I don't know how good it was but I gave it everything I had and brought it in on deadline.

I was a known writer, a book writer, and I was being given a piece of the action by the real movers and shakers in the town—but strictly as a favor. When I went into the Studio City office, we didn't hit it off. I had known these guys in prep school—in essence fraternity boys—and we hadn't hit it off then.

Hollywood is full of people who are too smart to be good. I don't mean that I'm good, or that I'm dumb either, I'm just not on that Richter Scale at all. Goethe said that talent is nurtured in solitude, and character in society. The artist needs to strike a balance somehow between the two poles to genuinely enter the discourse of his day.

These guys were giving me a chance and money. After I delivered the first draft, they called me in again and gave me all new beats for a second draft. The fee for the second draft was about a third of what the first draft paid. But they didn't ask for a polish—they wanted a whole new ball game.

So I took it home to write again, grateful to be getting the opportunity, after all. We lived on Poplar Crest in Thousand Oaks, and although the bubble in a level might have registered even inside the house, when you looked out on the street, we were on a steep, which gave our lives a haphazard feeling that I think my son Luther picked up.

He was outside all day, compulsively into his bike, then his skate-board, and it wouldn't be long before he was getting into drugs.

I'd started going to Al Anon meetings in my frustration with Luther's addiction. Addicts go over the top. Or maybe they go under. I was a cautious control freak by comparison, at the other end of the spectrum, but let me not forget that I'd chosen to do the impossible. I was a writer in a country that scarcely admitted there was such a thing.

The telemarketer who was born into the wrong house in the right neighborhood in Sherman Oaks, brought up a lot of bad feelings in me: feelings of inadequacy related to my own situation that I'd tried to tamp down into my guts. I imagined I didn't have this guy's problems.

"People don't like you for a very good reason," Donna told me in bed one night.

"It's because my mind is a speed boat," I said.

"Because you're snooty. You think you're hot. You haven't got any money. You want to go to the Hollywood Bowl and hear Stephane Grappelli like it's this big event. Everybody knows it's a very cheap date. The Hollywood Bowl is for goddam wetbacks."

For some reason I started laughing. Wetbacks—only a redhaired Irish fortysomething woman could come up with that, at this late date.

We were in her bedroom. It was a Wednesday, and we'd

come back from We-Tip. Tony had taken Paula out for a late supper or something. Do they have a late supper at Denny's? I'm kidding. He may have taken her somewhere fancy, which was more than I had done for her mother.

The boys at *Public Law* had pulled a fast one after I delivered the second draft. They gave me teleplay credit, and paid me, and then they wrote a completely new script.

I wasn't even humiliated–just shocked. Humiliated happens when someone you respect doesn't respect you. But I don't mean it didn't hurt, it did.

They wouldn't pay me again. Then too, you had the writers' strike happen just then, and that cut into my chances of parlaying the bone Fontaine threw me into a career.

Grand Street

ONE NIGHT A FEW YEARS AGO, when we were living in Santa Monica, our kids grown up and gone, I got a Voice Mail message from someone who said he knew me thirty-five years ago in New York. The man had a solid sounding voice, with a slight New York cast to it, nothing pronounced, and I started trying to figure out who he was. His name was Steve Erman, he said on the message, which didn't quite ring a bell, though it seemed to carry some far-off echo. I kept trying to give a face to the voice and eventually came up with one. A tall black dude who, I remembered, rolled the thinnest joints–and this long before sensamilla, a few tokes of which knock you into the stratosphere.

The other thing I remembered was that he once told me a girl I'd taken home to her apartment and had a nice time with, though it stopped well short of making it, was a nymphomaniac. Was she? I said, and he shrug-nodded genially.

When I finally spoke to Steve Erman it turned out he wasn't this fellow–he wasn't tall, he told me, and not black either, I gathered–and we got to talking about everybody from those days. I have a vague idea who he is now, though I can scarcely tell whether I remember him or invented him.

More or less incidentally during our conversation, Steve

Erman swept back the curtain on a mystery of those long-ago years, one involving an old friend who had died two decades before.

I first met Tom Roberts when I was still living at home with my mother and step-father and younger sister in a big apartment on West End Avenue and going to high school at Trinity. During the course of an evening at home, when I tangled with my mother, the first words out of her mouth always seemed to be, "Get out of my house!" I knew she didn't really mean it–or not for more than an hour or two–but I often took a perverse pleasure in taking her at her word.

Knowing Tom Roberts–who had come to Manhattan from Trenton when he was still perhaps shy of twenty years old and started an early crash pad down on Grand Street–I now had the option of walking out of the apartment, taking the subway down to Grand Street and spending the night.

It was the period in which one saw the first stirrings of the sixties and Tom was at the center of it even if he would tend to deflect any spotlight. A big burly fellow with a beard that he kept neatly trimmed, he was the son of the warden of a prison in New Jersey, I eventually learned. Grand Street, as we all referred to it, was a railroad flat–the third floor rooms strung like boxcars, one after another, from one end of an old brownstone to the other–and there was always an assortment of people around my age or a little older, variously asleep and awake, some with a friend of the opposite sex, having something to drink, or passing around a joint. It was the first place I ever tried marijuana, which at first didn't seem to affect me.

Tom was, by general consensus and by his own inclination, the host–graciously presiding, as my poet friend Ted Keeley would put it wryly some years later, long after Grand Street, when Tom was staying in a house in Cambridge that I shared with a couple of roomates. At that point, he was on the lam from New York to avoid a drug bust for dealing. The irony of it all–the son of the penitentiary warden...like a bad novel.

These days, with what we've learned in the intervening decades, we would identify Tom as an alcoholic, pure and simple, and I think that fairly early on he must have suspected as much of himself. My father rented me a midtown Manhattan studio after I dropped out of college, and on at least one occasion, Tom passed out in it and sonorously slept through to the next morning.

What I haven't mentioned is the particular gentility, in strong contrast to his physical bulk, with which he did everything but his actual job—running the offset printing press at Academy Typing Service, a business on the second floor of a small building on the corner of Sixth Avenue and Fourteenth Street. The summer I was eighteen, before going off for a single semester at the University of Chicago, we worked there together. On Tom's recommendation I'd been hired as a messenger by Barbara Foley, whose business it was.

Tom had a characteristic gesture of putting his fingers to his mouth when he broke into a smile that might have been, by his lights, an impropriety of some kind. He was, it seemed to me, with those he perceived to be worth his time, perhaps insecure, and he appeared eager to establish his own trustworthiness and social utility, via Grand Street and the range of his social contacts. Barbara Foley's son, a taciturn teenager who periodically appeared at the office, would in time grow up to be *the* big movie star of our generation, and Tom, in contrast to the deference which he bestowed on many, took delight in referring to Jake Foley as if he were already a sad also-ran in our midst. I'd like to say I discerned his mistake, but at the time my worry was that I, too, might be a sad also-ran, and I didn't notice.

By the time he came up to Cambridge, Tom had the manners and habits of someone much older than his years. The alcoholic chemistry had in effect preempted his destiny. Still, in Cambridge he began to live with a petite young blond woman named Cathy.

One's twenties can be a time in which the circuitry—the stations, touchstones and flashpoints—of one's adulthood are being appointed and anointed, and all systems are go. Alcohol and drugs are in themselves systems, too, of course, and what I was discovering in my own experimentation with marijuana, for instance, was that the drug had its own set of rules which were not necessarily a perfect match with life at large. The room became very vivid when you smoked a joint, but one might also wish to remain in its exact contours and colors longer than if one hadn't smoked.

There were drugs, then—and, alternatively, some comparable all-consuming program, such as ambition. To be a movie star like Jake Foley, for instance. During these years, every time I ran into him, he was different. From being this closed chrysalis, he was opening out. He became a handsome presence—quick to offer his hand when he could. Once I stayed with Ann, whom I was eventually to marry, in Jake's girlfriend's apartment for several weeks, entirely due to his generosity. By now, I had begun as a playwright, so there was a certain connection between us but no more than I had with many others who never extended themselves that way.

After Ann and I were married, we moved for a summer to Marblehead, Massachusetts. It was the zenith of my youth, a would-be Shakespeare in that sea-bright town of ecstatic birdsong. "Birds make bow-ties of sound," I uttered on the morning air. My wife, who was beautiful and shy, was pregnant. We were eating a macrobiotic diet. I discovered a gathering force in my work, my first full-length play, that paralleled Ann's creation in her belly. A pregnant woman is as sexy as a woman can be, at times, and that summer we were happy, I think: our lives had begun to open.

One Saturday, Cathy, the girl who lived with Tom, came up from Cambridge for a visit by herself, and the afternoon turned into a gruesome recital of the perversity of life with Tom, a chilling tour of his sexual peccadillos with this willing but now pasty-faced, self-loathing collaborator. Fairly early on, I perceived that the visit comprised an implicit act of violence perpetrated on the innocent young married couple by this classic passive-aggressive. She kept up a stream of ludicrous and repellent confession that had me on the verge of ordering her from the premises, and made Ann perhaps even more enraged—but we both kept silent. It was all about water-sports, sexual nomenclature I never properly researched.

That Cathy wanted to rub our noses in shit was clear as the small pale nose on her face. Youth feels such violation with the intensity of its social virginity. When Cathy left, Ann threw up, and I worried that some permanent damage might have been done to the baby. We felt violated indeed in the presence of this wan vessel, disgorging the obscenities of her bathroom life with this man I had known, it seemed, a very long time ago.

I lost touch with Tom then, as I did with Jake Foley too. But Jake I could see in the movies, where I could observe his aging and the advancing stages of his art. Each Christmas I exchanged cards with Barbara Foley, and it was through her, one year, that I heard that Tom was in prison for a drug bust. Was he in the prison his father ran, I wondered idly. Several years later, I learned with a jolt that he had been involved in an automobile accident and died. It was as if his life had a kind of reverse trajectory, an advancing implosion eventually culminated in early death.

Steve Erman told me over the phone that he'd attended Tom Roberts funeral and discovered, somehow or other, perhaps through a family member, that Tom had had a physical complication, his genitals en-cauled at birth so that they didn't develop normally. Hearing this startled me and seemed to throw Tom's life into relief.

I don't recall ever seeing him less than completely clothed. He passed out with trousers and even shoes still on. I can see him now, making the gesture of his hand before his laughing mouth, as if putting away an indiscretion he couldn't help at the same time sharing. He liked to laugh, and the characteristic gesture seemed to apologize in advance for that. When I go back in memory now to the rooms at Grand Street, among the first of my own life, I see a different figure in Tom than I knew at the time—a figure with an intimation of the difficult particular that seemed to defeat him, and which remained to all intents and purposes a secret, one that even Cathy didn't disclose.

Chloe

IT SEEMED TO KLEIN that, existentially speaking–was it existential? he wasn't sure–there was no difference between yesterday and, say, twenty years ago.

You remembered it–and there it was. It didn't take any longer to retrieve an older file, as it were. In fact it was short term memory that went down from time to time.

I can't remember where I live.

What's your name?

Give me a minute, it's right on the tip of my tongue.

"You must read this chapter on the Bibliothèque Nationale," Klein's wife Sheila sitting on the ottoman in their living room said to him. Klein was at his station in the corner of the room, at one end of the sofa, where he read by lamplight or watched the fire.

He had been watching the fire.

"I will," he said.

A moment later he got up and went into the kitchen where the penultimate–or perhaps ultimate–task of the day struck him. Washing the dishes. It was a small source of pride to him that he never retired on a disaster area of a kitchen–an invitation to bugs, he understood.

In the condo where they'd lived in Santa Monica before

moving to Village Green in Los Angeles, he had discovered a large cockroach one after-midnight, positioned about midway on the straw matting runner on the floor of their elongated pullman kitchen. He'd switched the light on. The thing had been big, New York-size, and he wondered how such a benign, beachy environs could foster such a coarse behemoth.

"Get the hell out of here," he told the bug; and, awakened from its samadhi state, the thing had scuttled beneath the sink.

Chloe, their middle child, called on her cellular one night and said that driving home from work in the Valley, she'd had a blowout on the 405 North as it turned into the 101. Klein was getting the car out of the garage when Sheila returned from a homeowners' planning meeting.

"Where are *you* going?" she said playfully in the darkness at the open end of the garage as Klein, behind the wheel, pressed the ignition.

It was January and Sheila brought a blanket to the car in case Chloe had gotten cold. They drove to the place where their daughter's car appeared on a narrow shoulder and drew up behind her, cars whizzing beside them.

On the way, they had stopped at an earlier accident, thinking Chloe's car might be there, and as Klein turned back onto the freeway, a car careened and honked and Klein pulled the car swiftly back onto the shoulder.

Chloe drove home to Oak Park after Klein summoned Triple A, and the man who responded to the scene, an Iranian who could barely speak English, changed the tire, illuminated by the lights of their Volvo.

Later that night he realized how close he had come to an accident, turning back onto the freeway at their mistaken first stop.

It could happen at any time. Alan Pakula, who directed *All the President's Men*, had been killed on the Long Island Expressway, just shy of seventy years old.

In his youth he had been harshly judgmental of people, while also tending to take their failings personally. You are not the target, he'd read at one point with a sense of relief.

For Sheila and him, children of the sixties who had cut their ties with the social moorings of the previous generation, much had been learned from scratch—their own children, in fact, had played a major role in their socialization, in lieu of the world they rejected.

Chloe was for Klein a great gift and conundrum. She was so unworldly that it was a source of worry, and at the same time perhaps the most endearing person he had ever known. Balancing her check book seemed not in the realm of possibility, and she had cultivated a relationship with Urgent Money, a franchise of fantastically overpriced loan sharks, that appalled him.

A year before Klein had endeavored to give Chloe the gift of his knowledge of checkbook balancing. It would, he believed, set her life on course. Instead, an evening that was to involve the clean and orderly transfer of this indispensible life knowledge had ended with Klein screaming in frustration at the byzantine complexity of his daughter's notations—with multiple unexplained ellipses—in her check register, and the collapse of his beautifully laid plans. Yet even as it happened, he couldn't help but admire Chloe's wonderfully fluid and expressive handwriting.

It had taken weeks for normalcy to be restored after Klein's outburst—weeks of his remorse, with flare-ups of resentment within the remorse.

One afternoon Sheila called up to him at the computer in their second floor bedroom to look out the window. He turned his head to the windows that ran the length of the room. It had been raining and now the sun was shining on the grass and the still-wet winter trees. It was celestial.

"Jesus," Klein called from his chair.

"I'm going to photograph it," Sheila said.

Klein had written his second play, *General Electric*, in the early seventies while living in Marin County on welfare. Those days had been among the most glorious of his life, a dense unfolding as rain and sunlight punctuated one another.

He would make regular visits to the county Civic Center building in San Rafael to meet with his case worker, a person who was constantly being replaced.

Klein would explain to the man or woman that he was pursuing gainful employment but that it had momentarily eluded him. On occasion he would be required to take part in a county work project like digging a ditch at the Audubon Canyon Ranch in Stinson Beach for several days, which was both a distraction and a tonic.

The play was working. Klein knew he had struck something valuable and drew all his energies to the task, although it involved only an hour or two of actual writing each day. His life concentrated and pulled everything tighter in its gravitational field. A wild man of their town, Bill De Loach, borrowed five dollars from him one day on the fly, and Klein managed to receive it back from him in a timely fashion, which was unheard of.

Leaving the Civic Center after an appointment with his case worker, Klein took the stairs and in essence flew down the flights, his hand referring once or twice to the bannister for slight balancing adjustments while his feet never touched the ground.

On Fairfax, near the Hollywood Farmers Market, an old woman walked toward Klein, going the other way on the sidewalk. The woman was having trouble walking, her body pitching and dragging laboriously. She looked up at him and said something that sounded like "Old age makes trouble."

As he approached her immediate vicinity, Klein slowed down and leaned toward her as she continued to look sourly at him.

"English?" she said.

"What?" he said, not knowing what she meant.

"Yiddish or English?"

"English," he said.

"Old age makes trouble," she said, frowning, and trundled on.

It crossed Klein's mind that Chloe could be a kind of spiritual teacher to him by virtue of her difficulty with issues that seemed as clear as day to him. His clarity was mismatched, so the circuitry had to re-route itself. His daughter was as much the person he loved by virtue of her failings as her strengths.

"Do you want to try these chips," Chloe said, offering him a bag she held in her hand, with a closed container of Starbucks coffee in the other hand, as she came in the front door.

"Maybe later," he said. "Be careful about crumbs."

"Oh, I will," she said.

The Dead

SOME YEARS AGO I COORDINATED a memorial reading of the works of a poet friend who had died in his forties. He was ten years older than I, but now I was older than the age at which he had died. He was very much actualized, so his age, per se, wasn't a real issue. The occasion for the memorial reading was the publication of his selected poems. It was to be at Beyond Baroque in Venice, and I'd enlisted two others who had been his friends to be co-readers, in the process conferring several times with Beyond Baroque's director, a young man of perhaps thirty.

It only recently dawned on me that there was an unspoken parallel in the fact that the director's father, a well-known Los Angeles artist, had died at fifty, when his son was barely out of his teens. I wasn't familiar with the artist's life. Although I'd known he was no longer alive, I didn't know the specifics of his death, the result of an automobile accident, I learned recently.

The evening of the reading there was a memorable feeling in the room. There were 50 or so people, and, in addition to the director, his mother, the artist's widow, also attended. She looked kind, but stricken–and this a decade after her husband's death. The son told me after the first half, at intermission, that he didn't want to jinx the reading but he felt that so far it had gone perfectly. After the intermission, the three of us who were reading shared the stage to read alternate sections of a long work, and then the evening ended.

I didn't think the second part had gone as well as the first part. Earlier, the widow had smiled tentatively and now she was gone. Nor have I seen the son since that night—he left Beyond Baroque soon afterwards for a different job.

The other evening I picked up a catalog of his father's work that I'd received in the mail and read a bit about him and what he was doing. It was complicated and interesting in the way of an artist gone early. After looking over the catalog, I found that I couldn't remember who else was there that night aside from the three of us who read, and the son and the wife of the artist—and, it seemed to me, the artist's spirit hovering in his two loved ones, more palpable even than the spirit of my poet friend.

The Shape of Jazz to Come

YEARS AGO THE MUSIC SOUND TRACK that accompanied a movie was more or less seamlessly continuous. It was there underneath the dialogue when it wasn't in more brilliant evidence, and it made a movie a different sort of experience than it is today. These days a movie is a bigger, bolder event in one's life but not as relaxing and revitalizing. One no longer thinks in terms of double features because they would be too emotionally and psychologically exhausting. When the music sound track was continuous, no matter what kind of emotional crescendo occurred, there was still that musical continuity underlying it, and it invited one to mull one's own life simultaneously as the picture unfolded. It was as if things happened more slowly, like opera, where emotions sometimes appear to happen in a slow motion that allows time for a beautiful aria.

I remember seeing *Marjorie Morningstar,* a very long movie that had the density of real life without intruding too deeply into one's consciousness, at least not mine. Gene Kelly played a heel in a summer stock theater troupe, as I remember, and I identify the movie with the summer of 1965, when I was twenty one and roomed with two young actors who were interning at the Woodstock Summer Theater in Woodstock, New York.

All kinds of things happened that summer when the sixties first began to hit their stride. A lovely red-haired waitress named Ruth at the Expresso Coffee House left her husband, who became bitter and grew physiognomically ugly over the course of a few weeks. An unprepossessing harmonica player with the Jim Kweskin Jug Band, Mel Lyman, took over the household of the unhappy couple, setting up shop as a guru of some sort.

Mason Hoffenberg, who had written *Candy* with Terry Southern, and I, who had written some rather short plays, decided one night that we were going to go and beat the shit out of Mel Lyman, but we chickened out as soon as we entered the house, in which there was too palpable a gel of adulation, as it were.

I remember a young man named Joe Pavanno, 28 to my 21, who had taken an apartment above Main Street in Woodstock a few months before I arrived with my two friends, or more accurately accompanied them to town, since I had no job to bring me there. Joe had written two short books of prose, and having gotten word that I edited a little magazine, eventually showed them to me.

They were literary equivalents of what Joe had found in the new jazz that was breaking at that time, although most of the public for the music had been usurped by the juggernaut of the Beatles, the Rolling Stones, and the "new" Bob Dylan, a Woodstock resident who had gone electric that spring at the Newport Folk Festival to the chagrin of the die-hard folk purists and the delight of a huge new audience.

Jazz was being forgotten just then, although Ornette Coleman, Cecil Taylor, Archie Shepp, and Albert Ayler, among others, were changing the music again. The New Thing was a step beyond bebop, and Joe had a friend, whom he'd grown up with in Philadelphia and idolized as a player of the new sound. Marion Brown, the black reed player, and Burton Greene, the white pianist, were both around town that summer, and Joe knew Burton, who had made a half-serious legend of himself as a tree lover, and, literally, tree hugger.

Joe's writing included long semi-abstract passages, but what impressed me most in it were realistic vignettes from his own life as a child in the City of Brotherly Love with his friend Smitty. The books were called just *Book One* and *Book Two*, and I quickly combed through them and eventually published a long excerpt in the final issue of my magazine that fall.

Back in Manhattan then, at the venue on the Lower East Side that less than a year later would be known as the Fillmore East, a landmark concert of the New Thing in jazz was promoted, and Joe, it turned out, was one of the people behind the scenes. The headliner and the big draw was Ornette Coleman, who made Charlie Parker's bebop into a melting clock of Texas R&B and a lot of other strains, held together by Coleman's ability to make all of it meld and swing. He was like Miles, Sonny Rollins, or Mingus, imbued with a rock-bottom musicality, albeit he was also the fastest sax in the West. *The Shape of Jazz to Come* was what he called one of his albums, which I found it salutary to listen to around midnight, when the colors in the room acquired an extra edge of brightness from one's tiredness, and Ornette slipped a whole new shimmer into the musical palette.

Also on the bill with this musical giant was Dave Smith, Joe's own Smitty, and given the number of worthy musicians who had been around and paid dues, this was an anomaly to say the least. Dave Smith was virtually unknown, had no record out on a major label, if in fact he had one at all. ESP was the avant-garde label in jazz at the time, and Albert Ayler, for instance, had more than one album out with them. Cecil Taylor was another figure of comparable stature, even then a kind of elder statesman of the avant-garde.

I attended the concert, wanting to see and hear Ornette and curious about Smitty, of course, too. Dave Smith, with a large group of sidemen, nine or ten of them seated in a bandstand line across the stage behind him, was the opening act. A small man standing front and center, he wore jeans and a blue embroidered shirt with a red bandana around his neck, a curiously Western touch for a Philadelphian–and those colors remain a memorable signature of his performance. He and his band played at least half a dozen rather short compositions, each of which framed a solo by him that seemed truncated, stunted, perhaps because it was played at breakneck speed. One had the sense that the small alto–which produced a tinny, toy-like sound–might at any moment come loose from his hands and fly across the stage. It was long before steroids but it was as if he had to be pumped to be on stage at all–an unknown white player on a bill with a legendary black artist at an event for which the audience was at least half black–and once on stage, he felt obliged to cut it short or risk ridicule. It was like hearing slices of music. The notes came fast and furious but without the musical leavening that allows the listener to relax and take pleasure in the work. In a word, having made bold to be on stage in the first place, he seemed frightened to be there. The set passed quickly, there was an intermission, and we headed back for the main event. Indeed, Dave Smith had been like the bantam weight opening bout on a bill with a heavyweight.

Ornette, backed by a small ensemble, was magisterial by contrast, simply in his element. His sound was big, authoritative, with its signature speed but with a full spectrum of colors, slides, peeps, glottal effects, shifts into slower tempos, and other surprises that were seamlessly encompassed by his commanding musicianship. In his famous white smock with clerical collar, it was indeed Doctor Ornette tending to the grateful house. For all its avant-garde notoriety, the music was a great pleasure to hear. The set went for a full hour, there were several encores, and we all filed out with smiles on our faces. I knew I'd witnessed some sort of parable, but what the gist of it was I'm still not sure.

Joe Pavanno died young, of a blood disease, only a few years after the concert. As far as I know, he never published a book–his appearance in my magazine may have been his major publication, small as the venue was.

A dozen years later, when my wife Ann and I and our children, were living in a barn-like house in Bolinas, I met a man one afternoon sitting at a table outside Gwen's sandwich shop who turned out to be Dave Smith. Our brief conversation comprised only oblique acknowledgment of Joe Pavanno, and none at all of the concert with Ornette Coleman. During the intervening years, he hadn't continued as a musician, and now had a number of small children with him, as well as a gentle dog to whom he had called, smiling, on first seeing me, "Bite him!" He seemed skittish, more than likely out of embarrassment at what had happened years ago, which was clearly out of another lifetime, perhaps more Joe Pavanno's lifetime, in the end, than his own. Indeed, our conversation that afternoon was as abrupt and truncated, in its way, as his playing had been at that strange event at the crossroads of the sixties. I never saw him again.

THE WAR

WARREN LANE HAD BEEN A HERO of Klein's youth, one of the brilliant young men of the late fifties and early sixties who seemed to have a new book out, or just about to come out, every year for a decade or more before the bottom fell out, or rather was cemented in, by the rise of the MBAs and the disappearance of the midlist book. The big corporations that bought the publishing houses discovered with shock and dismay that these businesses, the cultural custodians of Thomas Mann and Garcia Lorca, of Bernard Malamud and James Baldwin, were yielding less of a profit on their capital investment than would, say, an ordinary passbook account at the Bank of America.

And the walls came tumbling down. When Klein was sixteen, Lane published a lyrical evocation of his heartland albeit Jewish adolescence titled *Call and Response* that had a kinetic poetry, a sheer joy in being alive, that confirmed Klein's own intimations about both life and language. Lane was like a cubist who used a bit of real newspaper in his composition: it seemed to Klein that *Call and Response* was invested with patches of actual blue sky in its swarthy, wise-guy pastiche of prose-poetry. Delmore Schwartz gave it a rave blurb near the end of his tormented life.

The problem was, people got old, Klein reflected some forty years later on entering for the first time Lane's North Beach apartment. It was on Broadway up above the alternately fabled and tawdry environs down the hill—Enrico's, City Lights, Tosca's, and the All Nude! Shows that had endured through several generations. Carol Doda was an old lady somewhere now, trying to manage two silicone-injected behemoths—or perhaps she'd had the silicone removed.

"This apartment is temporary," Lane was saying as they walked down the corridor of the railroad-style flat ending in a caboose with a sofa that offered a nice view of the twin towers and the San Francisco Bay in the background. "It's just that I've had it now for forty years. I kept it through my marriage, when I bought a house. It's rent-controlled, thank God."

Klein smiled and looked out at the view from the bachelor chaos of the household. Too bad the marriage ended, he thought, and the many affairs; Lane needed a woman's touch and was no longer the handsome comer of the early jacket photos. He was an old writer, now, with no pension plan, still firing on all cylinders but getting a bit hard of hearing.

He had come to film him for a documentary about different people's experiences that moved out of the box of the ego-bound self for a moment. There was a film crew of three and Klein was the interviewer.

Lane sat on the sofa and Klein took a nearby chair. The place was unkempt. There was a dusty French edition of a novel by Lane from 25 years ago. Why didn't he hire a cleaning lady and put the place in order? Or did he like the dust? Like a preview of coming attractions.

"One time I was very low," Lane said in his deep baritone, reminiscent of Rod Serling's, as the camera rolled. "My marriage was over; it was all that messiness—all that emotion, blood and guts—and it seemed as if I'd never sleep again. I walked down to Polk Street at three in the morning. There's a regular 3 A.M. crew down there, I believe, misfits like me who can't sleep. And I went into an all-night diner—not to talk to anyone, but just to be in their presence. I guess I ate the

24-hour-a-day breakfast special, but having these tormented souls around me, around *my* tormented soul, restored me. I didn't feel alone. It was healing."

Lane was the last interview of the day, and after leaving the writer's apartment, Klein said goodbye to the crew and drove in his rental car over the Bay Bridge. It was late February and all day it had been raining on and off, with wondrous intervals of wet sunshine. He had an evening flight out of Oakland Airport in a couple of hours, but meanwhile thought he'd spend a little time in Berkeley.

Taking the Ashby exit he discovered an Arco station at the corner of Shattuck and decided to gas up for the rental car return at the airport, all the while aware that he was nearby the first place he and Sheila had lived after getting married in New York in the fall of 1968. Their Woolsey Street cottage—or half-cottage, since it was split with an older couple on the left side of the clapboard one story—was around the corner from the old Black Panther headquarters on Shattuck, just down the block, as he remembered.

After filling up, he pulled the car onto Shattuck and drove to Woolsey, several more streets south than he'd remembered, and hung a left. There it was, then, the street with its slightly run down three story buildings. Behind one of them had been their cottage. The lump in his throat seemed to occur simultaneously with recognizing the place, but it was Sheila he remembered. So closely held in herself, she was the bud of who she would become: a slim yellow rose, beautiful, straight and true.

It was drizzling again and he walked through a front gate back to a door that might have been theirs during the three months they had lived there, but he wasn't sure. He went back out the gate to the white Metro—it was beginning to darken—and drove to Telegraph Avenue and up toward the campus. He found a parking spot off Bancroft Way and decided to have dinner before looking into Moe's Books and driving to the airport.

At a Mexican restaurant on Telegraph he and Sheila had frequented over thirty years ago, he was seated at the first table of a row that ran down the center of the room. At the adjoining table were two young women, Berkeley students he imagined. The one diagonally across from him was blond, her face plump and young. While keeping his gaze averted, he heard a well-spoken, socially aware young woman. The university was still morally compromised by various associations, it seemed; Klein was happy that young people weren't letting it pass unremarked. He remembered a lunch that fall of '68 in this same restaurant, at a larger table abutting one wall, with a former prep school classmate, now long-haired and possessed of a violent political outlook and agenda that Klein had a hard time crediting with full seriousness. "Let's burn down a bank, okay? No, seriously!" Still, perhaps the young man had gone underground, or had been living a respectable life these past three decades under an assumed name, wanted by the FBI.

How lucky he had been to meet Sheila. Up to then, he hadn't really gotten along with anyone–male, female, family or friends. How wonderful to discover this person who echoed his own deepest intimations about life. Long before meeting each other, they had each loved *Silas Marner* when it was assigned in high school and everyone else seemed to detest it. It was the homely coziness of the world it depicted, Klein decided, that they'd each taken to heart.

Aware of time, and uncertain how long the drive to the airport would be, he ate his taco and flauta, rice and beans with focused efficiency while trying not to rush. Simultaneously, he was aware of the young woman talking to her female companion, who sat virtually next to Klein at the adjoining table and hence was out of view. She was now on the subject of her boy friend, and the uncertainty of the relationship. In another moment, it emerged that she had–with her boyfriend's seeming approval but secret, soon-to-be discovered dismay–indulged in a three-way with a couple at a party, a party the boyfriend deserted, she discovered, while she was upstairs with the couple.

Sheila would have been as appalled as he was, he knew: all those appendages in momentary heated congress. The Bush administration, so to speak. A terrible joke. He had a fleeting impulse to look up from his plate in the dimly lit restaurant and hold forth for a moment in a spirit of disinterested truth telling, to alert the young woman to her serious misjudgment of his gender.

"I wouldn't have done it, if I hadn't been drunk," she was saying. "I don't regret the experience as an experience, but I'm really sorry I hurt Paul."

Her invisible interlocutor was hard to read—surely not as shocked as Klein was, but he thought he discerned a new spaciousness between her punctuating assents.

At the Oakland Airport, his flight had been delayed. The rain was more serious in L.A. and air traffic control there was backed-up. He sat down in a row of anchored swivel seats near his gate and pulled from his carry-on bag a book on loan from the Santa Monica Library, a new selection of Lionel Trilling's essays, *The Moral Obligation to Be Intelligent.* It was a wonderful and appalling title from another vanished era.

He was reading an essay in which Wordsworth and the ancient rabbis were related across a chasm in a conceit that Klein, for one, couldn't credit, but God bless Trilling for trying. The Jews lacked the very thing Wordsworth found peace and fulfillment in—a Lake district of one's own, a tie to the sounds of the water, the trees, to the light in the trees.

The taxi from LAX let him off around midnight—the plane had been three hours late—in a downpour. He was back in the paradise he and Sheila had fortuitously discovered in Central Los Angeles six months ago, a development dating from the early forties, 68 acres, much of it greenbelt, in which cars were kept to the peripheries. The trees were now well over half a century old, just about Klein's age in fact, right outside the front door and windows. It was like having a town home in Central Park.

When he climbed the stairs and entered their bedroom,

Sheila was sitting up in bed, at her late night vigil with *The New York Times.*

"Hi," she said, smiling.

In the early morning dark, he woke up worried about everything. Would they have enough money to hold onto the place they'd found? Even if the world were coming apart, as the election of George W. Bush seemed to formally ratify, he knew there might be some wondrous design to it beyond his ken. He prayed for himself, for Sheila and their children, and then said an extra prayer for Warren Lane, now nearing the end of his earthly tenure, having lived it in good faith. Most of their ilk, after all, had been involved in a kind of undeclared war, a lifelong psychological and financial battle that, self-protectively, one might even hesitate to name.

Printed November 2001 in Santa Barbara
& Ann Arbor for the Black Sparrow Press by
Mackintosh Typography & Edwards Brothers Inc.
Text set in New Baskerville by Words Worth.
Design by Barbara Martin.
This first edition is published in paper wrappers;
there are 200 hardcover trade copies;
100 hardcover copies have been numbered & signed
by the author; & 20 copies lettered A–T
have been handbound in boards by
Earle Gray & signed by the author.

PHOTO: Gailyn Saroyan

ARAM SAROYAN was born in New York City, attended public and private schools on both the East and West coasts and graduated from Trinity School in Manhattan in 1962. After attending the University of Chicago, New York University, and Columbia, he started a literary magazine, *Lines*, in New York in 1964, publishing the work of Charles Olson, William Burroughs, Philip Whalen, Ian Hamilton Finlay, and Ted Berrigan, among others.

His one-word poem "lighght" became the subject of ongoing decades-long government and public debate after being chosen for a National Endowment for the Arts Poetry Award by Robert Duncan in 1968. His poetry has been widely anthologized and appears in many textbooks. Among the collections of his work are *Aram Saroyan, Pages, Day and Night: Bolinas Poems* (Black Sparrow Press, 1998), and *Artists in Trouble: New Stories* (Black Sparrow Press, 2001).

Saroyan's prose books include *Genesis Angels: The Saga of Lew Welch and the Beat Generation*; *Last Rites*, a book about the death of his father, the playwright and short story writer William Saroyan; *Trio: Oona Chaplin / Carol Matthau / Gloria Vanderbilt–Portrait of an Intimate Friendship*; *The Street* and *The Romantic*, novels; a memoir, *Friends in the World: The Education of a Writer*; and a true crime book Literary Guild selection, *Rancho Mirage: An American Tragedy of Manners, Madness and Murder.* His selected essays, *Starting Out in the Sixties,* was published in 2001. He is also the author of a series of plays, including *At the Beach House, Landslide,* and *The Evening Hour.*

A past president of PEN Center USA West, Saroyan is a faculty member of the Masters of Professional Writing Program at USC and a frequent speaker at universities. The father of three children, he lives in Los Angeles with his wife, the painter Gailyn Saroyan.